I0666544

Anything can happen when you let your guard down . . .

After receiving a violent threat on the heels of her father's disappearance from the town of Arrowhead Bay, Devon Cole fears for her life—until Vigilance, a local private security agency, steps in to shield her from danger. Although she isn't usually quick to surrender her freedom, she has no problem stripping her defenses for her new sexy bodyguard . . .

Tortured by the painful memory of lost love, Logan Malik is determined not to risk his heart again. So when he's tasked with watching over Devon day and night, he's focused on doing his job. Day is no problem, but as tensions rise at night, nothing can protect them from giving in to unbridled passion . . .

Visit us at www.kensingtonbooks.com

Books by Desiree Holt

Finding Julia

Game On Series
Forward Pass
Line of Scrimmage
Pass Interference
Fourth Down

Vigilance Series
Hide and Seek

Published by Kensington Publishing Corporation

Hide and Seek

A Vigilance Novel

Desiree Holt

LYRICAL PRESS
Kensington Publishing Corp.
www.kensingtonbooks.com

Lyrical Press books are published by
Kensington Publishing Corp. 119 West 40th Street New York, NY 10018

Copyright © 2017 by Desiree Holt

All rights reserved. No part of this book may be reproduced in any form or by any means without the prior written consent of the Publisher, excepting brief quotes used in reviews.

All Kensington titles, imprints, and distributed lines are available at special quantity discounts for bulk purchases for sales promotion, premiums, fundraising, and educational or institutional use.

To the extent that the image or images on the cover of this book depict a person or persons, such person or persons are merely models, and are not intended to portray any character or characters featured in the book.

Special book excerpts or customized printings can also be created to fit specific needs. For details, write or phone the office of the Kensington Special Sales Manager:
Kensington Publishing Corp.
119 West 40th Street
New York, NY 10018
Attn. Special Sales Department. Phone: 1-800-221-2647.

Kensington and the K logo Reg. U.S. Pat. & TM Off.
LYRICAL PRESS Reg. U.S. Pat. & TM Off.
Lyrical Press and the L logo are trademarks of Kensington Publishing Corp.

First Electronic Edition: October 2017
eISBN-13: 1978-1-5161-0367-6
eISBN-10: -5161-0367-X

First Print Edition: October 2017
ISBN-13: 978-1-5161-0370-6
ISBN-10: 1-5161-0370-X

Printed in the United States of America

To Joseph Patrick Trainor, who has become my go-to guy on all things law enforcement and special operations. Thank you for all your patience and for answering my millions of questions

Author's Foreword

From Desiree

Writing a book is a solitary experience but it never comes to the bookshelves, virtual or other, alone. For me it starts with my treasured friend and beta reader extraordinaire, Margie Hager, who has the best eagle eye in the world. Thank you, Margie my love, for all the hours you put in to help me bring my stories to life. And for your friendship, which is a highlight of my life. And to Janet Rodman who always looks out for me.

Then there is my family. Do they read my books? Absolutely not! But they are the best public relations team in the world. From my daughter Amy who tells all her clients about me to my son Steve who makes sure he lets everyone he knows when I have a book released to my younger daughter Suzanne who is my good right hand and my granddaughter Kayla who is my wonderful left hand. Guys, I could not do it without you. If you see me at a convention, Suzanne will not be far from my side.

My cats, of course, keep me company while I write, especially Bast who thinks she should get coauthor credit!

Thanks to all the people who answer my endless questions, from SEALs to Force Recon Marines to Delta Force soldiers to local law enforcement to sports experts. The time you continue to give me is very special.

Last but very far from least are all of you, my wonderful readers, who send me such great e-mails and posts and are so faithful. A special shout-out to Phuong Phen, Fedora Chen, Shirley Long, and Patricia Sager who have been with me since my journey started and in frustrating times give me the inspiration to push ahead.

I love you so much. You are my extended family and I send you all many hugs.

There are a lot more stories to come. Please stay tuned.

I love to hear from my readers. You can write to me at desireeholt@desireeholt.com and I hope you will do that.

Where else can you find me?
www.desireeholt.com
www.desireeholttellsall.com

Facebook: www.facebook.com/authordesireeholt
Twitter: @desireeholt
Pinterest: www.pinterest.com/desiree02holt
I look forward to hearing from all of you.

Desiree

Acknowledgments

Thank you to Marine Brig General Thomas V. Draude, who helped me in my information gathering

Prologue

Graham Cole clutched his cell phone, barely restraining himself from throwing it against the wall. Where the hell was Vince? Everything was falling apart and they needed to get the hell out of Dodge.

How had they even gotten to this point?

A drug cartel. He was laundering money for a drug cartel.

It had all started so slowly.

"We think if you changed these suppliers, you'd help your bottom line."

"If you switched distributors for these products, you'd be in a lot better shape."

"These people are the cause of all that red ink. Get rid of them."

When Graham had discovered the true source of the funds he'd used to save his business, and wanted to pull out, Vince had convinced him it was too dangerous. Vince had been right. No one ever walked away from a cartel.

Still, he'd been determined to see if there was a way out of the chokehold. Somehow—he had no idea how—word had gotten through to Cruz Moreno, head of the vicious Moreno cartel, that Graham wanted out. He was told to take his money and shut up.

"They could go after Devon, too," Vince had told him.

God! On top of everything else he'd made both Vince and Devon targets of these miserable assholes.

In the end the only answer he'd come up with was to disappear. Maybe without him there, they'd leave Vince and Devon alone. Giving up the lifestyle he'd worked so hard to build wasn't even a factor. If he stayed, things would be a lot worse. If he was arrested, Moreno could use a threat to Devon to keep him from testifying. If he was gone, he was no longer a threat and she'd be safe.

He hoped.

El Jefe had laid it out plain and simple. *"We own you, compadre. Never forget that. And don't screw me over."*

So he'd made his plans, quietly and under the radar.

He leaned back in his chair, rubbing his chest, feeling the acid burn of indigestion. He hoped to hell he wasn't having a heart attack.

As always, the television in his office was on so he could skim the day's headlines, keeping an eye on the financial reports for anything that might affect the conglomerate. Old habits die hard. Now, a running news story caught his attention.

"That's all the information we have at the moment. Repeating, Vincent Pellegrino, vice president of corporate finance for Cole International, has been found dead in his car on Interstate 75. It appears he swerved for some reason, crashed through a barrier on a curve, and went over the side. Authorities are calling it a one-car accident but they are still investigating. We'll bring you more information as it becomes available."

Vince dead?

Jesus Christ on a crutch.

Beads of sweat formed all over his body. He rewound the story twice but the details never changed. What the hell had happened? Had Moreno somehow found out what he was planning and killed Vince as a warning? For the first time in a long time, he knew real fear. What had once seemed like the answer to a prayer now felt like an octopus wrapping its tentacles around him, choking the life out of him. They could be coming for him any minute. Who knew that when he attempted to repay the money, he was inviting a possible death sentence?

Now he needed to get the fuck out of here before Moreno's men showed up at his doorstep. But he was damn sure taking all the evidence with him. He might need a bargaining chip.

He checked the desktop computer one more time for the feed from the security cameras. Nothing. He'd triple-checked before getting ready that the alarm system was still on. Also good to go.

Satisfied he was still safe, he unplugged the external hard drive from his desktop computer and stuck it in his briefcase along with the laptop and the portfolio. Then he opened the tower, removed the internal hard drive, and shoved it into his briefcase, too. When he got to sea, he'd deep-six the internal one along with the laptop. Even if he wiped it, a good technician could restore everything, and who knows what would lead them to him. As long as he had the external he was all set. He was almost ready now, heading for the one person he could trust, to a place where he could set himself up with a new computer and figure out how to best use this stuff as leverage.

He sent a quick text to a prearranged burner phone, then took a moment to restore his phone to factory settings. His briefcase was locked, so he stuck the phone in his pocket. He was planning to toss it anyway. As soon as he was away from the harbor he'd chuck it overboard. Anyone trying to find him with a GPS locator would have a hell of a hard time doing it. Let them stick that up their collective ass. He'd be long gone by then.

If he had one regret, it was for Devon, the daughter he was leaving behind, and the damage he'd done to their relationship. He considered leaving a note for her or sending her a text, but he didn't want anything that could connect her to this. Too dangerous. Still, it saddened him greatly that he'd probably never see her again. He hadn't been the best father in the world the past couple of years. Once he got to his new location, he'd keep track of her through the Internet, Googling her name, and checking the newspapers as well.

He thought again of Vince's so-called accident, and nausea bubbled. But right now he needed to get the fuck out of here. Blotting the sweat on his forehead with the sleeve of his shirt, he unlocked a drawer in his desk and pulled out a slim portfolio. Then he grabbed his Glock 9mm from another drawer and stuck it in his pocket. He didn't have much time, needed to move right now.

He lifted the briefcase and headed for the garage. A sound caught his attention as he opened the inside door. It sounded like it came from the kitchen and his stomach knotted. No, no, no. Impossible. There was no one here. He was imagining things. He'd given the housekeeper and groundskeeper the week off. The alarm should let him know if someone was trying to break in.

I'm imagining things. That's what happens when you put yourself in a dangerous position, screwing over dangerous people.

He needed to calm down or he'd stroke out before he even got out of here.

Then he heard it again. A squeak, as if someone walked on the highly polished hardwood floors. He held his breath, straining to hear. Was that yet another one? His heart pounded so hard he thought it would beat itself out of his chest, his fear so strong he smelled it.

He hadn't seen anything on the security cameras, but why hadn't the alarm sounded? No, he was imagining things. It was his state of mind. Edging up to the door, he peeked out into the hallway, looking one way, then the other. At this time of day, the house was filled with sunlight. Surely he'd see anyone if there was someone to see.

I'm driving myself nuts. I need get the hell out of here. I'm running out of time.

Letting his breath out, he turned once more toward the garage door, stopping when again he thought he heard another sound. He grabbed his gun and started to turn around, but a hard, muscular arm locked itself around his neck. A hand yanked the gun from his grip as if it were nothing more than a feather duster and pressed it into the small of his back.

Fuck! Double fuck.

His legs had turned so rubbery he wasn't sure he could stand if the man released his hold. If only Vince hadn't cried wolf so many times before, Graham would have paid more careful attention to his warnings. If only he'd left earlier. If only he'd been more careful. If only a lot of things.

"Going someplace?" A guttural voice ground out the words in his ear, hot breath singeing his skin.

Real fear crept through him, paralyzing him. He hadn't made it. His escape was so close but exactly what he feared had happened. His timing sucked. Was this it? Was this how it was all going to end for him?

"H-How did you get in?" What had happened to his high-priced alarm system?

"You're not quite as safe as you think you are, asshole. A strong radio frequency can knock out even the best alarms."

"You're choking me." Graham could hardly get the words out as the stranger pressed harder on his windpipe and dragged him along the floor. He was sweating so badly now he could smell it on his body. How would he ever get out of this? He'd been so close, so very close.

"We're going to take a little trip, you and I," the man went on, "along with whatever is in that briefcase. Mr. Moreno says you're unhappy, *amigo.* He wants to meet with you and make sure you understand nothing is to change. Your friend, Vincenzo, tried to run, too. Unfortunately in his haste he met an untimely demise before he could give us all the information we want."

Vince. Goddamn.

"Let's move." The man urged him forward, still exerting the pressure on his neck and nudging him with the gun.

He couldn't let Moreno's thug get him past the front door. Graham dragged his feet and looked around wildly for something, anything, any option to get him out of this. Whatever it was, he'd have only a few seconds to make it happen. Then, in the hallway, he spotted something that gave him a faint ray of hope, if he could get hold of it.

"I—I can't breathe." He made his voice as faint as possible, and sagged against the man behind him.

"Too bad."

"If you deliver a dead body," Graham gasped, "Moreno won't be very happy with you."

He could have sworn the man growled, but he finally loosened his hold. Knowing he'd have scant seconds to do anything, Graham yanked on the man's arm and ducked beneath it. In one desperate movement he spun around, grabbed a bronze statue from the hall table, and hit the man over the head. For an endless moment nothing happened, and he was afraid he'd misjudged. Then the man toppled to the floor, nearly taking Graham with him.

He had no idea if he'd killed the man or merely knocked him out, but he didn't stop to find out. If the man was dead, in a few days his housekeeper would find the body, somewhat rancid by then. If it was the latter, he was short on time to get the fuck out of here.

He picked up the gun and the briefcase that he'd dropped and raced for the garage. He was sweating profusely and shaking so much he bumped into the car, the briefcase slamming into the fender. He yanked his keys from his pocket, hoping he was steady enough to drive. He jumped into the most innocuous of his vehicles, a gray Mercedes, and hauled ass down the driveway to the road.

When he made the turn onto the highway, he spotted a black utility vehicle parked near the trees with a man in the front seat.

Fuck!

The driver, spotting Graham's car, pulled out onto the road just as his partner, wobbling slightly, came racing down the driveway.

I should have hit him harder.

Lucky for Graham the few seconds the driver stopped so his partner could jump in gave him a miniscule lead, but not much. Graham punched the accelerator and hauled ass down Seacliff Road. He had a small window of opportunity to get the fuck out of here, and he wasn't wasting any of it. That SUV would be on his tail any minute.

Faster! Faster!

He glanced at the speedometer and saw he was doing a hundred. He hoped he didn't wreck the car and kill himself just when he was nearly out of here. He was so focused on reaching the marina that it wasn't until he touched his pocket that he realized his cell phone wasn't there. Fuck again! What the hell had happened to it? If the wrong person found it and managed to restore it, his ass would be grass. Of course, first they'd have to find him. Right?

Breathe, he told himself. *Just breathe. Almost there.*

All the way to the harbor he kept checking the rearview and side-view mirrors. The road twisted and turned around the shoreline so at times his view of the rear disappeared. There. Was that a black SUV? No. No, it was a pickup and it turned off into a strip center before it caught up to him. He was definitely going to vomit first chance he had.

Jesus, Graham, don't lose it now.

Or any more than he already had. He just had to get to the boat before they caught up with him. Then he'd be safe. He always kept the smaller of his two boats provisioned and ready for anything, as part of his emergency plan. Just in case. He also made sure he had all the equipment on board he'd need.

Don't think about it. Don't think about it. Too late now.

He rounded a curve in the road and there was the marina up ahead. He could see *Princess Devon* now, its twin hulls bobbing in the water at its berth. Almost there. Still no SUV in his rearview mirror, but it could appear around the curve at any moment if those two guys had gotten their shit together.

At last he was parked and headed down the pier where the boats were docked. All he needed was another few minutes. A few more steps…

Chapter 1

"Your father is missing."

Devon Cole tightened her grip on her cell phone and tried to make sense of what Sheridan March had just told her, as fear swept through her. Maybe she hadn't heard right.

"What do you mean, missing?"

"The Coast Guard found the *Princess Devon* drifting five miles offshore early this morning," the Arrowhead Bay chief of police explained. "But there's no sign of him anywhere. And no clue to anything in the house. We went through every inch of it. The alarm was fried, probably needs to be replaced, but otherwise the place was clean as a whistle."

Devon clutched the phone. "Was there anything on the boat? Something he might have had with him that could give us a clue?"

"Nada."

"Where's the boat now? Would the Coast Guard hold on to it?"

"In its slip at the Bayside Marina. After the Guard went over every inch of it, they had one of the men on the cutter bring it back in and berth it. I have the keys."

Devon swallowed to ease the tightness in her throat. "When was the last time anyone saw him?"

"Sunday," Sheri told her. "As soon as I got the word from the Coast Guard we began checking with his friends. The last time anyone saw him was when Cash Breeland had lunch with him at the Driftwood."

"That's the same day I talked to him." She rubbed her hand nervously on her jeans. "He didn't say a word about going anywhere. Did the Moorlands say anything about seeing him?"

Ginny and Hank Moorland owned both the Driftwood Restaurant and Bayside Marina.

"Hank was in Miami for a couple of days but Ginny was there. She said she never laid eyes on him."

"And Gary at Bayside? Did he see anything?"

Sheri made a rude noise. "I talked to him myself but he's usually so off in his own world a marching band could have taken off and he'd never notice. I swear I don't know why Hank doesn't can his ass. Besides, it was a Sunday, so the marina was jammed with people arriving and leaving and some just working on their boats. He did say a couple of guys were asking about him, but he thought they were just friends."

"Did you talk to anyone who has a boat in a slip near his?"

"The ones we could find."

"God." Devon tamped back the rising fear. "I can't believe this could happen. He's an avid sailor and very, very safety conscious."

Her father had been sailing for as long as she remembered. When he still lived in Tampa he was out on the water every Saturday, sailing down the coast, sometimes with business associates but more often with her mother. That was how he'd discovered Arrowhead Bay. But he almost never went out during the week. Saturdays were his days on the water. And, after her mother passed away, sometimes on Sundays. It was something both her parents had enjoyed, and Devon often thought it was a way for him to recapture her presence.

"I know," Sheri agreed. "Everyone knows that about him."

"And the other boat?" Devon asked. "The *Lady Hannah*?"

"Still here. There's not even a sign anyone was on it." She paused. "We know he's an excellent sailor. The Coast Guard thought maybe he'd fallen overboard, but—"

"I guess that's possible, except he was a nut about water safety. He'd be careful."

"That's what I told them," Sheri agreed.

"The Coast Guard started searching immediately, right?"

"Yes, but it's a big ocean. They brought in another cutter to search as well as one of their Dolphin helicopters. I promise you it's a full-out search and rescue operation. And there's another thing."

"What?" What else could there be?

"I don't know if you caught it, but there was a story on the national news yesterday that Vincent Pellegrino, one of your father's vice presidents, was killed in a one-car accident."

Ice chilled her blood. "Are you saying the two things could be related? That my father didn't just fall overboard?"

"I'm saying we have to look at all possibilities. This is too much of a coincidence to ignore."

"Did you call his office? Ask his admin if he'd decided to take an unannounced vacation?"

"I did, but she knew nothing. And they are all in a turmoil over Pellegrino's death."

"But who would want to kill him?" Nausea bubbled up in her throat. "Either of them?"

"We don't know, and that may not be it at all. I'll just have to connect all the dots."

"Holy crap, Sheri."

"One other thing. His house was meticulously clean, as if someone had gone through and sanitized it. But—this is weird—his computer was on his desk but the internal hard drive has been removed."

"What? What the hell?"

"My thoughts exactly."

"What about the external hard drive? It should be right next to it."

"Nada," Sheri told her. "Gone, gone, gone."

Even as she tried to dial back the sick feeling creeping through her, Devon was already dragging her suitcase out and pulling things out of her drawers and closet. She ran through her mind all the projects she had in process, which could be put on hold, who she needed to try to renegotiate deadlines with.

"I'm coming down there right now. I can't just sit here and wait around. I'll finish packing as soon as we hang up and be on the road right away."

"Good. I think you need to be here. Corporate is sending some people down here and I know they'll want to talk to you, too. Call me or come see me as soon as you get here." Sheri paused. "We're all over it, Devon. I just wish we had more to go on."

"I know. It's just…" Just that she'd already lost one parent and didn't know if she could deal with losing another. "I think I'll go to the house first and take a look around."

"Sounds good. I'll wait to hear from you."

The minute she hung up from Sheri's call, she packed the suitcase and threw it and her computer stuff into her car. Less than thirty minutes later she was headed south from Tampa on Interstate 75. She alternated between the threat of tears and full-blown panic as the conversation replayed like a looping tape in her head as she ate up the miles.

While she drove, she kept trying to reach her father. She had both the cell phone and the house phone on speed dial, but she got nothing. Where the hell was he? She'd been on the road for about an hour when her cell rang. The readout showed Sheri's name so she pushed the remote button to answer.

"Have you found him?" she asked, forgoing any kind of greeting.

"I wish. No, I just wanted to give you a heads-up."

Now what?

"What's going on?"

"We've got a couple of reporters sniffing around here, asking about your father's disappearance."

"How did they find out so fast?" Devon asked.

"A million ways. This is the age of the Internet. Maybe they were after your father to ask him about the death of his executive. I wouldn't put it past them to rent a boat and go check on the search."

"Damn, damn, damn." Devon pounded a fist against the steering wheel.

"You said it," Sheri agreed. "Anyway, I'll bet anything the first story will hit the newspaper tomorrow and they're looking for more details."

"Oh my God. Sheri, I can't talk to them now."

"Don't worry. I'll keep them off your back. But it's possible if they give it a big play, someone seeing it might remember something."

"You're right," Devon agreed. "I'm just not good with stuff like that and right now my mind's in too much of a whirl to even speak coherently. I'll probably say the wrong thing and make the situation worse."

"I understand. We can't shut them out, and but I will do my best to keep them off your back for as long as I can."

"Thanks." Devon blew out a breath.

"If they catch you, the best thing is to tell them no comment. I'm sure they'll hit the Cole International offices in Tampa. Just let the people there make any statements."

"Sounds good to me."

"Don't forget. Call me or come by as soon as you get here."

"I will."

She disconnected the call and stuck the phone in the console.

Great. Just great. Reporters, looking for juicy scandal about the disappearance of a business giant.

Oh, Dad, how could you do this to me?

The fact was, she'd been worried about him for the past several months. Her mother's death five years ago had thrown him for a loop. Piled on top of that were problems with Cole International. He didn't discuss them with her but there was a hint here and there, and he was constantly on edge. Then, suddenly things seemed to be better.

She'd missed him when he moved to Arrowhead Bay, but she understood him wanting a change. The house was filled with too many memories of her mother. Plus her father said he was tired of city living.

On the trips to the little town while he was still living in Tampa, he met people. Made friends. The times she sailed down there with him she'd gotten to know people, too, and fallen in love with the small, sleepy Southern town. He was as happy as she'd seen him since her mother died.

She'd met Sheri March at one of the many festivals the town held and they'd connected at once, becoming good friends. Through Sheri she'd met a lot of other people, including the chief's sister, Avery, who ran a private security agency. With friends to hang with and her father almost himself again she'd begun to look forward to visiting him. He loved hearing about the growth of her graphics design business and praised her for what she accomplished.

Then he'd stopped asking her about it except on rare occasions.

She tried to pinpoint just when that had all started. *Almost two years ago*, she thought. The tenor of the visits had changed. *He* had changed, becoming more tense, edgier, sometimes even withdrawn. When she asked about it, he just brushed it off. She missed their tight relationship. They had always been close, so it bothered her more than she let on.

He was abruptly more preoccupied with the business than ever, even obsessed with its financial situation. It never made sense to her because Cole International was worth millions. Whenever she asked him what was wrong, he assured her everything was fine. Just some pesky business details, he told her, that were taking a little more of his attention.

She'd continued to make sporadic visits, hoping to recapture the tight sense of family they'd had. After all, it was just the two of them now. But no matter how hard she tried, she'd felt them drifting apart more and more. There was a wall of some kind around the man she just could not breach.

When she noticed the change in him, she tried to question Cash Breeland about it. Cash was the president of the locally owned Arrowhead Bay Bank. Devon didn't know him all that well, but he and her father had become friends even before the big move. In fact, it was Cash who had introduced her father to friends of his and drawn him into their social circle. But Cash just downplayed her questions.

"I know your daddy's been preoccupied some," he drawled when she asked him to meet her for coffee. "He's just working through some knotty business problems. With all this overseas competition, some of his units aren't performin' the way they should. He'll pull out of it as soon as there's an uptick in trade."

But he hadn't and now he was gone.

Missing.

The word gave birth to a lot of speculation and none of it good.

She spotted the highway signs for Arrowhead Bay and gave herself a mental shake. She needed to clear the garbage out of her head until she could find out for sure what was going on.

She took the farthest exit for the town, the one that took her to the road where her father's house was. He had built at the far end of town in the area known as Seacliff. More land, larger homes. He liked space, he'd told her. Cole International board members and executives routinely visited him there. And from his side patio he had a magnificent view of Arrowhead Bay and the harbor.

His house was the next to last one on Seacliff Road, and in minutes the familiar gateposts came into view. She gave silent thanks that there were no reporters around. They must have taken Sheri literally. She pulled up in the driveway and shoved the car into park, then stared at the house for a long moment. Automatically she reached into the half-empty bag of red licorice bites on her console and popped a couple in her mouth.

Sitting there now, chewing on the candy, she remembered the last time she'd seen him, a little more than a month ago. Their brief conversation played out in her head.

"You're leaving already?" He had looked up from his desk when she stopped in the doorway to the den.

"You're busy and I have work back in Tampa to take care of."

"I thought you brought your laptop with you."

"I did, but I think I'd be more comfortable at home."

For a fleeting moment, a pained expression crossed his face, one almost of sorrow.

"We should spend more time together."

She'd nearly snorted at that. They'd always been so close, especially after her mother died, but he'd withdrawn from her.

Still, he was her father and she loved him.

Was it possible this was voluntary? Had her father chosen to disappear so completely? No. *Too outrageous*, she thought. He was the epitome of the corporate icon. A mover and shaker. Winner of awards. Profiled in magazines. Business school graduates used him as their aspirational model. What on earth could make a man like that choose to vanish as if he'd never existed?

Even with his changes in personality and behavior, she could say this was 100 percent unlike him. What if he'd been grabbed by someone? But who? It could be a competitor, a disgruntled employee, someone on the bad end of a business deal. She knew very little about his business dealings. Would there be a ransom request? Would they contact her or his corporation? How would she get the money if the call came to her? How—

No. Sheri hadn't said anything about a kidnapping.

Another thought stabbed at her, one that chilled her. Had someone killed him and dumped the body overboard? But who? And why?

She would ask Sheri those questions as soon as she spoke to her again. Meanwhile, back to square one. If neither of those things turned out to be a reality, why had Graham Cole disappeared? What was going on with him?

Stop!

God, she was driving herself crazy.

She felt an unexpected rush of tears and a tightening of her throat. Despite the state of their relationship, he was her father. She still loved him and his disappearance frightened her.

Enough, missy. Get your ass into the house.

But the moment she climbed out of her car, a sudden chill raced down her spine and an ominous feeling gripped her. She stood there, gathering herself. Could a house be menacing?

Ridiculous. Stupid.

She wasn't the type of woman given to feelings like that. She was down to earth and practical. *Some might even say hardheaded*, she thought with a tiny smile.

Okay. I'm here. I should go inside and see if I can find anything the police might have missed. Or that would give me some kind of clue as to what had happened, something that would mean something only to me.

Go on. Don't be a chicken.

It was just bricks and stucco. What did she think was inside? A body? Not likely. The police had already searched the house. When she was sure she had herself under control, she hiked up the steps to the front door, for the moment leaving all her stuff in the car. As she slid the key for the front lock into place she wondered if it still worked. When the key turned and the lock clicked open, she breathed a sigh of relief.

Automatically, she reached for the alarm panel in the front hall, then remembered Sheri said it wasn't functioning. That a whole new one would need to be installed. How very weird. It was always on.

At least the air-conditioning had been left on, a blessedly cool change from the furnace that was Florida heat in the summer. Jingling the key ring, she walked through the house, looking around, although she had no idea what she expected to find.

The house was open and airy, with a wall of windows the length of one side that looked out to the lawn and beyond that to the bay itself. Her father had hired a decorator and given her free rein. The result was a tastefully decorated home that was open and welcoming.

As she walked from room to room, the same eerie feeling that gripped her when she'd stood in front of the house swept over her again. As if something very bad happened here. The chill racing over her skin had nothing to do with the artificially cooled air. She sensed a presence of evil in the air, and kept looking over her shoulder, as if expecting someone to pop out of a closet.

Stupid, stupid, stupid. I've been watching too much television.

She wandered into his den, seeking any kind of clue. Framed photos of herself and her mother and the three of them sat on the credenza but the desk was uncharacteristically bare. There was nothing on it, not an open book, a stack of papers, nothing. No sign of any activity, yet this was the room where he spent much of his time. How strange. Except...

Damn. Sheri was right. The computer was on his desk but the hard drive was gone. She checked all the drawers, although she was sure the police had already done this. No hard drive, internal or external, and no laptop. She'd forgotten to ask about that. Would he have taken all that with him? What did he plan to do with all his information if he'd decided to disappear? Could he run his business if no one knew where he was?

Again that icy feeling raced over her skin, the kind you got when people told ghost stories in the dark. As if strangers had been here, and not the ones investigating Graham Cole's disappearance. Could evil leave a sense of its presence?

Evil? Really?

Dramatic much, Devon?

She just couldn't shake the feeling something was off.

If only she'd forced the issue, made him talk to her. Fixed whatever barriers had been thrown up between them. Maybe she'd have a clue as to what was going on.

For a moment she considered the B and B in town, but why spend money she didn't have to? A house couldn't harm you, right?

A loud noise from the kitchen made her pulse leap and her heart thump. She grabbed a golf club leaning against the wall, tiptoed down the hall, and peered into the room. Nothing. No one. Should she step inside? What if someone was hiding in the alcove? With the alarm system not working anyone could come into the house.

Then the noise repeated, and she blew out a breath when she realized what it was. The icemaker in the refrigerator was disgorging cubes into the container.

Devon sat down at the breakfast bar, hands still shaking, and tried to steady herself. Maybe staying here wasn't such a good idea at all. Was she crazy to think someone had left an imprint here and it wasn't her father?

There's nothing here. Give your imagination a rest.

The landline on the kitchen wall rang, startling her. Who would be calling? Most of her father's calls had come in on his cell phone. Automatically she reached for it.

"Hello?"

Dead silence.

She waited, then, "Hello? Is someone there?"

Still silence. Why did the words *dead silence* come to mind? Then she heard it, the faint sound of someone breathing.

"If someone is there, speak up, or else I'm hanging up this phone."

When there was still no answer, she replaced the receiver, irritated. And troubled. She wanted to believe it was kids making prank calls, but with her father's disappearance it took on a more ominous feeling.

Right, Devon. Make this into some big deal. A lousy phone call. Probably just some wrong number and they were too embarrassed to say anything.

Maybe. She was not someone given to flights of fancy or premonitions. If anything, she was solidly grounded and practical to a fault. Only nothing had felt right to her since she walked in the front door, and the phone call had just added to the feeling of unease. She had a sudden need to get out of there, be with noise and crowds. Her stuff could wait until later. Right now she needed to be with people. A lot of people.

She had just headed out of the kitchen when the phone rang again. With a mixture of impatience and dread she picked up the receiver.

"Hello?"

Silence again.

"Listen. Whoever you are, either talk to me or I'm hanging up. If you call again, I won't be here."

She slammed the receiver back in the cradle. That did it for her. She needed to get out of here and find Sheri right away.

Her stomach chose that moment to grumble, reminding her she also needed food. She'd left Tampa two hours ago with only a large Starbucks in her stomach, and said stomach was now sending her signals. She remembered the housekeeper kept the fridge and the freezer stocked with basics so she could just fix herself something if she wanted to. But the eerie feeling wouldn't let go.

Sheri had said to call or come by as soon as she got into town, and right now seemed like a very good time to do that. Going straight to the police station seemed the best thing to do. She'd feel better seeing Sheri, anyway. Maybe she could help Devon put her feelings in perspective.

The police had gone over the house thoroughly. Surely if something was out of whack, they'd have found it and told her. Something besides the jacked alarm system.

I'm just letting my mind play tricks on me. That has to be it.

Okay. That was it. She was getting out of here for a while. She'd head right for the police station and try to find out where things stood. She should have gone there right away. And she wanted to know what the latest was with the Coast Guard. The whole thing was still so unreal to her.

She walked through the house to the garage, still carrying the golf club and peeking around doors and walls. And feeling like an idiot. She found the extra remotes for the garage door and grabbed one, then hurried back through the house and out the front door. Without understanding why, she checked three times to make sure the front door was locked. She also looked carefully around as she got into her car, as if expecting to see someone peeking at her from behind the garage or one of the many massive trees that dotted the place.

Damn. If reporters might be hanging around, she'd better get that alarm fixed in a hurry. Anyone could get onto the property if they wanted to.

She wasn't easily frightened but the whole situation spooked her. Maybe she *should* stay in town at the B and B until she figured out if she was needed for anything. Still, she'd be damned if she'd let anyone chase her out of her father's house.

Seacliff Road was sparsely populated, the homes built much farther apart than those in town. There was only one house on the road past her father's and after that was a dead end. The lack of traffic made her nervous, as did the thick growth of trees that lined the side opposite the houses. Probably no one was lying in wait for her—where had *that* thought come from?—but she'd feel a lot better being part of a crowd. She kept looking in her rearview mirror.

"Just in case," she whispered.

But in case of what? Besides, who even knew she was in town? She was letting the entire situation spook her. What she needed to do was get into town and talk to Sheri face-to-face. Once she got a better read on the situation, she'd settle down. At least she hoped she would.

Just as she came to a slight curve in the road she glanced in the rearview mirror and her heart nearly stopped beating. A black SUV that seemed to have come out of nowhere rode her bumper. Oh, God! Doing her best not to panic, she gripped the wheel and pressed down harder on the accelerator, but no matter how fast she went the car kept pace with her.

She navigated the next turn, hoping she could pick up a little speed and put distance between her and whoever this was. But then she felt a jolt as the SUV hit her rear bumper, just enough to scare her. Her engine was built for economy, not speed, and no matter how hard she pressed the accelerator she couldn't seem to outrun the vehicle riding her back end. Praying for someone to show up and help was useless. This was a thinly populated road where half the residents were snowbirds. Getting help right now was in the region of impossibilities.

In the next moment the other vehicle bumped her again, much harder, causing her car to lurch to the side. Suddenly she was losing control, no matter how she wrestled with the wheel, and she veered off the road. She came to a stop in the deep ditch that ran alongside the road. The SUV bumped her once more before it pulled up and stopped in front of her at an angle, blocking her even if she could move.

What the hell?

The first thing that popped into her mind was Vincent Pellegrino's so-called one-car accident. Was this what happened to him? She was equal parts scared and pissed off. Scared because it was obvious whoever this was meant her no good. Pissed off because her day just kept going downhill and she was sick of it. She grabbed her cell phone, but dropped it because her hand was shaking. By then a man had climbed out of the SUV and was instantly at her side of the car. Another man appeared at the passenger side, boxing her in.

The one next to her knocked on her window, startling her so she dropped her cell phone again. She reached down to get it but the man on the driver's side banged on her window once more.

"Open the window," he barked in a harsh voice.

She shook her head, double-checked to make sure the doors were locked, and reached down again for her phone. The next thing she knew something hit the passenger window, hard. The window cracked and shattered into what looked like a million pebble-sized chunks that flew across the seat. Startled, she let out a little scream and pushed back as hard as she could against the seat.

The man on the driver's side knocked on her window again.

"If you don't want me to break this one, roll it down," he growled.

Devon shook her head. She knew she should probably be cowering in fright, except that wasn't her style, even in a dangerous situation. Surely someone would come along on this road, right?

She closed her eyes for a moment and when she opened them, the man on her side knocked on the window again and held up an iron bar.

"I'm not going to kill you, bitch." His voice was a low monotone, slightly accented. "Not yet. This was just to get your attention. Next time it could be your legs. Tell me where he is and I'll leave you alone."

"Please. I—"

"Do you hear me? Where has he gone? When you talk to him, tell him we'll be happy to have you as our guest until he shows his face. We know where to find you."

Devon slid her gaze from one to the other. The two men looked as if they'd kill her before breakfast and still eat a hearty meal. She opened her mouth but no words came out. She pushed back against her seat again as the man on the right started to reach through the broken window to unlock the door.

At that moment a four-door pickup zipped around the curve behind them and slowed, the driver obviously spotting the tableau on the side of the road. The truck passed both of their vehicles, then pulled over across the road and stopped. Was this backup for the two men already bent on terrorizing her or could fickle fate be sending her a savior?

* * * *

Logan Malik slammed on his brakes. On the right-hand side of the road, a car leaned into the ditch, a black SUV parked in front of it. Two men stood on either side of the car, and he could see the window on one side had been smashed out.

Logan's instincts, created from long experience, told him they weren't offering to help. He parked his truck on the opposite shoulder, checked to make sure his gun was loaded before tucking it in the small of his back, and jogged across the road.

A woman was trapped inside the car. Damn!

The man on the driver's side turned toward him. They were dressed identically in black jeans and black all-weather jackets despite the heat. Heavy sunglasses obscured their faces and they wore black ball caps pulled low over their foreheads.

Their posture was decidedly unfriendly.

Okay, Logan, defuse, defuse, defuse.

He just hoped the woman was sharp enough to play along with him.

"We have this under control," the man on the driver's side said. "You can go on."

"Whoa, whoa, whoa." Logan held up a hand and looked through the window at the woman. "What happened, sweetheart? I told you I'd follow you to town. You should have waited for me to get off the phone."

The look he gave her said play along.

The expression on her face was a combination of anger and terror. She wet her lips. "I'm so sorry. I didn't want you to rush your phone call."

Thank God. At least she was no dummy. But how the hell had she gotten herself into this situation?

He looked from one man to the other, his face expressionless. What the fuck was going on here? "What happened, babe? Did you take that turn too fast?"

Keep it up, lady. We don't want full-out war with these guys.

She looked from him to the man standing next to him and back to Logan again. Her faced was taut with fear, but the look in her eyes told him she had smarts and was using them. Maybe she figured if he got rid of these two guys she could handle one man herself.

"I, um, skidded on the road and ended up in the ditch."

"We're helping her," the man beside him said, his Spanish accent evident.

Logan gave him a look he hoped said get the fuck out of here or I'll bust your balls. As an agent at a private security and protection agency and former Marine, he'd taken down more than one man at a time before, men who were sharper than these two.

"This is your wife?" one of them asked. His voice was heavy with skepticism. If she'd been targeted specifically, they'd know she wasn't married, but maybe this would scare them off.

"Sure is. Thanks for stopping, guys, but I've got it from here."

They two men exchanged a look, as if deciding whether or not to take him out.

Logan glanced into the car. "Damn, sugar, you've got that glass all over you. Let me get my phone out, call for help." He lifted his shirt to reach for his phone in his back pocket, deliberately exposing the gun in his waistband.

The man next to him took a step back. Good.

"Oh, oops." Logan grinned. "Sorry." He reached on the other side and pulled out his cell.

But the man shook his head once to his partner, who looked like he was spoiling for a fight, and they backed away. Good. They were smart enough at least not to start a firefight on a public road, no matter now sparsely traveled it was.

"Sorry," he said. "We just stopped to see if we could help."

They strode back toward their SUV.

Logan pulled out his cell phone and began snapping pictures of the two men and their vehicle. He had barely lowered the cell when the vehicle took off with a screech of tires.

Then he turned to give the woman a good look. Even shock from the situation didn't detract from her appeal. Rich, thick sable hair pulled back in a ponytail accented her face with its delicate cheekbones, full lips, and smoky gray eyes framed by the thickest eyelashes he'd ever seen. Her body, with rounded breasts and hips, was a wet dream walking. She was definitely all woman, something he'd noticed the moment he'd approached her car. One hell of a woman, if he was any judge.

Unexpectedly his cock stiffened.

For fuck's sake, Logan. Get your shit together.

He wasn't as much shocked by his physical reaction as by the fact that it happened at all. For a long time now, he'd managed to keep a clamp on his sex drive and take it out only when required, like taking aspirin for a headache.

"You're a smart woman," he said. "I didn't know if you'd play along with me."

She inhaled an unsteady breath and blew it out. "I took a chance. You could have been worse than they were."

"Still, that shows brains and quick thinking. Good for you." He studied the interior of her car. "Wow. They did a number with that window. Don't move. There's chunks and pebbles everywhere."

She stared at him, studying his face. "You promise you aren't the second wave? You know, like good cop, bad cop? The bad guys threaten me and you come along and win my confidence by helping me?"

"Nope. Scout's honor."

"I, uh, saw that you have a gun."

"So did those jackasses. I wanted them to see it." He smiled at her. "But I only use it as part of my job."

She caught her lower lip in her teeth. "They just came at me out of nowhere and ran me off the road. Then they boxed me in and smashed the window."

"Later I'll want all the details. Right now let's get you out of here."

"Do you know who they are? Those men?"

"No." His voice hardened. "But I know other garbage like them."

She swallowed. "So who are you, anyway?"

"Oh. Sorry." He winked at her, and the tension in her body visibly eased. "Logan Malik. Savior of women in danger."

"Devon Cole." She dug up a smile. "Woman in danger who needed saving."

"I'd shake hands with you but I think you should sit very still." He nodded at the glass sprinkled all over her. "You've got some scrapes where the chunks of glass hit your arms but fortunately they aren't sharp enough to do more than that." He studied her face. "Miraculously none of it flew at your head, so your face is clear."

She blinked.

"Oh." She looked down, taking in the glass scattered over her lap, the seat, and the floor of the car. Then she then lifted her arms and looked at them. The safety glass had splintered into pebbles of all sizes, and she had some scrapes and bruises where they'd hit the unprotected skin. When she lifted a hand to brush off the ones clinging to her T-shirt and thighs, she was shaking.

"Adrenaline crash. Been there, done that. Take some deep, slow breaths and in a minute you'll be steadier."

"I'm fine," she assured him, although he was sure that was a big exaggeration. "Do whatever you have to."

And she has guts. I sure hope I find something wrong with her before I make a big mistake.

With a slow, deliberate movement he pulled open her car door and stuck his head inside.

"Hold on." He made his voice sound as reassuring as possible. "I want to get you out of here before your car lurches any farther into the ditch."

She cleared her throat. "I'm going to need a tow truck. And I should call Chief March. I need to report this."

"I'll do it. I'll make both calls. Also, I got a picture of their car and license plate, which I will ask my boss to run for me." He looked at her front seat again. "Your cuts should be looked at. So let me get things going here."

"I'm fine, really. A tow truck and a little first aid and I'll be fine."

He gave her high marks for not falling apart. He'd feel better if someone checked her over but he agreed there wasn't anything serious enough to require medical attention. Alcohol, a hot shower, and maybe a few Band-Aids should take care of it. He scanned the interior of her car again.

"Okay, but we do need to get you out of here before this thing rolls over."

She sat very still while Logan unlatched her seat belt. When he shifted and turned his head, his gaze locked with hers. Something hot and dark and mysterious surged between them. For a moment that stretched into eternity, they stayed like that. Then, whatever it was disappeared and he concentrated on easing her from the car.

With a combination of gentleness and strength he lifted her from the car and carried her to where his truck was parked.

"Is this what you do, Logan Malik?" Her voice was shaky. "Go around rescuing women in distress?"

"If they're in trouble. Especially beautiful ones." He opened his passenger door, and guided her onto the seat. "Stay right there, okay?"

He pulled out his cell and punched in some numbers. He felt her eyes focus on him while he gave the location to the tow truck driver.

"Yeah, out on Seacliff Road," he said into his phone. "Okay, good." He hung up and punched in the number for Arrowhead Bay Police.

"Chief March, please. Hey, Sheri, it's Logan." He quickly outlined the situation. "Yeah, I already called for a tow but can you call up EMS? The driver has some injuries."

"No." Devon shouted the word. "Please, Logan, if I needed medical attention, I'd be smart enough to tell you."

He studied her for a moment, then nodded his head. "Forget EMS. Oh, and hey. Will you call Avery? She might as well find out now what I stuck my nose into. Thanks." He stuck the phone back into his pocket.

Devon looked at him, frowning. "Avery? Sheri's sister? Why are you calling her?"

He grinned. "She's my boss. She likes to know when I get myself into trouble."

"Oh." She bit her lip, pulling her full bottom lip between even, white teeth. "You work for Vigilance, the bodyguard agency?"

He laughed. "Among other things. Hence the gun." He winked. "You never know when you might need good protection." He sobered. "Do you have any idea who those assholes were?"

"No." She shook her head. "I've never seen them before."

"Do you happen to have an idea what they were after? This didn't look like your everyday roadside mugging. In fact, I'd say they're some pretty nasty characters."

"I think they were looking for my father, but I have no idea where he is." Pain slashed across her face.

Uh-oh.

Like everyone else in Arrowhead Bay, he was well aware that at dawn this morning a Coast Guard cutter on patrol had found Graham Cole's sweet catamaran, *Princess Devon,* floating unoccupied about five miles from shore. The Guard was well into an intensive search for a body.

"You have any idea what scum like that would be doing looking for him?"

"I wish." She did that thing with her bottom lip again, and Logan gritted his teeth against the surge of lust that powered through him. Holy hell. He was more disciplined than that.

"No worries," he assured her. "We'll get you taken care of and make sure you're safe."

"I think you're already doing that. Anyway, Chief March—Sheridan—called me this morning and here I am."

"How come you didn't leave your stuff at the house? I saw everything still in the back seat of your car."

"I, uh, decided I wanted to see Sheri first. I realized I should have stopped there before heading out this way."

"Probably a good idea." He leaned against the frame of the truck. "You sure didn't need this on top of everything else."

But she was certainly handling it well, he thought. She was understandably frightened and dealing with the shock of her father's disappearance, yet she was holding herself together with a strength that impressed him.

She looked up and gave him an obviously forced smile. "I don't know what you were doing on this road, but I'm sure glad you were here."

"Me, too."

Chapter 2

The shrill sound of sirens announced the arrival of the police. Two cars turned around and parked behind Logan's truck. A young patrol officer climbed out of the first one, followed by Sheri March, who had driven the second car.

Devon always thought how unlike a chief of police the woman looked. Standing five foot five, she had a lean, compact body and a heart-shaped face, topped by fiery red curls. A lot of people had been fooled by her appearance and refused to take her seriously, even dressed as she was today in the familiar khaki shirt and pants of the police department. Most of them were still regretting it. Right now Devon was beyond glad to see her.

Sheri jogged up to Logan's truck and gave Devon an assessing look before she said anything.

"You okay, Dev?"

Devon nodded once. "I think so." She hated the fact her voice was still so shaky. "Thanks to this nice man here."

"Nice man, huh?" Sheri grinned at Logan. "I'll pass that along to my sister."

He shrugged. "All in a day's work."

Devon looked at Sheri. "Have you heard any more from the Coast Guard?"

"Yes, and no. Yes, I heard from them and no, there is nothing new." Her eyes were filled with sympathy. "I know this is hard, Devon, but Commander John Schnelling is experienced and he's been doing search and rescue for a long time. If your father is out there, he can find him."

Devon rubbed her arms, suddenly chilled, ignoring the soreness left by the chunks and pebbles of glass.

"I know, I just—I— Thank you, Sheri."

"You know we're doing everything we can, right? And we'll keep on doing it."

"Want me to take the report on this, Chief?" The patrol officer had moved up to stand beside them.

"Just get some shots of the scene before they cart her car away. I'll get as much as I can from Logan and the rest from Devon later."

"Sheri, I can answer questions now," Devon protested, although she really, really wanted to get off this road. Even the house with its eerie feeling looked better to her.

"No. If you're positive you don't want us to take you to the clinic, then let's get you home." She looked at Logan. "I'm sure you got a license plate number. Right?"

"Yes, but I'll bet it will either come back stolen or we'll find it's a dead end."

Sheri made a face. "Of course. These are no amateurs. What did they look like?"

Logan gave them a brief description of the men, more detailed than Devon knew she'd be able to.

"Devon, did they say anything to you?"

She nodded her head. "They wanted to know where *he* was. I assume the *he* is my father. And I'd better tell them or worse would happen."

She was surprised her voice sounded as steady as it did, considering her heart was still pounding with a combination of fear and anger.

Logan squinted his eyes against the sun as he looked back up the asphalt ribbon of Seacliff Road. "You just got here. How did anyone even know you were coming? Or when you'd be here?"

"I have no idea." She'd wondered the same thing herself. "The only person I spoke to was Sheri, and I don't think these guys hang out in her office."

"They could have been watching the house," Sheri pointed out.

"So why not try to corner me there?" Devon asked.

"Maybe that's what they planned," Sheri suggested, "but then they saw you leave."

Devon snapped her fingers. "The phone calls."

Sheri and Logan looked at her and spoke in unison. "What phone calls?"

Devon told them about the two calls she'd received.

"Checking on you," Logan pointed out. "You told them you were leaving the house. They decided to follow you and trap you on the road. There's hardly any traffic out, and they knew at the curve they could run you off into the ditch and corner you."

"In any event," Sheri added, "let's watch what we say, who we say it to, and who's around when we do."

"No kidding." Devon rubbed her forehead, trying to ease the building headache. Damn it. She had to pull herself together. If only she had some answers. *Daddy, what's happened to you?* She felt her throat tighten as tears threatened and forced herself to swallow. Then she remembered something.

"Sheri?"

The chief of police turned to her. "Yes?"

"While I was driving here, I kept trying to call my dad. The landline has no answering machine, but he has voicemail on his cell. It didn't answer, though."

"That's because he doesn't have it."

Devon frowned. "What?"

"We found it on the floor in the garage, the only thing out of place."

"But it still would have gone to voicemail, wouldn't it?"

"We think your father might have dropped it when he was leaving." Sheri paused. "Devon, he restored it all to its original factory settings. That's a good indication of premeditation on his part."

"But why? Maybe he was planning to get a new one and just didn't have a chance to pick it up."

"Anything is possible," Sheri agreed. "We're looking at every angle, I promise you."

"So you couldn't get anything from it?" she persisted. "Texts? Numbers? Nothing?"

"There is a way to get past the factory wipe and restore all the data on it. We're working on that right now."

"Working how?" And how fast, she wanted to ask.

"One option is a warrant to do whatever is needed to dig out the information still hidden there."

"And the other?"

"I want to talk to Avery about it, which is why it's still locked in my evidence lockers. No matter what, we're going to find out what happened." She touched Devon's hand. "I promise you that."

Logan crouched down beside her and looked at her intently, his eyes assessing her. For the first time, she got a good look at him.

His eyes were grayish blue like the ocean on a stormy day. Eyes a woman could lose herself in. Eyes that gave away no secrets about the man. They were framed by sinfully thick lashes that matched hair blacker than midnight, which hung to his collar. His chiseled jaw had just the right amount of scruff. A thin, nearly invisible white scar that traveled from his eyebrow to his jaw. Firm lips that teased upward in a half smile. And a body, leaning squarely over her, that looked to be all hard muscle that strained the fabric of his black T-shirt and his jeans. It could have been created by a sculptor. He was the most darkly gorgeous man she'd ever seen. She stared at him and felt as if a lightning bolt had struck clean through her.

Oh, God. The sizzle between them was so hot she wondered it didn't crackle in the air. Did he feel it just as strongly?

Damn, Devon. This isn't the time for this.

Then she thought, *I can't let him see what a mess I am inside.*

Sheri moved up beside Logan. "Listen, guys, I hate to pour more hot oil on this, but we've got another problem here. One more reason to get the hell off this road and get Devon inside somewhere. You've seen the reporters in town, right?"

He nodded. "Like rats after dead meat. They were here when the Coast Guard report went out and they went on high alert. Suddenly it became more than chasing the story about Vince Pellegrino's so-called accident. I heard them talking in Fresh Roasted this morning. There are no secrets in Arrowhead Bay."

"Graham Cole is a story all by himself," she reminded him. "The death of his vice president was all over the news and just stirs the pot even more."

"What death?" Logan narrowed his eyes. "I make it my business to stay away from the news except when it has to do with a client. You think this all has something to do with Cole International?"

"With a corporation that size," Sheri said, "all kinds of things are possible. I chased away all but a couple of the jerks, but if they sniff out that Devon's here, and find out about this…episode, they'll be hot after her."

Devon listened to them, the nausea growing inside her.

"Well," Logan drawled, "we just won't let that happen."

He started to say something else when yet another car pulled up and Avery March popped out of it. "Hey, Devon. How's it going?"

Devon's laugh was slightly hysterical. "Oh, great, Avery. Best day of my life."

She laughed. "Sheri told me my star employee is managing to keep himself busy. I figured I'd check it out for myself."

"And right now being busy means getting Devon's stuff out of her car before the tow truck gets here," he told her.

Devon looked at Avery. "I get the feeling from the way he handled my little incident he's probably in a class by himself."

Avery nodded. "You've got that right. He was in the Marines before he hired on with Vigilance." She leaned closer to Devon. "Don't tell anyone, but he knows twenty different ways to kill a man." She winked.

Devon's eyes widened. "You're kidding."

"Uh-uh. I'd definitely want him on my side."

Devon silently blessed whatever act of the fates had sent Logan to her…

and by extension, Avery…at just the right time. He had saved her, and that feeling of being protected flashed through her every time she looked at him.

It took him two trips but Logan soon had everything out of her car and stashed it in his truck.

"Thank you." She gave him a grateful smile.

"No problem." He winked. "I live to serve."

The noise of a heavy vehicle sounded and the tow truck lumbered up to where they were. The driver hopped out and greeted Sheri and Avery before asking everyone to move their vehicles so he could hook up Devon's car.

Devon thought one of the nicest things about a small town like Arrowhead Bay was the camaraderie. Sheri had told her once that after you meet someone here they're no longer a stranger. Right now that small-town atmosphere was steadying her nerves.

Not that Logan Malik wasn't doing his share in that department.

"Chief?" The patrol officer materialized. "You want me to take statements or are you doing it?"

"You got the pictures?"

He nodded. "And a diagram."

"Excellent. You can head on back. I'll take care of getting all the statements." She turned to Devon. "I don't want to drag you into the office after all this."

"Thank you."

Avery gave her a studied look. "I think if we get some coffee into you, it might settle your nerves. Although I have to say, you've done a damn good job of not showing them."

Coffee. That sounded wonderful. She would kill for a cup right about now.

Clanking sounds echoed in the air and when she looked over she saw the driver hooking up her vehicle. Logan and the sisters were huddled in discussion. She wondered what that was all about.

More clanging and grinding from the tow truck got everyone's attention.

"I've got 'er all hooked up," the driver called out, "and I'm ready to leave. I've got your cell number, Miss Cole. I'll call you when the mechanic assesses the damage."

"Thank you. Listen, where can I rent a car in this town?"

She couldn't be without wheels. Right now she'd get one of them to give her a ride back to the house, and she'd make a call and take care of it. She pushed herself out of the truck, then had to lean against the open door, surprised to find she was lightheaded and unsteady on her feet.

Avery was next to her in a hurry, reaching out to steady her. "You're okay. Take a breath. Delayed shock, and probably adrenaline crash."

"That's what Logan said before. Holy Hannah!" She put a hand to her forehead.

Avery looked her over to make sure she was steady on her feet. "What's up?"

"I need a ride back to the house."

"Devon, you can't go back to that house alone." Avery looked at her sister. "Right, Sheri?"

"Absolutely. Until we know what the hell is going on with your father, it isn't safe for you to be there alone. Those guys from today aren't finished with you."

She'd been afraid of that. "So what am I supposed to do?"

"I'll stay with her." Logan's deep voice startled her.

Devon stared at him. "What?"

He grinned. "Looks like you need a bodyguard. That's part of my job."

"B-But I can't pay you," Devon protested.

"Did I say anything about money?" He glanced over at Avery. "I just finished a job and I have nothing up on the books right now. This okay with you?"

Avery shrugged. "Hey, it's your time. And I agree she needs protection. God knows who else is out there waiting for her. And let's not forget the reporters hanging around."

"I—I don't know what to say." Devon was independent but she wasn't stupid.

Logan's mouth curved in that killer smile again. "Say 'Thank you, Logan. I'd love to have you stay at my house with me.'"

A little shiver of anticipation raced along her spine, making her wonder if she'd truly lost her mind. She needed to focus on something besides how sexy her new bodyguard was. But then she thought about what had brought her to this point. The chill that raced over her had nothing to do with sexual awareness and everything to do with fear.

Chapter 3

"If this is all settled, we need to get moving." Logan pulled his keys out of his pocket. "Avery, I need to stop by my place and get some things." He looked at Devon. "Avery and Sheri will take you out to the house and I'll be there right after."

"Like I said before, we'll get some hot coffee into you," Sheri said. "Maybe some food. My guess is you haven't eaten a thing."

Devon shook her head. "I just jumped right in my car and hit the interstate. But there's plenty of food at the house."

Avery shook her head. "We'll take a look but you need to get some food into your system."

Devon shook her head. Suddenly her hunger had disappeared. "I don't know if I can eat anything."

"Try, okay?" Her lips curved in a kind smile. "We can't have you passing out."

"Logan, would you stop by Fresh From the Oven and get a dozen of those muffins with all the chocolate? Devon should eat something and the sugar is good to combat shock."

"Will do." He cranked the engine in his truck and pulled out onto the road.

Devon swallowed. "Sheri, when do you think we'll hear from the Coast Guard again?"

"I wish I could answer that." Sheri took her hands and squeezed them. "But be prepared. If they haven't found him after three days, they'll call off the search. That's protocol."

"It's just that not knowing is a bear." She nibbled on her bottom lip.

"Come on. Let's get going and get you up to the house. You'll ride with me."

Clutching her purse, Devon climbed into Sheri's copmobile. As they drove back up Seacliff Road, she sat with her fists clenched in her lap, looking out the windows wondering if the black SUV would appear out of nowhere again.

"They're gone," Sheri said, guessing what was on her mind. "For one thing, there's too much traffic here right now for them to try anything. For another, you and Logan both saw enough of their faces to make them regroup before they give it another shot. By the time they do, you'll be situated with Logan glued to your side."

Logan! In her house with her. Right. The thought of that made the butterflies resting in her stomach decide to do a tarantella. She must be crazy to be so affected by the man considering the situation she was in. A man she'd known for, what, three seconds? Damn!

The minute they were inside the house, Sheri headed for the single-serving coffeemaker on the counter, then rummaged in the cupboards until she found the mugs.

"Here, sit." She nudged Devon toward the table and set a full mug in front of her. "Drink this."

Sheri had just seated herself with her own mug when Avery arrived.

"Whew! The barbarians are at the gates already." At the raised eyebrows, she added, "Reporters."

Every muscle in Devon's body tightened. "Are they here? Outside?"

Avery nodded. "Two of them pulled up the driveway behind me. Devon, you'll have to talk to them eventually, but right now you have nothing to tell them. They can spend their time pestering the Coast Guard or asking questions in town. They'll do both, anyway."

"Damn." Devon closed her eyes and took a breath. "I keep thinking I'll wake up and find out this is all a mistake."

"We wish. Sheri, can you get that nice young patrolman to come out here and throw some muscle around? Just until I get a new security system in here?"

"On it." Sheri unclipped the radio from her belt and called in to the dispatcher with what she wanted.

Devon managed a weak smile. "Thanks."

"Oh, and before I forget…" Sheri reached into her pants pocket and brought out a key ring. "To the house and both boats. The Coast Guard gave them to me for safekeeping. They were still in *Princess Devon*'s ignition."

Devon wrinkled her forehead. "So isn't that a sign he was on the boat and fell overboard?"

"Honey, right now it's a sign of nothing. Let's wait until we have more information."

"Waiting. Right. Something I've never been very good at."

"Once Logan gets here," Avery added, "we'll talk about a new sophisticated alarm system. Plus, Logan won't hesitate to throw some muscle around if need be." She blew out a breath. "Let me fix myself some of the good-smelling coffee and we can talk."

She had just finished filling her mug when the landline rang. Devon got up and reached for the instrument, a reflex, but Avery grabbed her arm.

"You don't know who that is. You wouldn't be getting calls for yourself at this house, right?"

Devon shook her head.

"So it's either the thugs Logan ran off, or others like them, or a reporter."

Devon jerked her hand back. "What should I do?"

"Answer it, but hold the receiver so we can both hear."

She nodded. "Hello?" She frowned when no one answered. "Hello? Is anyone there?"

Avery grabbed the phone from her, still holding it so they both could hear. "Who is this?" Silence greeted them. Finally whoever was on the other end hung up. Avery looked at Devon. "Is that like the call you got this morning?"

She nodded. "Same thing."

"One thing it tells us," Shari told her. "Whoever this is, they don't have your father. Otherwise they wouldn't be looking for him. And they want him pretty damn bad."

"Or more than one group is after him," Avery added, "and these people are pissed. And we still don't know how the death of Vincent Pellegrino factors into this. It's too damn coincidental for it not to."

Devon's throat was so dry she had to swallow twice before she could get the next question out. "More than one group?"

"Anything is possible," Sheri reminded her. "If we had some idea what the hell this is all about we might have better answers. And this house is so immaculate there isn't a sniff of a clue. I hope to hell we can get something off that cell phone."

"Do you think they'll come up here looking for him again?" Devon was almost afraid to ask the question.

"That's always a possibility." She gave Devon a reassuring smile. "But that's why you'll have Logan, plus a lot of other safeguards."

"If these guys are the same two who were at the marina," Avery commented, "they sure don't seem like the kind of friends Graham Cole would have. Apparently Gary didn't see anything out of the ordinary in two dirtbags asking about one of the town's leading citizens. Asshole."

Sheri made a rude noise. "I'm sure Gary didn't even process that. He's so clueless he didn't even know *Princess Devon* wasn't in its slip. I don't know why the owners even keep him on."

"My question would be how did they know to ask at the marina and what time of day were they there?"

Sheri leaned back in her chair. "Dev, you think you can go ahead now and tell us what happened? I want to know everything, from the minute you got to the house, the calls, whatever you remember."

Devon did the best she could, trying to remember every detail.

"They scared me shitless," she said, "but I did the best I could not to let them see it."

"Smart and with guts." Sheri squeezed her hand. "We'll see what we can find when we put out a description. Also, I'll be checking around town to see if they've been asking about Graham. And do it without raising everyone's curiosity more than it already is."

"I suspect those two have been keeping a profile so low it's practically nonexistent, though," Avery told her. She looked at Devon. "The first thing I want Logan to do when he gets here is a complete security assessment, so he can call me with what we need for your new system. We'll monitor it from the office. A breech will also send an alarm to Logan's watch."

"His watch?" Devon blinked. "It must be some watch."

Avery smiled at her. "It is. Believe me."

"This is just a nightmare." Devon rubbed her forehead. "You talked to my dad's friends, right? What did they have to say? They might know something, especially Cash Breeland. He was pretty tight with him." She thought for a second. "Also Earl Flannery. And Roy Parker. He was pretty tight with all of them. I can't think who else."

"Spoke to all three," Sheri assured her. "They were all just as shocked as you are."

"God. You'd think someone would have a clue."

"Roy said he seemed a little distracted at their card game last week, but other than that, nothing."

Devon rubbed her face. She'd been fighting off reactions to everything, but her body was losing the battle. She ached as if she'd been in battle and her insides felt like jelly. She had to pull herself together.

Sheri touched her hand. "It's okay to fall apart. Anyone who had a day like this would be hanging on by a thread."

"I guess. It's just not who I am." Nor had it ever been. Not even when her mother died, or when her father backed away from their relationship for more than a year. She'd allowed herself the moment of grief, then pulled up her big girl pants and moved forward. She'd always been like that.

"Maybe, but right now you have to give yourself permission to let go."

Easier said than done.

"If we just had some idea of the what and why here." Devon braced her elbows on the table and rubbed her temples with her fingertips. "Nothing seems to fit. An experienced sailor just doesn't fall overboard. A high-profile business executive doesn't just disappear. Men like my father don't hang out with the kind of people who would run me off the road. God! I just wish I knew what the hell was going on."

"And we're going to find out," Sheri promised her. "We don't have to rely on just my small department, either. I can hit up the sheriff's department for additional manpower. But Avery has offered to do anything we need, and I think for this I'm taking her up on it."

Devon lifted an eyebrow. "Is that okay to do? Mix public and private like that?"

Avery grinned. "We do work for the United States government. I think we can handle Arrowhead Bay."

They all knew Vigilance had the resources to tap into things that weren't readily available to your typical police department.

Devon let out a long breath. "Thank you so much." Not that she didn't have the greatest admiration for Sheri, but Arrowhead Bay had just a six-person police force. The most difficult things they handled were speeding tourists and bar fights during football games. Surely for something like this they needed more help.

Avery looked over at her sister. "So I'm guessing first on your list is the cell phone?"

Sheri nodded. "You've got staff and equipment that is way above anything us ordinary mortals have. But time is critical here."

"No problem."

"Good. When we leave here, I'll run it right over to you." Avery got up to brew another cup of coffee for herself.

Devon was only half listening. She kept sliding glances toward the front door, tuned in for sounds of Logan's arrival. Safe! There was that word again, along with secure. Grounded. She'd felt it from the moment he'd jogged over from his truck. All those things. How could she feel that about a man she'd just met? Hadn't even known more than an hour?

And now she was going to be staying with him in this house, just the two of them. Her hormones seemed to be doing battle for first place with the little ball of fear in her stomach. Crazy, right? But just as inexplicable as everything else in this insane situation.

And then he was there, his presence filling the room.

"Muffins." He placed a bag from the bakery on the table in front of Devon.

She inhaled the aroma of the fresh muffins, the scents of chocolate and cinnamon teasing at her nose even before she opened the bag. Surprisingly, she discovered she was hungry.

"Yum. That smells wonderful."

"They cure almost anything," Avery told her with a smile. "Thanks, Logan."

* * * *

Logan smiled at his boss. "No problem."

Then he took a hard look at Devon, seated at the table with her fingers wrapped around a steaming mug of what he assumed was coffee. She was still pale, and the tension surrounding her was so strong it almost vibrated in the air.

Back on the highway he'd been worried about her. For a few minutes, he was afraid she was going to fall apart. Now, however, she looked a little bit better. Her color still wasn't great but she looked more in control of herself. He had to give her high points for the way she was handling herself. He was glad when Sheri got up, found a plate for the muffins, and set them in front of her.

"Coffee, Logan?" Avery was standing by the coffeemaker.

"Not right now. I want to get the stuff into the house. Devon, what's the deal with a remote for the garage door? I don't want to leave my truck sitting outside."

"There are some in the garage," she told him.

"Some?" He lifted an eyebrow. "Most people just have one."

"I know, but my father was obsessed with them. Every so often he'd change the codes. He showed me how to reprogram them and if I was coming to visit, he would give me the new code. I asked him about it once, and he said people coming to the house could clone the remote so he changed the code after every visit."

And wasn't that just interesting. People only did that if they had something to hide and wanted to control whoever had access to them. Logan had been through that before.

"What kind of visitors did he have?" Avery asked. "Do you know? And how long did it go on?"

Devon scrunched up her forehead. "Let me see. It started about two years after he built the house, and I haven't the foggiest about visitors, beyond Cole International people. He never discussed them with me. Why?"

"Because that shows a high level of paranoia. That could be when things took an unexpected turn for him."

"That's what we're going to find out."

"God." She swallowed. "Okay, the inside door to the garage is right off the front hall."

It took him a few trips to bring in all his and Devon's things from his truck. She pointed him to her room and he chose the one across from it for himself. Better surveillance, giving him a direct line into her room if he needed it.

By the time he came back into the kitchen, Devon had a fresh mug of coffee and was making an attempt to eat a muffin. Then he excused himself while he scoped out the rest of the house. What he found—or didn't find—troubled him.

"You're right," he told Avery. "This house could have been wiped by a professional. Something's way off here."

Avery had just handed him a mug of coffee when Sheri's phone signaled. She listened for a moment, shock suddenly freezing her face.

"What is it?" Logan demanded.

"The boat." The way she looked at each of them made every one of his warning signals go off. "The *Princess Devon* is on fire.*"*

Devon's face turned white.

"On fire? But—But…" She looked up at Logan, who had moved to stand behind her chair, his hands resting on her shoulders. "How? Why?"

"We don't know," Sheri told them, "but the Coast Guard has to be notified, and I need to get down to the marina. The fireboat from Almonte County Fire Department is already there."

"I'm going, too." Devon jumped up, almost knocking over her coffee.

"No." Logan tried to push her back into the chair. "You don't need to be there."

"Damn it." She pushed his hands away and leaped up, almost knocking over her chair. "That's my father's boat. He disappears and suddenly his boat catches fire? Something doesn't add up, and I want to know what the hell is going on. Please, Logan."

"Devon, you've got a big target painted on your back," Avery reminded her. "What if someone did this to draw you out? Besides, you don't have a car."

"I don't care what you say," Devon snapped. "I'm going. Someone can take me or I'll walk."

Avery's *reasonable* voice wasn't going to work here. Logan could feel Devon vibrating like a tuning fork, and he was filled with an overwhelming need to protect her. Which might, considering the circumstances and her attitude, be a difficult job.

"I'll take her," he said. He'd rather have her glued to his side than running off even more recklessly. "She's going, so save your breath. We all need to get moving."

"Stay. Go. Whatever." Sheri threw up her hands. "I need to get down there." In seconds she was out the door.

Devon reached for her purse and turned back to Logan. "Well?"

"Okay." He held up a hand when Avery opened her mouth again. "Save it. I know when arguing is useless. Would you call the office and get a couple of our techs out here? Have them figure out the most complete security system we can install. And tell them to keep their eyes peeled."

"Done." She had already pressed speed dial for the office. "Go ahead. I'll meet you down there."

Logan could barely keep up with Devon as she raced into the garage and got into his truck. He had a feeling that if he hadn't punched the button to open the garage door, she'd have insisted he just drive through it.

"Hurry," she urged, hands clasped tightly in her lap.

Logan burned rubber backing out of the garage and heading down the driveway. Despite Devon's urging to hurry, he took care to look both ways and scope out the surrounding area as he reached the road. *And a damn good thing*, he thought, as he spotted a black SUV almost hidden in the trees across the road. When it pulled out behind them he grabbed his gun from his waist and pushed Devon's head down.

"Stay like that and don't move under any circumstance."

"What's happening? What—"

"Trouble. Just do me a favor and hang tight. Please."

He had to give her credit. She shut up and bent way down, just as he'd told her to do, even though he could feel the fear and anger vibrating from her. They hadn't gone fifty yards before something cracked against the rear of the truck cab, and he knew damn well it was a bullet. Last year he'd protected a very high-profile oilman whose life had been threatened. He'd taken his truck to Tactical Armoring Corporation in San Antonio and had it fixed up inside and out. Now he had bulletproof tires, and a vehicle reinforced against everything up to and including armor-piercing rifles.

He pressed harder on the accelerator, keeping one eye on the road and the other on the side-view mirror. If they could make it to the end of the road and take the turn to the marina, he figured they'd be okay because then they'd be in traffic. He hoped these idiots weren't stupid enough to engage in a firefight with a bunch of other people around.

A heavy thud sounded against the back of the cab, and Logan knew from the sound it was an armor-piercing bullet. Whoever these guys were, they came well equipped.

He watched the speedometer creep up to eighty, then ninety, then a hundred. He was sure the men behind them wanted to pull up alongside and try for the windows, but he kept ahead of them with his powerful engine. They were almost to the end of Seacliff Road.

"Hang on. Brace yourself."

He wrenched the wheel around, skidding into the turn, and then they were on the busy road to the marina.

Traffic forced him to slow down and when he looked in his mirror, he saw the other vehicle had turned off the other way. Smart. They didn't want people around for what they had to do. He had to tell Avery so they could revisit the security needs. A high-end system might not be enough.

"You can sit up now," he told Devon.

When the SUV pulled out behind them, she hadn't freaked, or panicked, or done anything he might have expected. She just did what he told her and left him to take care of business. He was afraid that wouldn't work at the marina, though, with tension rolling off her in waves.

As they neared the marina the traffic became thicker, and when they turned into the parking lot, he saw a thick cloud of black smoke rising into the air. The place was jammed, and not just with boat owners. Things like this drew everyone in this tiny little town. He managed to squeeze the truck into a narrow space but before he'd even shut off the ignition, Devon was already out. He barely caught her as he leaped out of the truck.

"Hold it. You don't move two inches without me. Someone just shot at us, remember?"

Every bit of color leached from her face. "They want to kill me."

He shook his head. "I think they want to kill me and get their hands on you. So for the immediate future, we're stuck together with glue."

Two of Sheri's patrolmen were barricading the gate that opened out onto the docks and doing their best to hold back the shouting crowd. In a moment two men he recognized as Vigilance agents joined them.

"It's okay," he told Deacon Broder, one of the Vigilance men. "The boat on fire is her dad's. Let us through."

That took a lot of squeezing to get past the pushing and shoving.

"Who are these people?" Logan asked.

"Some of them have boats in the slips near *Princess Devon*. We told them they can't go out on the dock yet, but they're maniacs."

"Yeah, I can see they're upset. I'll get Sheri to calm them down."

Devon was already running down the dock to where flames licked the air, mingled with the thick black cloud. Logan jogged down to catch her.

As soon as he neared the fire he could see that the boat was destroyed. Not even the hull was intact, floating in blackened pieces in the water. A small fireboat was in the water between the docks spraying the *Princess Devon* and *Lady Hannah*. Men in board shorts and Arrowhead Bay T-shirts were on the dock with hoses hooked up to spigots, spraying all the other boats in the area.

What a fucking mess.

Sheri was talking to a tall man in a uniform who he assumed was with the Coast Guard. He hated to interrupt her but she had to do some damage control.

"Sorry to interrupt, but Sheri, you need to calm the beasts down back there. Let them know when they can get to their boats."

She glanced back to the gate and nodded. "Okay. Logan, this is Lieutenant Commandeer Russell Deering of the Coast Guard. He's our new liaison while we wait to see what search and rescue does or does not turn up. Russell, Logan Malik is a top Vigilance agent. You can tell him anything."

"Hold on a sec, Sheri." Logan shook hands with the man and introduced Devon to him. "Could you keep an eye on her for a second? This is her dad's boat."

Deering lifted a quizzical eyebrow but nodded. "Sure."

Logan guided Sheri a few feet away. In concise sentences, he told her about the car chasing them down Seacliff Road and shooting at them.

"I think they were making another try at Devon. If they got rid of me in the process, so much the better." He rubbed the back of his neck. "I just can't believe how stupid they are to try something with the same vehicle. Although neither of them would win a contest for brains. We all need to be extra alert."

She nodded. "Did you tell Avery yet?"

He shook his head. "Haven't seen her but I will."

"Good." Then she turned and hurried down the dock to the demanding crowd.

Devon had been doing her best to get as close to the edge of the dock as she could, despite Deering's best efforts to keep her from it.

Logan grabbed her and pulled her back. "Don't want you falling in the water."

"He's right," Deering agreed. "Sorry about your boat, ma'am. But I do need you to stand back from the slip. That fire's not out yet and sparks are still flying."

Devon did as he asked, backing right up against Logan. She had her arms wrapped around herself as if shielding her body from the cold, even though it was in the nineties. She stood there, rigid, unmoving, just watching. Logan didn't give a fuck who was watching. He wrapped his arms around her, heartened when she didn't try to move away, and pulled her against his body. It was as much to give her warmth as it was to protect her.

He was busy every minute scanning the crowd, looking for the two men from this morning or anyone like them. He recognized some of the people. After all, he'd been living in Arrowhead Bay for two years. He was more interested in strangers, anyone who looked like they didn't belong. With all the snowbirds that was a little more difficult, but his eyes were trained to pick up nuances in stance and body movement. He also relied on his well-honed instincts. They hadn't failed him yet.

And all the time he was hyperaware of Devon's very appealing body pressed against his.

Deliberately he put all thought of her body out of his mind and concentrated on the here and now.

He was still convinced the fire was to draw her out of the house. Maybe they hoped in the crowd they could snatch her. Of course, it occurred to him whoever was behind this could hire a couple of locals to grab her, too. He was pretty sure they didn't want her dead until they found out where her father was. He'd be overly careful whenever they were out of the house.

At last Russell Deering, who had been watching and checking on things, walked back over to where they were standing, a look of sympathy on his face as he spoke to Devon.

"I'm sure I don't have to tell you the *Princess Devon* is a total loss. *Lady Hannah* can probably be salvaged but she'll need a lot of work."

"Do you know how the fire started?" Logan asked.

"Not yet. But we'll have a crew looking at what's left of it as soon as the fire is completely out. Miss Cole, we'll get a report to you as quick as we can for your insurance company."

"Insurance?" She tensed in Logan's arms.

"Yes. You'll need to file a claim for both boats." He looked at Logan, then back at her. "I know we have search and rescue out looking for your father. We still don't have any new information for you. We're still searching, but I'm sorry to say I'm not hopeful."

Devon drew in a deep breath and let it out slowly. "Thank you for keeping me informed."

"I want to go on board *Lady Hannah*," she told him as soon as Deering had walked away.

"I don't think that's a good idea right now. There are still sparks flying everywhere so the danger of fire isn't really over."

She bit her lower lip, a habit that tended to make him hard as a spike. "Do you think it will be all right sitting here like this?"

"Yes. There are too many official figures and too much of a crowd around here today. They might not even let you on it right now. Tomorrow would be better. You have the keys Sheri gave you, right?"

She nodded.

"Then I think we should go home and come back tomorrow. All you've had to eat today is a muffin and you don't want to get sick. Plus, I want to get you out of this crowd as soon as possible."

She shuddered. "Yes. All right. But—"

"But what?"

"What if *they're* waiting for us on the road?"

"Here comes Avery." He tilted his head at the figure walking down the dock. "We'll get her to send a follow car with us."

"A follow car for what?" Avery stopped next to them.

"A black SUV popped out of the trees across from the house and tried to shoot us off the road." He gave Avery a half grin. "Just in case they're waiting to try again, we need someone to follow us and cover our asses on the way back to the house."

"Okay. Good thing we're light on assignments this week. The crew is at the house working on the new security system. I told them to bring everything they could think of with them so they could get started right away."

"Good deal. Then I'll go ahead and take Devon home. Maybe I can even get some food into her."

"Everyone wants to feed me," she snapped, "but I don't have an appetite."

"Doesn't matter. You eat so you don't get sick. Come on. You'll only upset yourself more standing around here."

When he took her hand to lead her off the dock, he was pleased she didn't pull it away.

I'm just holding on to her for her protection.

Yeah, he could tell himself that all he wanted but he knew the real truth. And in the intimacy of the house he wasn't sure what would happen. He had a hard and fast rule—never, ever mix business and pleasure. But as a fellow Marine once told him on leave, rules were made to be broken.

Chapter 4

Logan took a good look at his truck when they reached it. There were some small dents but the armoring had held, thank God. He also took a minute to check the tires but again, as advertised, they were still intact.

"Damn good thing we had Tactical Armoring do their job last year."

Avery gave a mirthless laugh. "Of course, we never expected we'd need it in Arrowhead Bay. Okay, I'll have someone here in five."

He insisted Devon get into the truck, where she sat ramrod straight, her hands again clutched in her lap. He could tell she was holding herself together by a very short thread.

As soon as the Vigilance agents showed up he cautiously pulled onto the road, checking all angles. No black SUV or other vehicle that made his senses tickle. And no one shot at them on the way home, no doubt thanks to the tail car. Still, he kept his eyes peeled for any sign of anything the least out of place.

Three black vans were parked in front of the house and the techs from Vigilance were everywhere. As soon as he climbed out of the truck, Mike Bell, the crew chief, walked over to him.

"We're in warp speed here, Logan, just so you know. Avery said it has to be done yesterday."

"Thanks, Mike. I appreciate it." He turned to help Devon out. "Security system," he explained. "I think they'll have it finished today."

"'Kay." She looked and sounded as if in a trance. The moment they walked into the house it seemed all the starch melted from her body. She collapsed into one of the chairs at the table.

"I can't believe the boat caught fire."

"Not to add to your stress," Logan told her, making his tone as even as possible, "but it's possible it was actually blown up."

Every bit of color drained from her face. "Blown up?"

"We've got people shooting at us, Devon. That's not such a stretch of the imagination."

"It wouldn't be my father." She shook her head. "He loved that boat. Both of them."

"Desperate people do desperate things. But let's wait until we get a report. Meanwhile, I think you need to lie down." He waited to see if she gave him an argument.

"Okay." Her voice was so soft he could barely hear the word.

"Come on." He took her hand and guided her to her room, worried she'd pass out before they got there. "Let me help you."

"No, I can take care of myself. Really."

"I know you can," he agreed in a soft voice.

Devon Cole had a spine and grit and didn't fall apart in critical situations. But everyone had their tipping point, especially when people were shooting at them. He wondered when she'd reach hers. He figured he'd better be prepared for the meltdown.

She kicked off her shoes, dug in her suitcase, and pulled out some items of clothing before carrying them to the en suite bathroom. When she came out, she was wearing sleep shorts and a tank top, which did absolutely nothing for either his hormones or his control. He couldn't help noticing how firm and toned her legs were, her nicely rounded thighs. He had to tear his eyes away from all that wonderful flesh that peeked out below the hem of her top.

For fuck's sake, Malik. Take a step back.

When he pulled back the covers on the bed, she gave him a weak grin.

"I think I can handle this myself, Logan."

"Indulge me, okay? Let me just make sure you're settled."

She just looked so fragile, doing her best to pretend she was fine when they both knew she wasn't. He wanted so badly to wrap his arms around her and pull her tight to his body. Tell her everything would be all right. There were a couple of things wrong with that. One, she was a client, and two, he had no idea if that was the truth. Oh, and then there was three—his vow never to get involved again. That might be the hardest to keep.

She slid down in the bed and pulled the covers up to her chin, covering everything but her face. That was better. Temptation eliminated. She'd get some rest and he'd get a little distance from her.

Fooling yourself much, idiot?

He stood there and watched her close her eyes, eyes that made him feel as if he'd fallen into a pool of molten lava that scorched his body. In a moment her breathing evened out and she was asleep. Good. When she woke up he'd get some soup into her. Despite her condition, he'd have to ask her a lot of questions about her father. And he wanted her fortified. It was often the smallest, least significant details that held the most important clue.

In the kitchen he found a pot and dumped in the container of homemade soup he'd brought from home with his other stuff. He'd learned a long time ago that between missions he needed something that was a total change, something that got his mind away from bloodshed and mayhem and man's inhumanity to man. He'd started it when he was a Marine, whenever they were on base and he had a kitchen to use. It eased the stress of their assignments. After his buddies finished ragging him about it, they'd been more than happy to eat whatever he cooked as a change from the mess hall. He'd kept it up when he left the Marines, always making double batches of everything and freezing part of it.

As he stirred he thought about Devon's reaction today, the way she handled a bad situation. She reminded him of a different woman in another time and another place. The same intelligence. The same bravery, the same determination not to lose control. The same sense of independence. The same instant, deep connection.

Amanda.

God!

Her death had nearly destroyed him, leaving him wrapped in guilt that his own actions had prevented him from saving her life. He hadn't felt or wanted a connection to another woman since then.

When he left the military, he took the job at Vigilance, one he dedicated himself to with the same force as the Marine Corps. The job was a perfect fit for him. The work satisfied him and made use of the skills he'd acquired in the service: reconnaissance, situational assessment, and combat operations. He was pretty sure there weren't too many places looking for people who were expert marksmen, knew at least two dozen ways to kill a man, and had skills that fit the bill for most black ops agencies.

Of course, he had no personal life, so he was free to take any and all assignments. That left him less time to think about the past and remember things he couldn't seem to forget. Been there, done that, and still carried the pain. If he did have free time, he used it working out in the Vigilance gym or practicing on the gun range.

I sure am a well-rounded person.

He snorted at the thought.

Not having a personal life worked to his advantage. Nothing to distract him when he was on the job, and no one he had to worry about. For him those days were long past. He never, ever entertained even the tiniest thought of becoming involved with anyone in his care. Not with his body and certainly not with his heart.

And now, here was Devon, about to turn his life upside down.

Logan knew all about her family situation. Everyone in Arrowhead Bay did. Until six years ago, the Cole family lived in Tampa. Devon still lived there. But then her mother passed away and a year after that Cole International had gone through a huge cash crunch. Many said it was because with the death of his wife, Graham had lost his focus on the business. Then, miraculously, he'd acquired a new partner, a silent one, and everything turned around.

So what had kicked off the current situation? Who was after him? Who had him? Where the fuck was he?

Avery would already have people running a search on Graham Cole so thorough they could even tell you how many hairs he had on his ass. Vigilance had the best of everything—sophisticated electronics, weapons, training sites, personnel. When Avery March approached him about joining Vigilance, she had sold him after one visit. He'd never regretted signing on.

He was glad Sheri had turned over the cell phone to Avery. She'd put one of her best techs on it right away. Time was at a premium. There was no telling when these assholes would make another try at Devon, and they needed some idea of what they were dealing with.

When the doorbell sounded, he turned the soup down and hurried to answer it before Devon woke. Through the peephole, he saw Mike Bell.

"How about coming out to eyeball this?" he asked.

"Sure. Let's take a look."

Logan figured even the richest oil baron would be safe in this place when his guys got through. Sensors on all the windows and around the door, motion sensors around the perimeter, plus scattered on the wide lawn, cameras at every possible place. And three high-tech computers to receive the feeds.

"Think that'll do it?" Mike asked, holding the diagram for him to see.

"Damn straight. How long until it's in working order?"

Mike looked at his watch. "Most of it before dark tonight. We'll finish up the odds and ends in the morning."

"None of those odds and ends would let someone in overnight, would they?"

Mike chuckled. "In their dreams. Even at half-mast, we're good to go."

"Great. Thanks. And tell Avery thanks."

He filled a mug with coffee and went to stand at the window, letting everything he knew—which was damn little—roll around in his head. What if that whole thing with the boat had been staged? What if someone went to a lot of trouble to make sure it looked like a voluntary disappearance? That someone would have to be smart and used to doing things like that. He thought about the house alarm system being disabled. That was easy enough to do, even from a distance if it wasn't sophisticated enough. Electromagnetic pulse systems, EMPs, had become common tools for such jobs. Had Graham done it, to throw people off the track?

If it wasn't him and it wasn't whoever owned the guys from the highway, did that mean there was a third player? Who the fuck was it? What did he want with Graham Cole? If there was indeed an unknown player here, that could mean Devon was in even more danger.

He turned off the soup on the stove and decided to do a more thorough room-by-room search while she slept. You never knew what you'd find. A lot of people dismissed the idea that houses had "feelings" in them, a sense of good or evil. Logan believed in them, in his gut reaction to things. This house had a bad feeling in the air.

He checked every inch of the closets, the shelves, the furniture, even under the beds. He took the time to go through the clothes hanging in the bedroom closet, searching for anything that might have been left in a pocket. He'd learned through experience that even when people thought they'd been thorough, they invariably left something behind.

He even pulled out the drawers in Graham Cole's desk to see if there was anything hidden there. His efforts turned up a big fat zero. There was nothing. A black ops team couldn't have sanitized this place better. He was sure Cole was the one who'd done it. The two idiots who ran Devon off the road couldn't find their asses with both hands.

He'd left nothing containing any information at all. Not even on paper. If he was that thorough, he was either in deep shit or running from some very bad people or both. The only aberration was that he'd dropped his cell phone and hadn't realized it. Logan could only guess that something drastic had happened to make the man leave in such a hurry that he'd made a mistake like that.

As Logan cleared each room, the feeling of evil intensified. He wasn't a person given to supernatural things by any means. But in the Marines, he'd learned to trust his instincts about everything. That sense had saved his life more than once. Something bad had happened here. Maybe more than one something. Whatever Graham Cole had done, whatever happened the day he disappeared, it left its imprint here.

He spent another fifteen minutes checking out the garage. There was room enough for four vehicles. Right now it held a Porsche as well as a motorcycle. There was a slot for the Mercedes that had been impounded and one open slot he assumed Devon used when she was here. Or any visitors he had. That was another thing. Who visited him here? Did he have out-of-town company? Devon said he told her he held business meetings here but with who? What kind of business? He wanted to make sure he wasn't missing anything.

It galled him that the man had left his daughter to deal with the fallout. Didn't he think whoever was after him would shift the focus to her when they couldn't find him?

He wondered for one brief moment if Devon could possibly be involved. Then he brushed it aside. He didn't believe it. Even more, he didn't *want* to believe it. She hadn't given off any vibes that indicated she was. Certainly today's episode should be a good indication she wasn't. Still, in the back of his mind he knew he had to at least entertain the idea that she was a part of this, of the man's disappearance. From day one in the Marines he'd been taught the detail you missed was the one that could kill you. So he always examined all angles.

His phone rang just as he finished. He looked at the readout. Avery.

"They're really humping it getting the alarm system installed," he told her. "Thanks for getting right on it."

"I told them it was urgent. These guys are fast. You know that."

"Did you learn any more at the dock?"

The sound she made was close to a snort. "I wish. Russell Deering and I know the fire chief, so they'll fax reports over to me as soon as they have anything to tell. I think you're right. The fire was set to draw Devon out, especially given what happened on the way to the marina. But just in case there's something else going on here, I've got Angel hanging out on the dock, in his board shorts and T-shirt, helping with the hoses and cleanup."

"Good, good." With his Hispanic ancestry, in a state with a heavy Hispanic population and cultural influence, Angel Cabrera easily blended into any place she sent him. He had a gift for getting people to tell him things without realizing it.

"And we're working on the backgrounds of the Cole International execs. Do you have everything there you need?"

Logan had his own personal weapons with him—a Glock 19, a Ruger LCP, and his Ka-Bar knife. They were like old friends, and he could handle anything with them.

"No, I'm good. I'm hoping we don't get into an all-out shooting war. How are you coming with the phone?"

"We've just gotten started with it. First of all, it's not an ordinary cell phone. It's made by a company like the one that makes ours."

"So it's ten times as hard to crack."

"That's right. We got past the factory restore and there's data on it, but it also seems to have multiple passwords."

Logan snorted. "Can you say paranoid? Now I'm sure there's shit on it we need."

"I've got Del on it. He's got it hooked up to a bunch of different programs at the same time. If anyone can break it, that would be him."

"Okay. Keep me in the loop on that."

"Ginger's been digging into Graham Cole with an electronic shovel. I want to know everything from the past ten years, personal and corporate. There's a clue somewhere and I mean for us to find it. I'll bet we find a lot of unpleasant crap there."

"I hope we find something soon," he told her. "I don't think they're near done with her."

"And that's why you're there, Mr. Marine."

"Ooh rah."

Avery laughed. "How is she, anyway?"

"Sleeping. I hope you get into that cell phone pretty damn quick. I have the feeling it holds the key to a lot of things."

"We're working on it. Just like I said two minutes ago."

"I know, I know." He raked his hand over his hair. "I just have this hinky feeling there is something dangerous we need to be prepared for."

"If it forced Graham Cole to disappear, you can damn well be sure it's dangerous. I'll keep you posted."

"When you have something, I think we need to show it to Devon, too."

"Okay. Sure." There was silence for a moment. "Are we sure we want her to see whatever we find out?"

"I think she has to know," Logan told her. "She's smart and no shy violet. Whatever it is, she can handle it."

"I agree. Whenever I've spent time with her, I got that same impression. That lady's really got her act together. I'm sending a file on her to your laptop. Check it in a few minutes."

Logan lifted his eyebrows. "A file on Devon? You have one already?"

Avery chuckled. "Logan, there wasn't much info to gather. She leads a pretty normal life."

Of course she did.

"And Logan?"

"Yeah?"

"Keep her safe."

"Count on it."

He stashed the cell and decided to go check on Devon. As he headed toward the bedrooms he heard retching and followed it to her en suite bathroom. The door was partially closed so he eased it open the rest of the way. She was on her knees at the toilet, dry heaving, her body shuddering. He wasn't at all surprised. She'd held it together remarkably well, when many other women would have been basket cases. A meltdown was not at all unexpected. He grabbed a washcloth from a towel rack and wet it, handed it to her, and hit the flush lever.

"Here." He spoke in a soft voice. "You'll need this."

"Oh, God." She looked up at him. "Thank you. I think I'm too sick to be embarrassed."

"Nothing to be embarrassed about. Delayed reaction. Happens to all of us."

She gave him a weak smile. "Even former Marines?"

"Even." He ran water into a cup, took the washcloth from her, and handed her the drink. "Swish this in your mouth. It helps."

Her body shook so much he had to steady her with his arm. He managed to get her to rinse her mouth before lifting her to her feet and bracing her with his arm. He wet the washcloth again, ran it over her face, then lifted her in his arms.

"So much for the muffins and coffee."

He had to give her points for trying to make a joke.

"Okay, then. Let's get you back to bed."

She shook her head. "You can put me down. I won't fall on my face. Honest."

"Promise?" He winked at her, trying to lighten the atmosphere.

She held up three fingers. "Scout's honor. I'm afraid if I crawl back under the covers, I won't get out until morning, and I know I need to eat. Are you cooking something in the kitchen? Whatever it is smells fabulous."

"Logan Malik's famous chicken noodle soup."

"Mmmm. Sounds good. But first I need to take something for this headache."

He sat her on the edge of the tub while he found aspirin and made her swallow two of them. She drained the glass, then splashed water on her face, inhaled, and let the breath out slowly. She patted her face dry with a towel and tried to smile at him.

Logan made a silent vow he would do his damnedest to make sure she was safe and to help her through this. Too bad for him what he really wanted was to wrap his arms around her and hold her tight against him.

As a comfort, he told himself silently.

Yeah, right. Fooling yourself much, Malik?

"Okay." Her lips curved in a tiny smile. "Heat up the soup. I'll be out in a minute."

Chapter 5

Devon's sleep had been anything but restful. If she hadn't been worn out from the shock of what happened, she might have slept longer. But the black SUV and the two men kept intruding into her dreams. One minute they were running her off the road, and the next they were chasing her and Logan and shooting at them.

She looked at herself in her bathroom mirror and made a face. She was paler than a hospital sheet, and fear had stamped dark shadows beneath her eyes.

"Pull up your big girl panties," she ordered herself, and headed into her bedroom.

The clothes she'd worn carried the odor of smoke and burning oil from the docks so she tossed them onto the floor of the closet to wash later. She pulled on a fresh pair of jeans and a soft cotton long-sleeved shirt, brushed her hair, and pulled it into a neat ponytail. She looked in the mirror again and made a face. Better but not much.

The pleasant aroma of the soup tickled her nose and her stomach grumbled. The soup sounded better and better. As she made her way into the kitchen she heard Logan's voice. Was someone here? God. How many people would she have to face before she had her act together? But when she walked into the kitchen, she saw he had his cell phone to his ear.

"Devon's up," he told whoever was on the other end of the conversation. "Gotta go." He stuck his phone in his pocket and looked her over. "Much better."

She made a face. "And you're a big fat liar, but thanks. Who was on the phone?"

"Avery. Here. Come sit down." He guided her to a chair at the table. "Let me dish up some soup for you."

"The housekeeper always keeps the pantry fully stocked, although I'm not sure who eats half the food. But I'm pretty sure we won't starve while we're here."

"I'll check it out and see what we can find for dinner." He found a bowl in one of the cupboards, filled it with soup, and placed it on the table with a spoon.

His smile threatened to curl her toes.

"Chef Logan's award-winning chicken noodle soup for you."

She stared at him, eyes wide. "You really made this?"

He shrugged. "Everyone needs a hobby. A long time ago I discovered fiddling with recipes was the best stress reliever I could find. I always have stuff in my freezer. I figured with the way things were going this might just be what you need."

She would have kissed him if she wasn't so stressed out, and worried what he might think. Or not think. Instead she just wet her bottom lip, gave him a smile, and whispered, "Thank you."

The soup was everything he said it would be—just a tad spicy and loaded with tender chunks of chicken and broad noodles.

"Okay, what did Avery say?"

He sat down at the table at an angle to her. "Please promise me you will not freak."

"Oh, God." She dropped her spoon in the bowl. "Don't you know that's guaranteed to make me freak?"

"Sorry." He captured her free hand with his warm one. "Just take a breath, okay?"

She drew in a deep breath and let it out, willing herself not to shake. "Okay. Let's have it."

"The divers salvaged several pieces in the water. Devon, they found a few small remnants of a timer. That boat was blown up on purpose."

For a desperate moment, Devon was afraid the small amount of soup she'd eaten would come back up in a rush. She swallowed hard and took another breath.

"Blown up. With a bomb."

"Yes. Avery tried to get all the pieces so she could get her people on it, but the Coast Guard claimed it. Deering promised Sheri and Avery to get them info as fast as he could."

"Can they trace anything with as little as they have?"

Logan shrugged. "Sometimes that's all you need. It depends. But we're on top of it, I promise you."

"Logan, you know what that means?"

"It means a couple of things. I don't believe your dad blew up his own boat. Either whoever is controlling our favorite thugs did it to send him a message, or there's a third player in the game and we don't know who that is."

"God." She closed her eyes and rubbed her face. "This just gets worse and worse."

"But at least we're collecting more threads to pull." The smile he gave her took the edge off her nerves. "And the crew outside is almost finished with the new security system. At least we won't have to worry about people sneaking up on us here. By the time your soup is gone, they'll be ready for me to give you the tour. Now eat, and that's an order."

Finishing the soup was no hardship. So Logan was a cook. She'd never have imagined that. She guessed everyone had their own surprises. If he was this good, maybe she could talk him into cooking for them while he was here. Lord knew her own culinary skills left much to be desired. Whatever she ate had one requirement, easy and fast to fix.

She had just finished the last spoonful when the landline rang again, startling her. She dropped the spoon in her bowl with a clatter and stared at the offending instrument.

Logan wrapped his fingers around her wrist. "Don't answer that."

"Don't worry. I have no intention of it."

He lifted the receiver and barked, "Hello?" Pause. "Hello? Listen, if you have something to say, spit it out. Otherwise quit calling." Another pause. "Hello? Okay, we're done."

He placed the receiver back in the cradle with a deliberate motion.

"Was that—"

"An asshole who thinks he can intimidate you."

She chuffed an unsteady laugh. "He's not far from wrong."

"Don't worry about him. I'll take care of it." Logan looked at her soup bowl. "Good. Come on, I'll show you what's going on."

She carried her empty bowl to the sink, rinsed it, and stuck it in the dishwasher. When Logan took her hand to lead her outside, she didn't protest. His hand was strong and warm and the contact made her feel more secure than she had since she'd received the first call about her father.

The same vans were still parked in front of the house, the men in jeans and black Vigilance T-shirts busy with whatever they were doing. She wondered for a crazy moment if she'd fallen into a reality television show where all the men dressed in black. God! What was wrong with her mind?

"I told Avery I want the most complete security system she can install. We're placing rotating cameras at all corners of the house." Logan released her hand and pointed them out. "Some of them are long range. They'll catch anyone in the vicinity and approaching the house. And we have others located in trees." He pointed to one man up in a tall palm tree and another crawling around on the roof of the house. "Everything will feed into the house to three high-tech computers—one in the kitchen, one in the den, and one in my bedroom."

"Your bedroom? Really?"

He pointed to two more men crawling around on the ground, each with a large canvas bag. "Sensors. Anyone steps foot on the property anywhere, the sensors will trigger the alarm system. If by some electronic miracle, they get past those, I'm also placing sensors on all the windows and doors. If someone tries to get in at night and I'm already in my room, I want immediate access to the cameras to see who it is."

Devon shivered and wrapped her arms around herself.

"Cold?" Logan looked at her. "Need a jacket?"

She shook her head. "It's at least ninety-five outside. I'm just having a hard time with the reality of the situation. All this"—she swept her hand to indicate the grounds—"the equipment, the phone calls, everything that happened today. I keep getting the sense I'm trapped in a nightmare. If my father did this deliberately, didn't he know how it would affect me? I can't imagine what kind of trouble he could be in that would make him do this."

"When people are pushed to the wall with no place to go, they do desperate things," he reminded her. "The question is what devil is he running from?"

She looked up at him and frowned. "I wish I had the answer."

"We'll find it," he assured her. "If anyone can, Vigilance will get the answers." He studied her face. "So, just to cover all bases, is there a strange face that might be showing up here that I should keep from shooting?"

"Strange face?" Devon pinched her eyebrows together. "I don't understand what you mean."

"You know, someone special in your life? Semi-special?"

Devon laughed. She couldn't help it. The men she dated always told her she was too wrapped up in her work, or too independent, or too…something. Translated, she didn't fawn all over them or show proper appreciation for their prowess in bed. Obviously she had a knack for making poor choices where men were concerned.

"No, no one special. No one at all."

God. Could she have sounded any more pathetic? And was that a tiny smile twitching at the corners of Logan's mouth?

"Good to know." He cupped her elbow. "Let's take a look at the rest of this."

When they were through walking the outside, he guided her back into the house. Two men were in the front hall. They had removed the panel from the old security system and were in the process of installing one that looked capable of flying a spaceship.

Devon gave a nervous giggle. "I hope I can figure out how to use that thing."

"No worries. I'll make sure of it. I—" His cell rang, cutting off whatever else he was going to say. "Yeah? Uh-huh. No kidding. Uh-huh. All right. We'll be ready for them."

"What?" Devon asked when he hung up. "Who was that?"

"Sheri. Two guys in very expensive suits from Cole International just left her office. They're on their way here."

"What did she say about them?" Devon worried her lower lip between her teeth.

He snorted, a derisive sound.

"They're typical corporate stuffed shirts who look like they have a stick up their collective asses. They asked a ton of questions, told her absolutely nothing, and weren't very friendly."

Devon frowned. "I just thought of something. They might have a copy of the insurance papers for the boats. Russell Deering was right. I'll have to file a claim and I have no clue who insures them or anything."

"Let's get more information before you worry about filing claims." He squeezed her hand again. "Maybe we'll be lucky and your dad will turn up by then."

"God. Don't I wish."

"Anyway, Sheri gave them a copy of the Coast Guard report from this morning and any other information she had, and they took off like their pants were on fire."

"Lovely. I can hardly wait to meet them. I'm sure they'll be a gigantic pain in the ass, especially since I have nothing I can tell them."

"Ahhh, but they might have something to tell you," he pointed out. "I'm damn well going to pump them as much as I can."

"Well, bring it on." She got up to make some coffee. "Want some?" she asked over her shoulder.

"I think I'll wait until our visitors leave."

"Okay, but I'm stoking on caffeine." She took a sip of the hot liquid, aware she needed to be tough. This meeting wouldn't be any picnic.

As if she'd conjured them up from her mind, the doorbell rang.

"Okay, Devon. Here we go. If anyone asks, I'm your security detail." She giggled. "Okay."

In an unexpected move, he pulled her against him and wrapped his arms around her.

"Your body is humming like a high-tension wire. It'll be fine," he promised. "You can handle it. You're a tough cookie."

The doorbell rang again, twice, as if the person pushing it was impatient.

"I guess they don't like to be kept waiting," she joked. "I'm good." That seemed to be turning into her favorite mantra.

When Logan opened the front door, she saw two men standing there, men who could have popped from the same factory. Both were tall, well groomed, dressed in dark suits with fine linen shirts and silk ties and carrying expensive-looking leather briefcases. Working for Cole International obviously paid well.

"We're here to see Devon Cole," the one on the right said.

"Identification, please."

Logan made it a statement, an order, not a question or a request. After this morning's episode, Devon was glad he wasn't letting anyone in the house without some verification of who they were.

He took the business cards they handed him and studied them carefully. Then he stepped back and gestured them inside but only as far as the foyer.

"I'm Craig Alford," the one on the right said. "And this is Wilson Bodine. Corporate attorneys for Cole International. We weren't aware there was anyone in the house besides Miss Cole." He glanced toward the living room where Devon was sitting.

"Is that a problem?" Logan's voice and face were expressionless.

Devon wondered what they might have to say that made them so picky about who heard it.

"No problem at all." Wilson Bodine shook his head. "Of course not. But under the circumstances we have to be careful who we discuss anything with. I'm sure you understand it's a delicate situation. We've already had to deal with some of the media who got wind of this. This is very bad publicity for Cole International."

"Which is why we need to understand your role here," Alford added in a stiff voice.

"I'm her security detail."

"Her what?" Alford's voice almost squeaked the word.

"Security detail?" Bodine repeated. "How about some identification from *you*, just to be sure you're who you say you are?"

Devon stifled a snicker at their outrage.

Logan flipped open his wallet and showed them his Vigilance identification.

"Then I'm guessing," Bodine said, "you have something to do with all those people outside?"

Logan nodded. "New security system."

"Is there something here that we aren't aware of?" Alford asked.

"I'm sure there are a lot of things," Logan told him. "But first, how about telling us why you're here."

Bodine, who seemed to be the one in charge, stepped forward. "If we could sit down, we could discuss this more privately."

"Yes, of course. Come in and have a seat."

Devon was more than grateful for the security of Logan's quiet presence as he introduced the two men to her. They carried an air of hostility that she didn't understand and it immediately put her on the defensive. What did they have to be hostile to her about? They had questions? She had a few of her own. She sat stoically on the edge of her seat, hands folded in her lap, watching as they seated themselves across from her. She was glad Logan didn't ask them if they wanted coffee. She certainly wasn't about to play hostess.

"What can I do for you, gentlemen?" She looked from one to the other. "This is a very difficult time for me, as I'm sure you can understand."

"And for Cole International," Alford told her.

"I have no connection with my father's corporation. I barely know anything about it. But I'm his daughter, so this situation is particularly upsetting for me."

The two men exchanged another look.

"When was the last time you saw your father?" Craig Alford asked.

"Three weeks ago. Why?"

"Did he discuss any problems he was having? Anything that was bothering him?"

Devon frowned. "Like what? You probably spoke to him more than I do. I was hoping you could tell *me* something that would help me understand what this was all about. That's not why you're here?"

"Anything you can remember at all, Miss Cole," Bodine persisted, ignoring her comment. "Any little fact you can think of."

"If there's something specific," Logan broke in, "maybe you could dial us in on it and we could be more help."

Craig Alford cleared his throat. "I'm more interested in anything he might have told you. Something he might not have discussed at the office, or with his executives. Anything he might have given you to hold for him."

Devon looked from one to the other. "I'm not sure I understand what you're looking for."

"Okay." Logan leaned forward. "You want to let us in on what the hell is really going on here? What aren't you telling us?"

Devon thought if Alford and Bodine exchanged one more look she might smash their faces.

"Please understand what we're dealing with here." Bodine was obviously choosing his words carefully. "Cole International is a business of some significance. We came down here specifically to ask you what you know about your father's disappearance and what information you can give us. Any personal papers or anything he gave you for safekeeping. On top of Vincent Pellegrino's death, we're dealing with some very precarious things."

"What precarious things?" she demanded.

"I'm sure you understand there are things we can't discuss. We—"

"If you can't discuss them," Logan said, "then what the hell are you doing here upsetting Miss Cole? We thought you were here to see if you could be of any help."

"We're sorry," Bodine said in a stiff voice. "But we need whatever information she can give us."

"I don't have any." She held out her hands, palms up. "Don't you understand? You probably know more than I do."

"Perhaps," Alford said, "if we could look through your father's office to see if he left anything that would point us in the right direction, that would help us all. Maybe even give us some answers about the fire. We heard about that from Chief March." He shook his head. "Terrible, terrible thing."

Devon stared at them, stunned. "You want to go through his private things? I think not. Surely everything dealing with Cole International is available in his office at corporate."

"Yes, well." Bodine pressed his lips together.

"What aren't you telling us?"

"Look, Miss Cole." Craig Alford's voice had softened. "We don't mean to make things unpleasant here. We appreciate your emotional distress and we're sorry we have to bother you right now. But there are things going on that aren't for public information. If Graham Cole did a disappearing act with critical information, we have a real problem."

Her eyes widened. "You don't think—"

"We don't think anything. Right now we're looking for answers."

"Well, I have none to give you." Devon clenched her fists. "I thought maybe you were here to see if you could help me."

Logan covered her clenched fists with his large hand and gave them a gentle squeeze.

"Never mind, Devon. We're not getting anywhere here. They aren't going to tell us anything, anyway." He paused. "Are you aware Miss Cole was attacked on the road on her way into town to see the police? Maybe the two situations are related. Would you happen to know anything about that? I'm very concerned for her safety."

If she hadn't been looking, Devon might not have caught the look of shock on their faces replaced by one of anger and then quickly wiped away.

"That's damn insulting," the one named Bodine growled. "Why would we know?"

Devon caught the underlying tone of panic. *Interesting*, she thought.

Logan shrugged. "I don't know. You tell me."

"Dial it back, Wilson." Alford cleared his throat. "Of course it's a given that her safety is important. I assume, Malik, that's why you're on the job?"

"It is. To protect her from everyone." His voice was edged with sarcasm.

"It's just important that we get on top of this," Bodine told her. "I'm sure I don't have to tell you how critical that is. Your father is the face of Cole International. His disappearance raises a lot of questions with everyone. We can't just leave things hanging." He paused. "For example, do you have his power of attorney?"

Shock ratcheted through her. "Power of attorney? Why would I have that? Wouldn't it more likely be someone at Cole International? One of you as the corporate attorneys? Or maybe his personal one?"

Alford shifted uncomfortably.

"Mr. Cole recently changed personal attorneys. We discovered it when we contacted the one he's had for years. Graham gave him a written request for all the files, both print and digital."

Logan frowned. "And he wouldn't tell you where he sent them?"

"Graham took them with him." Bodine practically spat the words. "He had all the digital files copied onto a thumb drive and then stood there while a paralegal erased them from the server."

Devon couldn't help the tiny smile that tilted the corners of her mouth. "Apparently he no longer trusted anyone with his personal papers."

"He hardly trusted anyone," Logan added, "if neither of you has his power of attorney. Would you happen to know why that is?"

The men exchanged one of their many looks.

"He set it up to be good for one year, renewed annually." Alford cleared his throat. "Last week I reminded him the one we had expired. I was unable to pin him down to sign the new one."

"It makes things damn difficult," Bodine insisted. "We can only operate for so long without it. That's why we were hoping you had copies of everything and can provide us with them."

Devon had to bite down on her anger, to keep from telling them her father's disappearance was more important to her than any of their priorities or business contacts. "I'll say this once more so please listen carefully to me. I just found out about everything this morning. I don't know where my father has gone or why. I don't have any information. I don't have any papers. I can't say that any more plainly."

Logan rested a hand on her shoulder, or she would have jumped up and smacked the guy. "Okay. That's it. We're done here. Now." He rose to his feet. "If you want updates, I suggest you keep in touch with Chief March."

Alford looked as if he had something else to say but his companion shook his head.

"Let's go." Bodine looked at Devon. "We're sorry to have disturbed you."

Yeah, I'll bet.

Devon also stood up, doing her best to keep a lid on her anger. "Mr. Malik will show you to the door."

She turned her back and walked out of the room. In the kitchen she took a long moment to steady herself, to fight back the anger seething through her. The jackasses hadn't even asked if she was okay or if the company could do anything for her. She heard Logan ushering the men to the door, their voices protesting one last time. Then he was right beside her, his arm around her shoulders, giving her a slight squeeze.

"You okay?" His deep voice rolled over her like warm molasses.

"I'm mad more than anything else." She curled her hands into fists. "They're lucky I didn't punch one of them in the nose."

He laughed, and the sound sent heat surging through her. "That I'd pay to see. But good. Mad is good."

"I thought maybe they had information they could share with us," she told him. "But that's not why they came here. They never even asked how I was holding up or anything."

"I don't like those guys. Devon, my antennae are vibrating here. I've met men like that before. Been on the other side of the table from them. What's driving them is more than just concern for the business. Something doesn't add up here."

"What do you mean, other than the obvious?"

"They were in a panic about your father's personal papers or anything relating to the company he might have had here. More than just standard operating procedure. They were fishing for something. CEOs die all the time, and even without a power of attorney the companies keep functioning while it all gets sorted out. They have a hidden agenda and I damn well want to find out what it is."

The phone rang again, interrupting him.

Logan yanked the receiver from the cradle. "Yes? What? Oh." His voice lowered. "Sorry. Just a minute." He handed the phone to Devon. "Cash Breeland."

She took the receiver from him. "Cash? What can I do for you?"

"Shouldn't I be asking that question?" The man spoke in a warm southern drawl. "I hear you ran into some trouble today. Twice."

"News really travels fast here."

He chuckled. "Arrowhead Bay is gossip central."

"Well, I'm okay. And Vigilance is taking care of my security until we know what's going on."

"Good, that's good. Well, Devon, honey, if you need anything at all, you just give me a ring. Your daddy and I are good friends."

She wanted to ask him if they were such good friends, how come he didn't know what happened. But she swallowed her words. Cash probably didn't know any more than she did.

"Thanks for calling." She handed the phone back to Logan.

"You might want to think about asking Cash Breeland if he knows who your father's new attorney is," Logan suggested.

"That's a thought, but I'd rather not give him the opportunity to ask questions I don't want to answer. Let's wait until Avery digs up whatever facts she can and go from there."

He was about to hang up the phone when it rang again.

Devon threw up her hands. "Oh, my sweet fucking Lord. What is with all the phone calls?"

"I'll get it," Logan told her.

"I want to listen," she insisted, "in case it's another one of my father's friends. Maybe, finally, we'll find out who it is and what they want."

"Let's find out." Logan held the receiver so they both could hear. "Hello?"

"We want to know where he is." The voice was a monotone, obviously disguised.

"Where who is?" he asked. "Who do you want? Who is this? Who are you looking for?"

"You know. You'd better be prepared to tell us. We'll do whatever we need to get that information. I'll get back to you, and this time I want the *senorita* on the phone."

"Forget it," he snapped. "She's got nothing for you so don't call again."

"Too bad." The line went dead.

Logan stood there, holding the receiver, frowning.

Devon felt chilled again and took another sip of her coffee. "What do they want?"

"I think, like us, they're looking for your father. The difference is they don't seem to be quite as friendly. Or have his welfare in mind, any more than the corporate suits do."

"If I don't know where he is, what will they do to me?" She cleared her throat to get rid of the little quiver in her voice.

"Nothing," he assured her. "That's why you have me."

Devon picked up the remote for the big flat-screen television on the wall and clicked it on.

"What are you doing?" Logan tried to take the remote from her.

"I want to see what's being said."

"It will probably only upset you."

"Maybe, but I'm already upset and I'd really like to see this for myself." She looked at her watch. "It's about time for the local news."

She selected one of the local channels. She was curious if they thought this was worthy of a cut-in. The picture that came up was of a news commentator in the studio.

"Police in Arrowhead Bay are still looking into the disappearance of wealthy business entrepreneur Graham Cole. His boat was found by the Coast Guard floating offshore of Arrowhead Bay where he lives. It is feared he fell overboard and drowned. Several hours of searching has turned up nothing, but the Coast Guard will continue their search.

"Cole's catamaran, Princess Devon, *was destroyed by fire today. So far the origin is unknown but an investigation is ongoing. Meanwhile, Cole International is still reeling from the death of their vice president for corporate finance, Vincent Pellegrino, in a one-car accident.*

"Adding to the situation, we've learned that Cole's daughter, who rushed to Arrowhead Bay from her Tampa home, was run off the road and attacked by two unidentified men. Police are investigating to determine if all the events are connected.

"Stay tuned for further updates."

Devon felt sick as she watched the report, and not just because she was having to hear about Vince's death again.

"Logan?" She turned to him. "They showed pictures of me, too. My face is plastered all over the place."

Logan took the remote from her nerveless fingers and shut off the television.

"Everything is out there on the Internet if you know where to look for it. News outlets have access to just about anything. Come on. You don't need to see that anymore."

"What if he's done something that would send him to jail? God, Logan." She shivered.

It seemed the most natural thing for Logan to take her hand and tug her in close to him.

"Just keep in mind that anyone who tries to get to you has to go through me," he reminded her in a fierce tone of voice. "I'm not going to let anything happen to you."

She absorbed the strength from his body, his clean masculine scent surrounding her. They stood like that for a moment, as if he knew she needed to be grounded. To find her balance in a world gone crazy around her.

"Just so you know," Logan murmured against her hair, "this is not one of my usual bodyguard duties."

She smiled, even though he couldn't see it. "I would hope not."

Maybe, she thought, today would end on a good note after all.

Then Logan's cell phone rang. He looked at the readout.

"It's Avery. What's up?" He listened for a moment. "Yeah, they just left here. And let me tell you, something smells there. Yeah, I know. Uh-huh. Well, I'm not letting her out of my sight."

Whatever he might have planned to say was cut off by the ringing of the doorbell.

"Fuck," he said. "What now? If a damn reporter has made his way out here, this may be the last story he'll ever do. You don't need that right now."

But when he opened the front door, they got an unpleasant surprise. Craig Alford was standing there, reaching for the doorbell again, an angry glint in his eyes.

"What now?" Logan growled. "I thought I made it plain I wanted you both to leave."

"I'm sorry, but we have one last thing." He looked at Devon, a hard, almost angry look that made her nerves jangle. "We want to remind Miss Cole not to say a word to any of the press. We're releasing our official statement. I'll fax you a copy." He looked at Logan. "You have my card if you have any questions, but we'll be controlling the situation from here on out."

He climbed into the passenger seat of a Lexus and the car pulled down the driveway.

Devon looked at Logan.

"What could possibly happen next?"

He grunted. "Don't ask. That's when shit comes out of the corner. Come on, let's see what we can fix for dinner. That soup will only hold you so long. Meanwhile, let's see if we can even the odds a little." He pulled out his cell phone and pressed a speed dial number. "Hey, Avery? Since you guys aren't doing all that much around there, add this to your laundry list. Get me everything you can find on Wilson Bodine and Craig Alford, attorneys

with Cole International. And throw in Vincent Pellegrino. Yeah. I know."
He chuckled. "I owe you everything. But you love me, right? Thanks."

"Wow." Devon grinned at him,

"Let's see if we can level the playing field a little."

Chapter 6

Graham Cole stood at the front of the fishing boat, watching as the captain, Dan Mulroney, skillfully guided it from the waters of the Atlantic Ocean into the harbor at Sentinel Island, Maine. The desperate flight from his house at Arrowhead Bay, the business with the *Princess Devon,* then the disjointed journey from Florida to Maine, broken up to avoid leaving a trace, had been both physically and mentally exhausting. After all the hours on the boat he was sure he carried the aroma of fish with him, but he didn't care. His journey was almost over.

He stood now on the deck of this boat wearing new clothes that suited his new personality and new name. If he had set out to deliberately find a place as his safe haven, this would have been his perfect choice. The island was a tiny spit of land in the Atlantic Ocean within throwing distance of Eastport, the northernmost port on the East Coast, settled by a family from England more than three hundred years ago who had originally thought they'd reached the mainland. When they discovered they were a few casting reels short of their destination, they decided to call the place Sentinel Island, standing guard over those ports actually part of the mainland.

The population of just over one thousand souls had been static for the past one hundred years. There was always someone from one of the families who stayed to fish the waters of the North Atlantic or guide the tourists who came to whale watch or ferry a batch of half-drunk fishermen out for the big catch.

Most of the men wore their hair a little shaggy, hugging their shirt collars, and a beard of some kind, to keep their faces warm in the chilly weather of winter, which seemed to stretch for ten months. A tourist, taking pictures, had once said if you lined all the men up side by side you'd never be able to tell who was who or which was which. That was exactly what Graham wanted.

When his corporation had begun to bleed red ink after his wife's death, Graham hadn't known what to do. It was accounting whiz Vince who'd suggested Cole International get an investor. On a Saturday sail, he'd shown Graham all the benefits and how it could save the corporation. And suggested he quietly look around, maybe with someone he trusted, to find such a person.

When Graham had discovered the true source of the money and wanted to pull out, Vince had convinced him that was too dangerous. He'd reminded him of news stories detailing the way cartels dealt with people who crossed or displeased them.

He didn't fool himself into thinking his problem was solved this easily. Moreno would never stop looking for him. His only recourse was to use what he had to take the man and his cartel down. Even then there would always be people looking for him. He just hoped that between now and then he'd buried his old identity so deeply they could not trace it.

With a steady hand, Mulroney eased the boat up to the dock at Darling's Marina, one in a line of four that hugged the little harbor, and into the skip he rented. Graham was no stranger to marinas. He'd kept both his boats at the one in Arrowhead Bay and had been both a sailor and a fastboat owner for a good portion of his adult life. Darling's could have been Bayside Marina moved north, with its floating docks, the mixed bag of boats in their slips, and the parking lot where the docks hit land.

Beyond it he could see the town itself, the flat streets of the commercial area rising to the hills where the residential area was. The sun was shining and there wasn't a cloud in the sky. Graham took that as a good omen. For the first time since he'd started on this trip from Arrowhead Bay first by speedboat, then helicopter, and finally the trawler, he drew in a deep breath and released it.

He had stuffed the external hard drive from his computer into his bag, dumping the internal one, along with his laptop, overboard when they were well at sea. Every bit of information on Cole International and on the Moreno cartel was stored on it. Whatever happened, whatever ammunition he needed, whether it was to get Moreno or anyone else off his back, he had it stored there.

He also had several burner phones along with pay-as-you go cards so he didn't need to subscribe to a service. He'd acquired the phones from a variety of far-flung locations. On the off chance someone was ever able to find and trace them, none of them tracked back to him. Plus they had the ability for him to change numbers frequently.

Now he was ready for the town…and the person who waited there for him.

The engines slowed, then stopped altogether. The two men who worked the boat with the captain jumped onto the dock, grabbed thick, heavy ropes, and began the process of tying down.

"Hey, Dan." A medium height, thickset man in jeans and a plaid shirt jogged slowly down the dock. "Get a good haul, did you?"

Mulroney shook his head. "I think they were hiding today."

"Must be your aftershave," the man joked.

But Graham knew the real reason was the boat had done no fishing at all. Their work today was to pick up Graham and deliver him to the owner of the marina. They'd worked their way down the coast to the tiny town where the helicopter had dropped him off. Then they headed straight back to Sentinel Island. Dan had greeted him with a mug of hot coffee, then left him to his own devices, a man obviously not given much to conversation. Graham was just as happy not to have to answer any questions. He was having enough trouble trying to sort everything out in his mind.

Had he gotten clean away? Had he left any trace at all that someone could follow? Had he stripped the house of anything that either the police or Moreno could use to find him? Although it was Vince's death that propelled his quick departure, he had been planning it for weeks.

For a moment sadness bit him as he thought about Devon. His one regret was the fallout that she would have to deal with. Now she'd be in the middle of this mess and probably end up hating him. No more than he deserved. The main reason he'd been distancing himself from her for the past few years was to keep her isolated from his situation. He just hoped one day he might be able to make amends, although that wasn't too likely. He just prayed that Moreno would leave her alone. But just in case, once he got settled, he'd make sure Moreno knew what would happen if he harmed Devon at all.

Two days after he'd left the *Princess Devon* drifting in the waters of the Gulf of Mexico, Graham Cole had disappeared. It was Grey Callahan who walked down the dock to the little office at the end.

He gave one brief thought to that boat, to the name. From the day she was born he'd seen Devon as his princess. How sad that when he had the money to buy the boat he named for her, his life had turned upside down and he'd had to cut her out of it.

When he opened the door the woman behind the desk let out a little squeak, jumped up, and threw her arms around him.

"You made it." Leslie smoothed her hands over his hair and his two-day scruff of beard in gentle strokes, as if she'd never get enough of touching him. "I've been checking the clock and watching the horizon since I got here this morning."

He chuffed a laugh. "It was a little touch and go, but yes, I made it. I'm here."

He wrapped his arms around her and held her close to his body, his anchor in the storm that his life had become. God, it felt so good just to hold her. Her rich auburn hair was like silk against his cheek, her skin as smooth as satin, and the scent she always wore, like cinnamon and jasmine, pricked pleasantly at his senses. At five foot six she fit nicely against him, her head coming to just past his chin, her soft breasts pressing into his hard chest. If he hadn't been afraid someone would walk in on them, he'd have run his hands over every familiar curve of her body.

What a blessing she was. This whole thing hadn't been easy, and he wondered what he would have done, where he would have gone, if he hadn't spilled his drink on Leslie Moore that night in the bar of a Philadelphia hotel. It still amazed him that even after he'd made a full confession to her she still wanted him.

"You got away from the *Princess Devon* without any trouble?" She tilted her head back to look up at him, worry lines creasing her forehead.

He nodded. He had no intention of telling her how he almost hadn't made it out of his house.

"Josh showed up right on time with the cruiser, the helicopter picked me up at the right spot, and the fishing boat was waiting for me where you said it would be." He cupped her cheeks in his large palms. "I should probably be killed for getting you involved in this."

"It was my choice, remember?"

He had told her everything, the good, the bad, and the ugly. And even knowing all the things he'd done, she was still willing to accept him into her life. Did he love her? He wasn't sure he even knew what love was anymore. But he did know that he and Leslie had clicked at once. That they had met two or three times a year at remote locations and formed a lasting bond. And that he was sure there wasn't another woman in the world who would open up her life to him under these circumstances and help him rebuild with a new persona.

"Your laptop came," she told him. "It's up at the house."

"Great. After I get settled I'll need to set it up. Thanks for doing this."

The last time they'd been together he'd given her cash and asked her to order a laptop with one of her credit cards.

"So there will be no trace to me," he'd explained.

"No problem. I got exactly what you wanted. But, Grey?"

"Yeah?" He'd asked her to practice using his new name so there wouldn't be any slipups.

"It's a very expensive, very fancy laptop. Are you sure you wanted to spend that kind of money?"

"It was necessary for what I need." He cupped her chin. "And money will not be a problem. As soon as I get things set up I'll be able to show an income that looks like it's coming from a retirement fund."

She studied his face. "You've been planning this for a long time, haven't you?"

He nodded. "I knew I'd have to get out and I needed to prepare. I must have been crazy to get involved with that maniac in the first place."

"Desperate times call for desperate measures." She patted his cheek. "But here you are. At last."

"Anyone asking you too many questions?" he asked.

"No." She shook her head. "My friends were so excited I was finally interested in someone again you could probably have three heads and they wouldn't care. When I told them you were retiring and coming here to live with me they wanted to throw a party."

"No parties." He was dead serious. "I mean it, Leslie. It's so important to keep everything very low key. We discussed this."

God. What if after all this careful planning, it fell apart at the last minute?

"I know. Believe me, I know. I was just teasing a little." She hugged him. "I told them you don't like that kind of fuss any more than I do."

"And no one's suspicious?" He had to make sure.

"Not at all. I promise."

"Did you get rid of the phone?" She'd bought a burner so he could text his message to her that he was on the way and to put things into motion.

She nodded. "Right away. Just like you told me to."

"I can't believe this actually worked." He blew out a breath.

They'd been setting this up ever since he made the decision that this was his only option. From the moment he knew he could trust her, that he felt something for her that she shared, they'd made careful plans.

He pulled her close and buried his face in her neck. "I hate bringing the possibility of this danger to you, sweetheart."

"We'll be fine, Grey. And look. I've been practicing your new name."

He cupped her face. "How did I get so lucky?"

"I think I'm the lucky one."

"Oh, yeah. Hooking up with a fugitive from a drug cartel. Real lucky."

"Grey." Her voice was serious. "We all make mistakes. We do things we regret later because sometimes we have no choice. That doesn't make you a bad man."

"I think a lot of people might argue that point with you. But enough of that for now. Maybe you should show me where we're living and I can put away my stuff. I had enough clothes on the boat so I'm good until we can do some shopping." He looked around the small marina office. "Or do you need to be here? Can you leave for a bit?"

"Of course. All the charters have been checked out for the morning and Eddie can handle anything else. He usually does the heavy lifting, anyway."

"Our story's good with him, too? No questions?

"None. I don't think Eddie has a curious bone in his body."

"Good." He sniffed the air. "And I think that's me with the fish smell in here. A fishing trawler smells like…well."

"Fish?" She grinned at him.

He chuckled. "That it does. I could use a shower along with a nice cup of coffee."

"Come on, then. Let's get you to the house and get you fixed up."

The town looked exactly as it did in the pictures Leslie had shown him. The downtown, such as it was, ran perpendicular to the marina where it dead ended. He noticed it took care of most of the main necessities in life. Leslie had told him for anything beyond that Eastport was just two miles across the causeway.

Her house, a typical saltbox with its steeply pitched roof, nestled into a hillside in a row of similar houses. How different everything was from the tropical environment he was used to, the Spanish style and Craftsman bungalows.

No palm trees either, he thought wryly. Instead there was a mix of maple and elm and yes, even the pine trees for which the state was known.

Everything is different now, including my name. Maybe getting back to the basics of life will help me straighten out the mess I've made of everything.

In the living room, he set down his suitcase and his briefcase and took a moment to look around. Leslie's house was small but neat, and decorated with a great deal of thought. Hardwood floors wore colorful rag rugs and their colors had been picked up by throw pillows on the couch. The paintings on the walls were few but chosen well. He had a feeling they were by local artists. No more bidding at auction on outrageously priced works. And now he saw that as a good thing.

He normally wouldn't spend much time taking stock of things like this. A house was a house, after all. Large, small, whatever. But he'd forgotten what a home was, a place where people lived and loved. God, he'd certainly fucked up his life.

Leslie stood there, watching him, twisting her hands with the first attack of nerves he'd ever seen from her. The worry lines were back on her forehead.

"It's nowhere near as grand as what you're probably used to." She wet her lips. "But it's very cozy and I'm comfortable here."

"Come here." He held out his hands to her and took her small ones in his. "It's perfect. Better than perfect because it looks and feels like you. What did the big house get me except in a lot of hot water?"

On his journey up from Florida he'd had a lot of time to think. Probably too much, allowing him to take painful stock of the life he'd walked away from. He wondered what would have happened if instead of letting Moreno put him in a box with his cash infusion, he'd downsized the company, sold off the less profitable units, and forged ahead from there. But greed was a terrible thing.

And look where it got me.

This was a whole new life for him. He would be comfortable here. Very comfortable. He'd make it work because he wanted to.

He gave her a quick hug. "I swear to you, Les. This is just perfect. New man, new name, new home." He kissed her cheek. "New woman. It's all good."

"Our bedroom is on the second floor."

He smiled at the sudden hint of shyness in her voice.

"Well, lead me to it."

The house, including the wall by the stairs, was a nice mixture of woods and wallpaper, creating an atmosphere of warmth. The bedroom was surprisingly large, with a four-poster, queen-sized bed, large dresser, and a picture window looking out at the backyard.

"I made room for your things in the closet and the dresser," she told him. "And there's fresh towels in the bathroom." Her eyes had a worried look to them. "You're sure this will be okay for you?"

"I'm looking forward to living here. To this. To you. To us." He gave her a smile he hoped was reassuring. He took her hands in his. "I would never have been able to do this without you. And this is what I want."

She blew out a breath and he saw the lines of tension on her face ease. "Okay, then. Take your shower. I'll be downstairs in the kitchen."

"One more thing. Do you have Internet here?"

"Of course." Her lips curved in a smile. "We're still in civilization here, Gra-Grey." Then her smile disappeared. "What do you need?"

"I just want to be able to monitor the fallout from this. Make sure my daughter's okay."

"Of course." Her voice was laced with sympathy. "That had to be the hardest part for you."

"I have to make sure they don't go after her. I was careful to keep her out of everything, even if it meant driving a wedge between us."

"No problem. I'll write the password down for you." Then she grinned. "Now go get rid of that fish stink."

"Yes, ma'am."

After he did that, he'd talk to Leslie about a place to hide a couple of things in his briefcase. Someplace no one would look for them. And he'd ask her to accept a heavy responsibility.

* * * *

Logan prided himself on being a disciplined Marine. Controlled in any and all situations. Removed from extraneous influences and able to focus completely on the task at hand. But he hadn't counted on Devon Cole walking into his life, the first woman in forever to awaken long dormant feelings and desires. To prick at the pain he'd kept hidden all these years. He was having a hard time telling his cock to behave where Devon Cole was concerned, not to mention his emotions. He *never* let his emotions into the game. Into anything, for that matter. Not anymore.

But almost twenty-four hours after he'd first laid eyes on her, he still couldn't get himself under control. He was consumed by a need to protect her. The fact that after being scared out of her wits and nearly killed she'd managed to pull herself together and not fall apart only increased and enhanced her appeal to him. He'd guarded a lot of women since joining Vigilance, but Devon was the first to remind him of Amanda. Same courage, same core of strength, same…everything.

He couldn't seem to take his mind off everything she did. Last night she'd barely slept. He was well aware of that fact, being across the hall from her and all. He slept with his door open and was conscious of every little sound. A little after midnight she'd gotten out of bed and opened her door. She stared into his room, as if trying to figure out if he was asleep or not.

"I'm awake," he told her.

"Don't you sleep?" Her voice had that soft, slightly cottony sound that told him just how uptight she was.

"As much as I need to."

She stood there in the doorway to her room for a long moment. He noticed that she'd put on long pants and a long-sleeved T-shirt and wondered if that was what she always slept in or was she just hiding from him?

"I'm going to leave my door open. Okay?"

"Works for me."

Another long pause.

"It's not that I'm afraid," she tried to assure him. "I just like sleeping with my door open."

"Whatever makes you comfortable."

What he'd wanted to say was he'd be happy to climb into her bed with her and keep her safe all night. Oh, and by the way, if he got to hold her and feel that soft body against his so much the better.

Dumbass.

He gave himself a mental smack in the head. Not once since he'd left the Marines and signed on with Vigilance had he even been tempted to mix it up with anyone, especially a client.

Of course half of his clients had been men so that reduced the list. Of the females he'd been assigned to for one reason or another, he liked most of them personally. But this thing with Devon was different, waking up feelings he'd forced himself to bury deep.

He'd promised himself if he ever felt anything for another woman, he wouldn't let boundaries prevent him from following through.

Of course, Devon Cole was still a client. He wasn't sure, despite the electricity crackling between them, if she'd welcome a move from him. Or if he had the right to make one. Or what would happen if he did. But having her walk into his life like this, a woman so like Amanda in every way, had to mean something.

Am I trying to convince myself of it? Make her into something she's not?

While there was always that possibility, he was pretty damn sure it wasn't the case.

He fixed a fresh cup of coffee for himself and carried it over to the floor-to-ceiling window in the living room. The sun was just making an appearance, and from the elevated site of the house he could see it cast its rays on Arrowhead Bay, the tiny body of water that gave the town its name. From his vantage point he could see the marina with its floating docks and the rows of boats in their slips. The Driftwood, the restaurant adjacent to the marina, wasn't open for business yet but the Coffee Pot was. The little diner that served coffee and fresh pastries and breakfast sandwiches for people going out in their boats, whether for business or pleasure, already had its lights on.

The ambience of Arrowhead Bay was a big portion of why he'd chosen to live here. He could get excitement anywhere in the world, on a job or on vacation. Vigilance agents weren't required to live here, only to show up for their assignments and at least a week of conditioning between jobs. But this place was special. Here was where he recharged his batteries and maintained his humanity, often after jobs he was afraid would rob him of it. Right now he hoped it would settle his brain and help him understand this situation with Devon.

The rule at Vigilance about involvement with clients was a minefield. Avery was very strong about that and he'd never stepped over the line. Not once. He had a well-earned rep for no involvement with anyone. Ginger Brody, the top computer expert at Vigilance, teased him by calling him Mr. Ice Box because she said he could keep his emotions locked down. Where was Mr. Ice Box now?

Gone, the moment Devon Cole barreled her way into his life. He'd never expected to meet someone again who hit him right where he lived physically and emotionally. The way Amanda had. Same latent sexuality, same courage and determination. And no, he wasn't substituting. He could have done that many times before. Either fate was giving him the famous fickle finger or he was being given another chance. He wished he knew which it was.

He still remembered the feel of Devon's body in his hands when he lifted her from her car. The way she fit against him when he carried her away from it. The light scent of whatever she shampooed her hair with. He'd had a lot of trouble hiding the fact his cock was hard as a spike.

Control, he urged himself. *Get your shit together.*

The last thing he wanted to do was fall on her like some sex-starved maniac, because this was about a whole lot more than just sex.

"That's one of the things I love about this house."

Devon's voice startled him. He gave himself a swift mental kick in the ass that he hadn't even heard her come up behind him. Some bodyguard he was. He was too busy thinking of doing other things to her body besides guarding it.

She moved to his side, holding her own mug of coffee. When he glanced sideways at her his unrepentant shaft raised its head and whispered, *My turn.* He hadn't realized it last night but whatever she slept in was made of thin, soft material that draped her body, outlining her breasts, her hips, and her most splendid ass. He wanted to coast his hands over her, feeling every dip and swell and curve.

Holy fucking shit.

Maybe he could hit himself on the head with a hammer.

"The view." She said it as if he was in some way mentally deficient and didn't know what she meant.

"Yes. The view. I can see why you'd love it so much."

"I'd come and stand here in this very spot," she went on, "looking out toward the water. I could almost feel the sun on my skin, and smell the salty breeze from the water. And somehow for those few minutes I could make myself believe that everything was okay. That my father hadn't turned into someone I no longer knew."

"I'm sorry." He didn't know what else to say.

She shrugged, then took a sip of her coffee. "Nothing you can do about it. Nothing *I* could do about it. He just closed himself off more and more, until there was no way for me to reach him."

"Yet you kept coming to see him," he reminded her.

"Yes. We'd been doing so great together and then suddenly it all went sideways. Because I kept hoping under all that remote exterior I'd somehow find my father. I didn't realize he'd already disappeared."

She sat heavily on the couch, placed her mug on a little side table, and dropped her head into her hands. Logan wasn't sure exactly what to do so he sat beside her, trying to take his cues from her. He was stunned when she leaned against him, resting her head on his shoulder, her face still buried in her hands. It was an automatic reaction for his arm to go around her and hold her against his body. His very misbehaving body.

She was soft and warm, and a faint scent of vanilla and jasmine clung to her. Without even realizing he was doing it, he touched his mouth to her temple and kissed it softly. He tensed at once, waiting for her to push him away or jump up and ask him what he was doing. She did neither of those things. Instead she pressed even closer to him, her breath whispering across the hollow of his throat where his pulse now pounded like a jackhammer.

"Devon, listen."

"Listen to what? Do you have answers for me? I hardly slept last night. I kept remembering those two men and what they wanted to do. And the phone calls, from someone equally as unfriendly. Just hold me for a little while, Logan. Okay?" She looked up at him. "Can that be part of your bodyguard duties?"

He swallowed a laugh. "Honey, what I'm thinking of has nothing to do with guarding your body."

She pressed a little closer to him. He stroked her upper arm, a gesture meant to give ease and comfort, but those were sure not things he was feeling. Apparently she wasn't, either, because she lifted her face to look at him, a question in her eyes.

As if she'd said the words out loud, Logan murmured, "If we don't get up from this couch right now, we're going to be in big trouble. I don't think I can be responsible for my actions."

She ran the tip of her tongue over her lower lip, a gesture that sent a message straight to his balls.

"Maybe responsibility is highly overrated. I've been responsible all my life."

"Devon," he began again.

She reached up and touched her fingertips to his mouth. "I'm tired of being sensible. Always doing the right thing. Never really letting go. Just for a while I want to forget about this disastrous mess I find myself in."

He was only human. He figured that could be his excuse as he threaded his fingers in her hair, tilted her face to his, and pressed his mouth to hers. He'd been fighting this since the minute he laid eyes on her. *You can't recreate the past*, he told himself. *Walk away*. But even as he thought the words he knew that was impossible.

Her lips were so soft and smooth he couldn't help swiping the tip of his tongue over them before he eased it into her mouth. And he was lost. God! She tasted like seven kinds of sin, hot and wet and welcoming. He wondered if every bit of her tasted just as good. Then he forced the thought from his mind. As turned on as he was from the built-up frustration, if he didn't get control of himself, he was liable to come in his pants like a horny teenager. Which was exactly how he felt. When her tongue moved to slide over his, it was like kissing a live electrical wire.

He tightened his hold on her head, tilting it first one way, then another to adjust the angle of their mouths. His tongue seemed to have taken on a life of its own, slipping over hers, licking the tender wet flesh inside, scraping over her teeth, then plunging as deep as it could. It only served to make his need to thrust his dick inside her stronger and more urgent.

Dragging his hands away from her face, he slid them beneath the flimsy long-sleeved T-shirt she wore and eased them up to cup her breasts. He squeezed the warm mounds that nestled in his palms. When he brushed his thumbs against her nipples, already stiffened peaks, she gasped, the movement sucking his tongue even deeper into her mouth. She pressed herself into his touch, a soft, sexy moan rumbling up from her throat.

Devon wriggled against him, tugging his T-shirt up so she could reach his bare skin and run her hands up and down his back. She eased her hands around to his chest, gliding them over the curls of chest hair and scraping her fingers over his nipples. Electricity shot straight to his groin and made him bite down on her tongue, drawing another gasp from her.

He broke the kiss at last, desperate to see her naked. He wanted to yank the T-shirt over her head, but he cursed himself for going at her like a starving idiot. With as much care as possible he eased the shirt over her head and tossed the garment to the side. He stared—just stared—at the perfection of her, the creamy skin and the plump breasts with nipples now a dark rose. He skated his hands over every visible inch, finally giving in to the temptation to dip his head and pull one distended nipple into his mouth and suck on it, hard.

The groan that bubbled from Devon's throat was surely one of the most erotic sounds he'd ever heard and only served to increase his rising need.

Slow. Go slow. Don't rush things.

Knowing this might be his one and only chance with her, that when reality returned she might even pretend it never happened, he was determined to make every second a memorable one, for both of them.

Devon was doing her own exploring, yanking on his T-shirt to signal him to get rid of it, then outlining every inch of his back and chest with her slender fingers. When she brushed the tips of her fingers over his flat nipples, he had to grit his teeth not to moan aloud or beg her to do more. This was for her, he told himself. Just for her.

Liar!

When he'd given the other nipple an equal amount of attention, he adjusted her position and leaned her back against the cushions. His conscience tried to tell him he should give her one last chance to change her mind, but he'd shoved that conscience into a dark hole the moment his mouth touched hers.

Only once before in his life had a woman had him as rattled with desire as Devon Cole. Or shaken his emotions so instantly. He'd never expected it to happen again and the fact that it did shocked him. Maybe this time...

Maybe this time.

His fingers were clumsy as he tugged the flimsy sleep pants down over the nicely rounded cheeks of her ass, her strong thighs, and the rest of her slender legs, before flinging them impatiently out of his way. His gaze locked on the tiny triangle of purple that barely covered her mound. Reaching down, he traced her slit through the fabric with the tip of his finger.

Devon moaned and opened her thighs more.

"Okay. We're not doing this on a couch like a couple of horny teenagers."

He swept her up in his arms and strode toward the bedrooms, then paused in the hallway as if uncertain which room to enter. Then, being the selfish bastard that he was, he decided on his, where her scent would linger on his sheets. At least he'd have that much of her.

He placed her gently on the bed, sucking in his breath when she opened her thighs wide again in obvious invitation. In seconds he was there, kneeling between her legs.

"That's it." He barely recognized his voice it was so thick with hunger and need. "Like that. Let me touch you. Feel you. Taste you."

He was stunned to see his hand shake as he reached out to touch her. He stroked her slit through the fabric, feeling the tiny purple scrap wet with her juices. Needing to see every inch of her flesh, he grasped the lace-edged top and tugged it down her body, then tossed it to the floor. Easing her around so her legs hung over the edge of the bed, he knelt between her thighs, draped those same legs over his shoulders, and opened her labia with his thumbs.

Holy shit!

What little control he hung on to was rapidly eroding. Her pussy was gorgeous, pretty and pink and glistening with her juices. Her clit had darkened and just begged for his touch. He used his tongue to follow the same place his fingers had, licking her from top to bottom, then swirling his tongue around her hard nub. She gasped and arched up to him, her thighs squeezing his head as she tried to close them.

But he was relentless. Holding her open while he lapped and licked and sucked and finally thrust his tongue inside her hot, waiting flesh. Her inner muscles clutched at him as he stroked his tongue in and out, the fingers of one hand toying with her clit, squeezing and tugging and pinching.

"Oh!" she cried, thrusting herself at him again. "Oh, oh, oh."

Her little cries only drove his need higher as he worked her with his mouth and hands. Then, with an arch of her body, her heels digging into his back, she came with an explosive force, pouring into his mouth, hips jerking, muscles tightening, her inner walls grabbing his tongue over and over again.

Finally the cries faded, the shudders eased, and she lay there, panting, eyes open looking at him and glazed with sensual heat. She did that little swipe across her lip with her tongue, nearly sending him into orbit, and her lips curved in a tiny smile. Without saying a word, he rose to his feet, stripped off his jeans and boxer briefs, grabbed the ever-ready condom from his wallet, and rolled it on, his hands less than steady.

Devon pushed herself upright and turned to arrange herself on the bed for him but he shook his head. He simply turned her over and pulled her to her knees. He waited for her to object, but the only sound he heard was the increased tempo of her breathing.

He took one long look at her body and gave in to temptation. Lowering his head, he placed kisses on both cheeks of her ass. She trembled at his touch, a delicious little shiver, so he did it again. Then, unable to hold back any longer, he spread her labia with his thumbs and slowly eased his cock inside her.

Holy fucking shit!

He had to clench his jaw to control himself. She was so hot and wet and tight it stole his breath. He took a moment to get himself under control. He wanted to give her more pleasure before he took his own satisfaction.

"Okay?" he murmured, bending over her and licking the edge of her ear. She nodded.

Her inner walls were already clenching around him, straining at his self-control.

He moved slowly, wanting to make sure he didn't rush her. That she was again completely ready for him. But oh, hell, that hot wet sheath just burned him with its heat. In and out, back and forth, he set up a steady rhythm, increasing the pace in small increments. Feeling his body racing to the finish line, he reached around her to find her clit. Pinching it between finger and thumb he tugged and rubbed, working her harder and harder as he stroked into her with increasing speed and force.

He thought he'd have a heart attack before he was certain she was ready again but then, there she was, right with him, exploding around him, her hot inner muscles clutching him and milking him. They spasmed together, again and again, bodies shaking with such force he wasn't even sure they'd survive the storm.

And then, at last, the shudders eased and slowed, his heartbeat dropped down to something below heart attack level, and he could pull a decent breath into his lungs. When he was sure Devon was okay, he eased from her body, turned her, and stretched her out on the bed.

"I'll be right back." His voice was so hoarse he almost didn't recognize it. Damn! Had he ever had sex that cataclysmic in his life? He had a sinking feeling Devon Cole was about to become a drug he was addicted to. Could he really chance it again? What if he failed yet another woman?

He disposed of the condom and hurried back to the bed. She was lying exactly as he'd left her. He eased his body in next to her and pulled her up against him.

He tucked her head beneath his chin and molded her body to his, his now soft cock nestled in the crevice of her ass.

"Logan?" Her voice was so soft he almost didn't hear it. He hated that it was filled with uncertainty. What had he done here?

"It's okay, Devon. I think we both needed something."

I certainly needed it, and a lot more. I am in such a pile of shit here.

"I don't want you to think—"

He touched two fingers to her lips. "It's okay. It was good, Devon. Very good. Let's hold on to that."

Now what, asshole?

For the first time in years he really *wanted* something. Every emotion he'd buried so deep all these years came screeching to the forefront. He'd made a promise to himself never to do this again. To keep his emotion locked away. He'd been a Force Recon Marine, for God's sake, who locked himself up tighter than a drum. He was protecting himself as much as anything else.

But the door had been opened and he wasn't sure if every bit of self-control he had, every bit of discipline, could slam it shut. Because one thing he knew for sure. As hard as it would be to keep his hands to himself from here on out, it would be a fucking damn sight harder to walk away from this woman. Fate was giving him another chance and this time he'd get it right. Avery would probably cut off his balls, but he'd figure out how to deal with it.

He kissed her temple. "Let's take a short nap before we hit the decks today."

"Logan?"

Damn. That shaky little voice was killing him.

"Uh-huh?"

"This, um, wasn't a, you know—" She seemed to be struggling with the words. "It wasn't a, you know, pity fuck, was it?"

Every muscle in his body tensed as shock raced through him. What the hell?

"Devon, listen to me. Whatever I feel for you...felt for you... Pity doesn't have a damn thing to do with it. Keeping my hands to myself after this is going to be damn fucking hard."

A soft little breath eased from her and her body relaxed.

"Good. Because I think it's the best I've ever had."

He was still replaying those words in his brain when he felt her body relax as she dropped into sleep.

Well, buddy boy, he told himself. *You've gone and done it now.* Thank God she hadn't told him it was all a mistake. What the hell was he planning to do about it? How did he plan to keep his hands to himself after this?

But hard as he thought, even as he drifted off to sleep, no answer presented itself.

Chapter 7

They were drinking coffee and eating the breakfast Logan had whipped up for them. Devon was unendingly grateful that he loved to cook, and did it well, because it wasn't one of her better skills. Simple foods and lots of takeout was her motto. But this morning he fixed omelets, bacon, and toast, all perfectly prepared.

"If anyone had told me I'd have a bodyguard who doubled as a premier chef, I'd have told them they were lying," she teased, swallowing the last bite of omelet.

He winked. "Just one of my many talents."

She certainly knew what some of the others were. She still felt the most incredible glow from their lovemaking. She only wished she knew what was going on in his mind. For her, making love with him had been epic. Cataclysmic, even. What was it for him? That look she'd seen in his eyes in unguarded moments...What was that all about? And the way he held her and kissed her afterward. There was more here than just sex. Or was it the artificial situation they were in that made everything seem larger than life?

She was glad he'd been already up and out of the bedroom when she awoke. She'd had no idea how she'd face him or how to act with him, sure he thought she was excessively needy. God! The way she'd fallen into bed with him, parking all her inhibitions at the door. She'd never been that way with any of her other lovers, few as they'd been. Of course, she thought, as she bit off a piece of the thick sandwich, maybe that was why none of them lasted. And why she hadn't cared.

Except for the last one. That had nearly been a train wreck and she still wasn't sure who was to blame. She just knew she'd made a vow to stay away from men for a good long while. Yet here she was, so intimate with Logan it made her tremble.

She could still feel Logan's mouth on her body, his lips and teeth on her clit and on her nipples, his very educated tongue as it drove her up and over into the maelstrom of a powerful release. His thick shaft filling her, taking her in a way that sent every one of her nerve endings into overdrive. The memory of it sent a hot flush through her body and she shivered.

She didn't know all that much about it, but she was pretty sure most bodyguards didn't become intimate with their charges. There was something deep here. She'd never believed all those stories about people meeting and their chemistry was hot enough to light up the sky. Not until Logan walked into her life. So now what? What did he expect? What did this mean to him?

Drive yourself crazy much, Devon?

"Devon?" Logan's voice cut into her reverie. "You okay there?"

She looked up, afraid she was blushing. From the look in his eyes she was sure he knew exactly what she was thinking.

Crap!

She gave herself a mental shake. "More than."

She picked up her tablet that she'd brought into the kitchen with her, thinking to distract herself. She wanted to check her e-mail while they ate, but first she wanted a look at *The Bay Bulletin*, Arrowhead Bay's daily online newspaper. Every Wednesday a print edition came out for those still addicted to paper, but for a newspaper on a shoestring budget this worked very well. She looked at the front page and groaned.

"Damn. I could have figured this."

Logan put down his mug. "What's the problem?"

"I'm front-page news in Arrowhead Bay." She handed the tablet over to him. "I guess I'm a local celebrity."

"*Local woman accosted on highway*," he read. "You could have figured that. Not much else going on around here."

"No kidding. Marybeth Hughes who runs the paper scrapes up every last detail of anything she gets a smell of. And this is big time for her. I'll bet she was a big gossip in school."

When Logan finished reading, he looked over at her. "They've got a big article on your dad's disappearance and the boat fire, too. This might make people more alert as far as strangers around here are concerned."

Devon lifted an eyebrow. "You're kidding, right? Snowbird season will be starting soon. Strangers will be swarming everywhere, all the time."

"One good thing." He tapped his finger on the screen. "There's a description of our two friends from the highway based on what you told Sheri. If the jerks happen to see that, maybe they'll change their minds about hanging around. They won't want to chance being recognized."

Logan finished his coffee and handed the tablet back to her. "Enough. Put this away until later. I think we should head down to the marina. I want to see what's going on today and look around. And I also think we should check out *Lady Hannah.* We couldn't take a look at her yesterday, as crazy as things were. I'll call Avery on the way and see if our agent she planted there picked anything up."

"Okay." She swallowed. "I'm almost afraid to see what we find out."

"Whatever it is," he said, "it's better than not knowing anything."

"Okay. You're right."

"Listen." He leaned forward. "I don't want you to—"

"Stop." She said the word louder than she intended. She didn't want to hear his apology or his explanation of the rules regarding bodyguards, if that was what he was getting ready to say. So she'd misread him. Big surprise. "It's okay. You don't have to say a word. We can just forget the whole thing, okay?"

She popped the last bite of toast into her mouth, concentrating on it as if it were the most important thing in her life. She waited for him to say something. Anything. But he just sat there, silent, drinking his coffee, watching her. Finally he set his mug down.

"No. We're not forgetting anything." His mysterious eyes studied her. "First, I need you to know that I never do this. Ever. I have a code where clients are concerned." He delivered the words with a hard edge.

Devon didn't think that was news. She was pretty damn sure Logan Malik didn't make a habit of this, yet here they were. She wanted to think this was special, that he hadn't just felt sorry for her because of her unfortunate circumstances. That look in his eyes, the way he touched her...

No, she could be practical about it and let him off the hook, if that was what he wanted. She just wished...

"Of course. I understand." She wet her lips. "So it's forgotten. Okay?" She'd figure out how to make herself forget it.

"You're misreading me, Devon. I don't want to forget it." He focused on her, his eyes boring into her. "And correct me if I'm wrong, but I don't think you do, either. Right?"

Devon looked across the table at him. That same pain she'd seen for a fleeting moment was back in his eyes, but there was something else with it, too. Something she couldn't define.

"No." She said the word in a quiet voice.

"So please don't jump to conclusions." And there was that look again, pain blunted by intense desire and hunger. "I want—" He stopped. "I think—" Another pause. "Later we're going to have some wine and talk."

"You don't have to make excuses to me," she insisted. "It's all right."

"No, it isn't, and no excuses. When I say we're going to talk, I mean it. And then we'll see where this takes us. There are things I need to tell you." He blew out a breath. "But later. Just understand there's no forgetting. At all."

"All right."

She'd hold on tight to that until they had a chance to talk. She'd never been hit so emotionally by something before and she wanted to know that this was more than a roll in the hay for Logan. That he broke his own personal code because he felt something very special for her.

When she looked across at him, his eyes were like twin lasers boring into hers, heat and hunger and something else flashing in them. Then, as if a broom had swept over his face, that same implacable expression swirled into place. His game face. He took a swallow of coffee and set his mug down.

"Let's get going."

She carried her plate and mug to the sink, stuck her dishes and Logan's in the dishwasher, and dusted her hands together. When she turned, she found herself body to body with him.

"Um, excuse me?"

She looked up at him. Bad move. The look he gave her felt as if it went clear through her. Their gazes locked for a long moment. There it was again, that mixture of pain and desire.

"Never mind. Let's go."

"Let me get my purse and the keys."

Logan was waiting for her in the foyer. "All set?" She nodded. "Let's go."

He checked everything on the new alarm system, punched in the code, and guided her toward the garage with his arm lightly at her waist. As soon as she had climbed into his truck and the garage door behind them rolled up, her entire body tensed.

What if someone was out there waiting to shoot at them again? What if the black SUV was out on the road? What if—

Oh, for God's sake.

But she'd been attacked on the road, she and Logan had been shot at, and someone had blown up *Princess Devon. This is stupid,* she told herself. They had a state-of-the-art security system in the house, and the bodyguard of her dreams beside her. What could happen?

Logan backed out of the garage, pressed the remote to close the garage door, and headed down the driveway. He paused at the foot of the driveway and she watched him scan the area.

He glanced over at her and covered her hands with one of his, giving her a gentle squeeze with his fingers.

"We're good, Devon. Nothing remotely visible out here. This is just force of habit for me. The one time I don't do it will turn into a disaster. Okay?"

"Okay." She blew out a breath. "I want you to know I am *not* some Silly Millie given to fainting spells and all that. I don't know what Avery or Sheri told you about me, but I handle my life pretty well. I even own my own business." She smacked her head. "But you know that. Avery probably sent you a file on me that even includes my birthmarks."

He glanced over at her, the corner of his mouth quirked in a tiny smile. "Birthmarks? I'm not sure I noticed any."

The same heat she'd felt earlier surged in her cheeks.

He shrugged. "And Avery sent me a file on you. She does that with every client. It's as much to protect us as it is to protect them."

"Oh. Of course." She should have figured that.

They turned onto the road and headed toward town. Despite Logan's reassurances, she couldn't help checking the side-view mirror every few seconds. No black SUVs appeared, thank the Lord. Or any other vehicle. They reached the bottom of the hilly road without incident and he made the turn that would take them to the marina.

There was little traffic today, but the marina parking lot was nearly full. The docks were filled with people working on their boats after yesterday's disaster. Devon even saw several boats from other slips in the water, bobbing just out of range of the disaster, watching as if this were a movie. *Bloodsuckers,* she thought, cursing their avid curiosity.

Logan parked and jogged around to open the door for Devon, his eyes busy scanning the area.

"You think those men might be here?" A knot twisted in her stomach.

"No, but I always check my surroundings. I don't like surprises."

"Neither do I."

As soon as they were out of the truck she was hit with the lingering scent of ash and gasoline and burnt matter. Logan held her hand as they walked along the dock, picking their way along the wet boards and skirting bits of debris. Devon looked at the sight and was heartsick. Who could have been vicious enough to do this kind of damage, with careless disregard for the other people who had their boats there?

"Don't get too near the edge," Logan warned her.

"I won't. I just…need to look."

She was vaguely aware when he stepped away from her. When she turned to look for him, she saw him talking to a young man with messy black hair dressed in board shorts and a T-shirt. She frowned, wondering why he was talking to someone who appeared to be a boat bum.

But then he moved back to stand beside her.

"Don't look back at him," he told her in a low voice. "That's Angel Cabrera, one of the Vigilance agents. Avery said she was keeping him here to check things out for a couple of days. I know he looks twelve but he's almost thirty. He's great for some undercover assignments."

"Oh my God," she whispered. "I'll bet. What did he say?"

"You aren't going to like this, but the guys from Cole International were here earlier nosing around."

Her stomach knotted. "They're doing all this stuff without keeping me in the loop."

Logan made a rude noise. "I have a strong feeling those guys are looking for something, just like your would-be kidnappers. The first thing that comes to mind is either of the computer drives."

"There must be something on there scaring the hell out of a lot of people."

"The suits are sure after something."

"Assholes," she muttered. "Did they talk to him, by any chance?"

He shook his head. "He isn't someone they'd pay attention to, which is why he's so good at his job. He did have some information, though."

"Like what?"

"Try not to react because we still have no idea who might be here watching. He said they tried to get on *Lady Hannah*. But—"

Her entire body went rigid, as both fear and anger washed through her. "What? They did what?"

"Wanted to get on the boat. But Avery had someone keeping people away from both of them, just in case of something like this."

"So what happened?"

He barked a laugh. "They were pissed as hell. Angel saw the whole thing. They tried throwing their muscle around. Said they were executives with Graham Cole's business and the boat was corporate property. They had every right to board it."

She clenched her fists at her sides, trying to control the rage bubbling inside her. "They are unbelievable."

"That's not true, is it?" he asked. "A lot of people put such purchases in the name of their business for tax purposes."

"Well, my father didn't. It's his name on the title, to both of them. Goddamn it." She swallowed, doing her best to get her anger under control. "Did they leave after that?"

"Not right away. Angel said they hung around a while watching the cleanup operation and I guess hoping the guard would be gone. But he stayed until it was dark. Angel left about an hour later. But you won't like what else he overheard."

"What now? I don't know how much more bad news I can take."

"They've checked into the B and B. They're staying until they find your father or whatever it is they're looking for."

"Great. Just great." She swallowed back the nausea. "I want to take some pictures of *Princess Devon.* I'll need them if I ever find out who the insurance company is. But first let's see what's on board *Lady Hannah* those douchebags might have been interested in. "

Logan grinned at her. "Douchebags, huh? Sounds right to me."

Getting on the boat was accomplished only after Logan borrowed a portable ladder from someone. He climbed on first, then opened the gate in the railing to help Devon. She stood on the deck, covered now with soot and ashes that had worked into an ungodly paste as it mixed with the water from the hoses. She looked around, feeling sick and depressed.

"This is a disaster." She felt tears gather in her eyes and tried to blink them back. "This was such a gorgeous boat, and my father kept her in immaculate condition. *Princess Devon* was a big catamaran but this one was Dad's snazzy sport fisherman. He loved taking out his friends." She tried to smile and failed. "Although I'm not sure how much fish they actually caught."

"Who's the *Lady Hannah* named for?"

"That was my mother's name." Her throat tightened. "I don't think he ever got over her death. Sometimes I wonder if whatever he got himself into that made him disappear had to do with his depression. He just really fell apart for a while."

"Which boat did you and he sail the most whenever you went out together?"

"Mostly *Lady Hannah.* She's what's called a day sailor and we never went very far. *Princess Devon* is what he used when he was sailing from Tampa to Arrowhead Bay and back again." Another wave of sadness swamped her. "Once when we went out on *Lady Hannah*, he talked with me about my mother. First time in what seemed like ages." She swallowed back the tears that just wouldn't go away. "And the last time. I'm pretty sure whatever he was into, he was already hip deep by then."

She saw Logan study the boat carefully, glancing now and then over what was left of *Princess Devon.*

"What?"

"If we go with the idea that that your father did a Houdini, why did he take the larger boat? I'd think the smaller, faster one would have been preferable."

"So maybe he wasn't trying to get away? Maybe he just went for a day sail and fell overboard like everyone thought at first?" She didn't know which solution she preferred at this point. A voluntary disappearance hurt her and left too many questions unanswered.

"I want to go over everything in this boat," Logan said, "starting with the cabin."

She gave him the keys and he climbed down the short flight of stairs to the cabin door. But when he went to unlock the door, she saw him scowl and crouch down. He wrapped his hand around the knob and before he could pull, it slammed open, knocking him back on his ass. Someone burst out of it, barreled up the steps, knocked Devon to the deck, and leaped off the boat. Before either of them could recover he was racing down the dock, weaving in and out among the people.

Logan jumped down and took off after him. Devon gripped the rail to still her trembling hands. How had someone gotten onto the boat and into the cabin? Who? Why? She watched, doing her best to keep her eyes on Logan. He was back in minutes, anger stamped on his face.

"He got away." He spit the words out in disgust.

"What? How? Where did he go?"

"It was a kid, a teenager. He was out of the parking lot before I could catch him. I'd guess there was a car waiting for him, hidden just down the road from the marina."

"Do you have any idea what he wanted? Or who sent him?" Then she shook her head. "Forget I said that. Of course you don't. I saw you stop and talk to Angel. Did he see anything?"

"No. He left about one in the morning, so the kid must have come aboard after that. He would have taken off with me chasing the kid, but I don't want to blow his cover. When we're done, I'll call Avery."

The cabin had another unpleasant surprise. Cushions were ripped, cupboard doors open and in some cases yanked off their hinges. Every single thing that could have been a hiding place had been destroyed in the search.

Devon dropped onto one of the torn cushions and put her head in her hands. The nausea that had been with her since Sheri's phone call came surging back and she had to swallow hard. She wished this was a nightmare and any minute she would wake up.

She was vaguely aware of Logan speaking to someone and looked up to see him with his phone clamped to his ear.

"Yeah. Everything. No, I have no idea how he got in but I'm damn sure going to find out. But Sheri? Whatever Cole took with him on those hard drives has got to be hotter than a pistol. Too many people are after it. I'd like to know what those thugs that keep going after Devon and the guys from Cole International have in common. Uh-huh. Uh-huh. You're right. Okay. I'll take some pictures, tell Angel to stay alert and head for the office."

He ended the call and crouched down beside Devon, taking her hands in his.

"What is it?" She cleared her throat. "Just tell me whatever it is."

"Devon, I wish I had answers for you but we just keep getting more questions."

"Tell me what you and Sheri think. I have to know."

"Okay." He sat down cross-legged in front of her. "It's obvious that kid in here was searching for something, and it's small enough to be hidden almost anywhere."

"Like a hard drive."

He nodded. "Whatever is on it—them—has to be pretty damaging to the people looking for it. What I can't figure out is what those guys with the guns and the men from CI have in common."

She rubbed her forehead. In addition to the nausea a headache was trying to break free.

"I swear to God, Logan, I have no idea what it could be."

"I believe you. That didn't even enter into our thoughts. But I'm less and less convinced your father fell overboard. I'm getting the feeling either your father disappeared on purpose or someone has him and everyone else wants him. And if he did do this on his own, he was very efficient. By the time his boat was discovered and a search started, he was already long gone from the *Princess Devon*."

She rubbed her forehead. "I'm really scared for him, Logan."

He nodded. "I'll bet. If he's running from someone, they may have caught wind of what he was planning and tried to stop him. Now their next point of attack is you."

"But who could have him and why are they keeping him?"

"All things we have to find out. Come on." He pushed himself to his feet and held out a hand to her. "Let's get some pictures of this boat and what's left of the other. Whenever you get insurance information, they'll want these. I'll have Sheri tell the Moorlands they have to stay like this while the investigation's going on. She can get the slips roped off, too."

Devon blew out a breath. "I can hardly believe I just got the phone call yesterday. So much has happened." She gave his hand an impulsive squeeze. "I'm glad you're here. With me. As my bodyguard."

Logan cupped her chin and tilted her face up to his. "I'm a lot more than your bodyguard, Devon." He looked as if he wanted to say something else but changed his mind. "Go on. Take your pictures."

Logan also snapped some pictures with his cell; then they stopped to take a hard look at *Princess Devon.*

"It's a total loss." Devon stared at the boat, sadness washing over her. "That beautiful, beautiful boat."

"Once the insurance pays off, if you want you can get another one," Logan pointed out.

She looked up at him. "Are you kidding? After this I may never want to get on another boat ever."

Logan took more pictures, then stuck the phone in his pocket.

"Let's go talk to the guy that runs this place."

"Gary Hopwood runs it for the Moorlands, although I think running it might be too loose a word for what he actually does."

"I want to check him out anyway, on the off chance he's not the doofus everyone says he is."

Devon wasn't sure exactly how old Gary was. With skin weathered by the elements and curly hair shot with gray, he could have been anywhere from forty to seventy. She knew that in the summer he worked alone, but in the winter months, when the snowbirds were roosting, he hired someone to help him. He'd be doing that shortly. She was aware he'd lived in Arrowhead Bay all his life and but that was as much as she knew about him.

Except when he helped people service their boats or move them into the big building that housed the repair shop and the dry slips, Gary spent his time in the small shack at the entrance to the floating docks. He looked up as Logan opened the door, setting aside his newspaper and taking his feet off the desk.

"Help you?" He gave them an inquiring look.

"Remember me?" Devon asked. "Graham Cole's daughter. We're just checking into his disappearance."

"Oh, yeah. Heard about that. Fell overboard, right?"

"We're not sure yet. The Coast Guard is still looking for him."

Gary looked from one to the other. "So what do you need from me?"

Logan took over so smoothly she hardly noticed it.

"We just have a few questions for you. I—"

Gary interrupted him. "Exactly who are you?"

"Logan Malik. I'm handling Miss Cole's security for the moment."

"Security?" Gary's eyebrows lifted. "Why the hell does she need security?" He shifted his gaze to her. "If he fell overboard why do you need protection?"

"We're just being cautious," Logan answered. "How late were you here yesterday?"

Gary's posture immediately became defensive. "Why? I didn't do anything wrong."

"We don't think you did," Devon assured him in what she hoped was a calm voice. "We're just curious about some things."

"What things?"

Crap, she thought. *Why can't he just answer the questions?*

"Oh, if you saw anyone hanging around yesterday that looked strange to you. Out of place."

"Listen, you two." He stood up, anger lining his face. "I run a good place here, but they don't pay me to be a guard. What with your pop's boat blowing up yesterday"—he turned his anger on Devon—"we had a lot of strange people here. I got nothing to tell you."

She would have pushed it but Logan took her hand and gave it a light squeeze.

"Well, thanks, Gary. You've been very helpful. You have a good day."

Gary eyed them with suspicion. "With all this shit going on here? As if." He dropped back into his chair and picked up his newspaper. Obviously the interview was over.

Devon let Logan take her outside and close the door.

"I don't know if he has no information or he's being paid to 'forget,' but our friend Gary knows a lot more than he's telling. We won't get anything from him today. We'll have to come at him from another angle."

"I want to scream," she told him.

"I know. Same here."

They had just reached the truck when someone called out to her.

"Devon? That you?"

She turned to see Cash Breeland hurrying over to them. "Hey, Cash."

He took her hands in his and gave her a sympathetic smile. "Honey, I'm glad I caught up with you in person. We're all so sorry about this thing with your dad."

"Yes, well, thank you." What could she say? She only knew him slightly, just from the few times she'd seen him with her father and then running into him in town.

"And that terrible thing that happened to you on the road?" He shook his head. "Hell, we never have stuff like that happening around here. Glad to see you're okay."

"Thanks for checking, but I'm fine."

"Uh, any word from the Coast Guard yet? Or did you maybe find some kind of note or something at the house?"

"No note, and no further word," she told him. "Did he happen to say anything to you?"

For a moment she thought she saw anger flash in his eyes. Then it was gone.

"I wish he had." He shifted his gaze to Logan. "Friend of yours?"

Logan held out his hand. "Logan Malik. I work for Vigilance. I'm Miss Cole's security."

"Security?" Cash's eyebrows rose nearly to his hairline. "Well, I guess after that incident she probably needs one." He looked at Devon again. "Honey, if you need anything, anything at all, you call me, you hear?"

"Well, there is one thing. I understand Daddy changed attorneys not too long ago. You wouldn't happen to know who he went to, would you?"

Again Devon thought she saw something in Cash's expression but as before, it was gone before she could figure it out.

"First I've heard of it. I can check around if you like."

"No, that's okay. I can do my own checking. I just thought you might know. Sorry to be rude, but we really need to get going here."

"Okay, then."

He looked as if he had something else to say but fortunately Logan hustled them both into the truck.

"Something's off about him, too." He turned the ignition. "I think we should stop by the office and run everything by Avery. And maybe she'll have some information for us by this time."

"Sounds good to me." She leaned back in her seat, wondering if this nightmare was ever going to end.

Chapter 8

Logan had just picked up his phone to call Avery and let her know they were on their way when it rang. He looked at the readout.

"Speak of the devil. It's Avery. Hold on. Yeah, boss. What's up? Uh-huh. Uh-huh. We just left the marina. No, nothing doing on the boats but Gary's still on my radar. And Angel's keeping an eye out on the scene. How about running a check on him? Uh-huh. Okay. Timing is great. We were just on our way, anyway."

Devon looked over at him. "Is it bad news?"

"Not necessarily. They've found a few things digging through your father's history and she has some questions."

"My father?" Her muscles tensed. "What did they find?"

"Don't know yet, but let's not borrow trouble until we have to. I told her I'd bring you right over." He slid a glance at her. "Take a breath. Try to relax."

"So Avery didn't give you even a little hint of what she wanted?"

"You heard this end of the conversation. Short and to the point. But we'll be there in just a few minutes and you can find out."

Devon had never been to the Vigilance offices, but then she'd never had a reason to. Whenever she'd seen Avery it had always been with Sheri. They'd meet at Fresh Roasted, the coffee shop with the mouthwatering pastries, or the Orange Blossom, a great restaurant for lunches. Or sometimes drinks and dinner at the Driftwood. She realized with a shock that the only socializing she'd done was coffee or meals with these two women. Sometimes one or two of their friends would join them but it wasn't as if she'd made an effort to create a social circle here. She considered herself damn lucky to have connected with these two women.

Logan reached over, took one of her hands, and squeezed it. "Just remember. Whatever Vigilance came up with is better than not knowing anything at all. Right?"

"I'm sure you're right. I still can't get my head around the fact my father could be involved in something dangerous."

"Let's just wait and hear what Avery has to say."

Instead of continuing on to Seacliff Road, he turned right onto a long narrow road that looked carved into a forested area. Thickets of trees lined both sides, the same kind of trees that grew on the bay side of Seacliff Road. Just as she wondered where the hell they were going, they came into a clearing, and she just stared. In the center of the clearing was a house with distinctive Key West architecture, painted white with a gabled roof and a wide front porch. Land that she hadn't even known existed stretched away behind it and to one side was a long two-story building that looked new. She wondered if they had cameras and sensors set up all the way in from the highway.

"Come on." Logan took her elbow and guided her up to the porch, where he tapped some numbers into an electronic keypad. "We can't tell other people how to be secure if we don't do it to ourselves. Look up." He pointed to the coach lights. "Cameras."

She shook her head as they stepped into a short, enclosed foyer. Logan pressed his thumb against a metal plate on the inner door and it swung open.

"Wow." She looked up at Logan. "You weren't kidding about taking your own security seriously."

"We have to." Avery came from an office to her left. "We have very high-profile clients."

Devon looked around, hoping her jaw hadn't dropped.

"I can't believe a place like this exists in a sleepy little town like Arrowhead Bay."

Avery laughed. "This town isn't as sleepy as you think it is. Our offices used to be in upstate New York, not far from the city, on property about as big as this. But the winters kept getting colder and I discovered being close to the Big Apple didn't give me any advantage. When my sister took the job as police chief here, she talked me into coming to visit and here we are."

"Not nearly as cold," Devon joked.

Avery nodded. "But security is still our number one priority. Almost everything we're involved in requires the utmost secrecy. For example, we don't want a stranger wandering in here while we're doing a complex electronic search on your father and his activities for the past ten years."

Devon stared at the other woman. "The past ten years?"

Avery nodded. "We may have to go back further, but we'll start with this chunk of time and see what we find. Logan told you I had some questions?"

She nodded. "But what, exactly, are you looking for? What is it you want to know?"

Logan wrapped his fingers around her elbow and urged her to follow Avery. "We hope to find out when and where he went off the rails, so we have to examine everything. It could have been some event that happened even twenty-five years ago that just came back to haunt him. But trust me, there's something that happened that led to this whole mess."

"Happens all the time," Avery told her. "Come on. Before we head to my office I'll show you the flight deck. People always get a kick out of it."

She frowned. "Flight deck?"

Logan laughed. "It certainly looks like one."

They were right. The room they took her into was probably forty by forty and filled with enough computers and monitors and screens to run the Starship Enterprise. A large semicircular desk, its surface dotted with keyboards, faced all the screens. Two people sat at the double console, their fingers moving over multiple keyboards, their eyes darting from screen to screen so fast Devon wondered how they remembered what they were doing.

Outlines of maps filled two of the largest screens, each one populated with a series of winking dots.

"Our active assignments," Avery explained. "We keep constant track of them. We have a daily report of activities and locations. If any of that changes without notice, we get ready to move a team into action."

Devon gave a nervous little laugh. "Sounds like you're planning for a war."

Avery nodded without smiling. "Sometimes that's just what it is, depending on who the client is." She pointed to a floor-to-ceiling row of smaller screens, each of them with photos of what looked like houses and yards. "These are the locations where we monitor security systems. We don't have eyes on them all the time, although we do regular checks. But if an alarm sounds, we can go right to the monitor and see what's happening."

Devon tried not to let her jaw drop or her astonishment show. She'd certainly seen enough movies and television shows with high-tech private security firms. But seeing it in the so-called flesh astounded her.

"If you look at that setup over there"—she pointed to a station in the corner where a man in a T-shirt and jeans was monitoring four screens at the same time—"that's Del. He's working on cracking the code on your father's phone. Like a lot of people, your father probably wasn't aware that even if a phone is wiped, the information can still be retrieved with the right software. But you still have to break the code and this is more complex than usual. He must have done a lot of research to set it up."

"Still can't get into it?" Logan asked.

Avery shook her head. "But we will. The code hasn't been written that Del can't break sooner or later. We're just hoping for sooner. But we're not waiting, of course. We're already into Cole International records, looking for anything in the past five years that jiggles the radar."

She took Devon's elbow and nudged her toward one side of the room where a woman sat at a desk with—count 'em—four computer screens and a stack of external hard drives.

"This is Ginger Brody. If it's out there in the Ethernet, Ginger can find it."

The woman looked like an elf. Devon was sure she wasn't more than five feet tall, if that. She had curly red hair pulled back in a messy ponytail and the greenest eyes Devon had ever seen. She was dressed in faded jeans and a T-shirt with the legend "Don't give me a Command, I byte." She looked about twelve.

Ginger hit the Save button on her keyboard and pushed out of her chair.

"Hi." She held out her hand to Devon. "Nice to put a face with my research." She grinned, then hopped into her chair again. In seconds her fingers were again flying over the keyboard.

"What's upstairs?" Devon asked. "Or is that classified?"

Avery chuckled. "To the right of the staircase are suites for the agents when they have to stay here. They don't all live in Arrowhead Bay but they come here for training and to be briefed on assignments." She glanced at Logan and grinned. "Mr. Marine here is the only one with no permanent residence. He lives here."

Devon's jaw dropped. "You're kidding, right?"

He shook his head, his face expressionless. "Haven't found a place I like yet well enough to buy."

"The entire floor to the left," Avery went on, "is my living quarters."

"You never get away from these guys," Devon said.

She laughed. "More like they can't get away from me. The other building out there is a combination gym and weight room, with a climbing wall, rappelling ropes, and plenty of space to practice hand-to-hand combat. Beyond that is the shooting range."

"That's why you have it so far from town."

Avery nodded. "I didn't think people would like guns going off in their backyards."

"I guess I never thought about what goes into being a bodyguard."

"Protective agent," Avery corrected her. "Floats better with our clients. Let's head to my office. We'll have coffee and see what's what."

As they walked out of what Devon wanted to call Space Station Central, she nearly bumped into a tall woman carrying a coffee mug.

"Oh. Sorry." The woman flashed a grin and held the mug up in the air to avoid spills. "Guess I was concentrating too hard. Did I spill?"

Avery chuckled. "Sam's always concentrating. That's what makes her such a good agent. Devon, meet Samantha Quenel. Sam."

So Vigilance had female agents, too. Devon studied the woman. She was tall, maybe five ten, and lean without being skinny. Her long blond hair was pulled back in a low ponytail and she wore jeans and a black T-shirt with a V on the sleeve. She wore no makeup and didn't look like she needed it. Devon almost hated her on sight.

"I do have a tendency to plow into people." Sam gave her an apologetic grin. Then she shifted her gaze back to Avery. "Anything you need me for? We wrapped that last one a week early so I'm at loose ends."

Avery laughed. "Did you ever hear the word vacation?"

"I'm waiting for the man of my dreams to take me on one." She grinned but Devon had the feeling she wasn't joking.

"Maybe. Just hang loose and we'll see."

Sam nodded and headed into the room, and Avery led them down the hall to her office.

Devon had expected a utilitarian office space, with basic furniture, tiled floor, and nothing on the walls. Everything else in the place seemed to be stripped down. She was shocked to find hardwood flooring, a woven area rug, and furniture with a Spanish flavor. Colorful prints brightened the walls, and in one corner a tall schefflera plant ruled over the room.

Avery saw the look on Devon's face and grinned. "It's my hideaway. Of necessity, everything else is bare essentials. I need warmth and color when I work."

She fixed them coffee, using mugs with the Vigilance logo. Devon took a sip of hers, hoping the hot liquid would soothe her nerves.

"Okay, you said you were on the way here." Avery looked from one to the other. "What's up?"

Logan told her about the incident on *Lady Hannah,* including a bare-bones description of the kid.

"Well, damn." Avery idly played with a pen on her desk. "That opens a lot more possibilities without giving us any answers."

"Someone's pulling the strings," Logan said, "and I don't think it's the two idiots that ran Devon off the road."

"You're right," Avery agreed. "Someone with brains is pulling strings and we need to know who and why."

"If it's dirty, please tell me it's Alford and Bodine. There's something off there. They were there to hassle Devon, which is weird. If they're attorneys in her father's corporation, I'd think they'd be there to offer her their help. Instead they all but accused her father of doing something illegal and suggested she was covering it up."

"I checked into them as you asked." Avery smiled at him, picked up her tablet, and tapped the screen. "I was getting ready to send this to you. Listen up. Guess where they cut their teeth as attorneys, learning the ropes?"

"I'm not going to like this, am I?" Devon asked.

"I'm sorry, but probably not. They cut their teeth working for a law firm in Arizona whose biggest client is—wait for it—Cruz Moreno."

Devon frowned. "Who's that?"

"No one good," Logan muttered.

Avery set her tablet down. "Cruz Moreno is the head of one of the biggest drug cartels in Mexico. They operate internationally."

"And how in hell," Logan asked, "did they get hired at Cole International with that on their record?"

"Please." She made a face. "Anybody can create a resume. I'm sure whoever answered any inquiries gave them a glowing recommendation. I wouldn't be surprised if Pellegrino was the one who brought them in. The report I have for you, unfortunately, is going to explain that."

"How?" Devon demanded. "What do you mean?"

Logan touched her cheek, the contact somehow soothing. "Let's hear the report." He looked at Avery. "Alford and Bodine are still in town," Logan told her.

Avery nodded. "They are, and staying at the B and B."

"And checking out the scene around the boats," Logan said. "You keeping Angel on the docks?"

"Yes. He's good at picking up gossip."

"I have a feeling Devon's in real danger until we get at the truth," Logan said. "If Cole's alive and not dead, and he's somehow mixed up with Moreno, someone could take it in their head to use her as leverage."

"Which is why you'll protect her as if she were the Queen of England."

He grinned. "Better than."

Oh, yes, Devon thought. *Definitely better than.*

"Also," he went on, "Gary at Bayside Marina is hiding something for sure. But for whatever reason, he didn't like me so I'll get diddly squat. Send someone else to shake him up."

Avery made a note on her tablet. "Duly noted." She looked at Devon. "First let me say how sorry I am that this has happened to you. We want to do everything we can to help find out what happened to your father."

"I appreciate that." Devon rubbed her temples, trying to stave off the headache blooming again. "So what have you found on the search you did on him and Cole International? Anything that will help me with this?"

The look Avery gave her was heavily tinged with sympathy. "Nothing that's going to make you happy. I'm sorry, but it doesn't look good."

Devon's head was beginning to feel like someone was pounding anvils inside. "Just—tell me what it is. At least I'll know what I'm facing if and when we find him."

Avery swiped to a page on her tablet. "In a situation like this it's always about the money. Follow the money is the golden rule, so that's where we started, with Cole International, the big money machine. We're just at the beginning but I want to fill in some blanks."

"Like?"

"There's just no good way to say this. Were you aware that your father had some financial difficulties a few years ago?"

Devon wet her lips. "Vaguely, but not the details. Cash crunch, he told me. He was very worried about it for a while. But I thought that was all straightened out. He got a private investor."

"Did he ever tell you who that was?"

"No, but it must have really helped." Devon dug back into her mind trying to remember. "That's when he decided to move down here, buy that land, and build that huge house. Is that important?"

"Just trying to put the pieces of the puzzle together. So you're saying that when he moved down here, you got the sense everything had been fixed?"

"Yes." Devon nodded her head, then decided that was a bad idea. The anvils were still clanging away. "He seemed a little more relaxed. Not quite as edgy. He said he needed to get away from Tampa and the house he and my mother lived in for so long. And he was tired of the city. I think he just needed the change. Losing her nearly destroyed him."

"That kind of loss can be devastating," Avery agreed.

"I was pretty sure the financial problems had been solved because he was relaxed again and taking some time to enjoy life. I even went sailing with him a few times."

"When you visited, did he introduce you to people?"

"A few." She wrinkled her forehead, trying to search her memory. "We usually had lunch at the Driftwood. That's where I first met Cash Breeland. The others came later."

"Okay." Logan's voice was soothing. "Just think for a minute. When did you notice a change in him again?"

Devon took a long swallow of her coffee, trying to straighten out her brain.

"Maybe about a year and a half ago. Now that I think of it, he was on edge a lot. Again."

Avery leaned forward. "Did he say anything to you?"

"Not much. When I asked what was wrong, he said just a little business problem he was wrestling with. He was sure he'd figure out a way to handle it. He'd always solved problems before so I had no reason to question him. I just tried to give him space. I didn't want him to shut off again like he did before he got the investor."

"You know his company was built with companies, not a specific product, right?"

"Excuse me?" Devon was confused. She hadn't ever really known a lot about her father's business. When he was first growing it, she'd of course been way too young to understand. As she got older she hadn't been all that interested. Teenage stuff was followed by college stuff and followed by her first two jobs and finally setting up her own business. For that she'd approached Graham to ask his advice, and he'd sent her to his attorney. She'd thought it strange at the time that he didn't sit down and discuss the ins and outs with her, but her mother smoothed it over by saying he had great demands on his time.

"It means," Logan said, "that he started out buying a company. Then another company became available for sale and he had the cash to acquire it. Then the next one, and pretty soon he'd laid the foundation for Cole International." He looked at Avery. "That right, boss?"

She nodded. "The problem with doing it that way is if one division falters, it can bring down the entire corporation unless it's handled properly. Four years ago when he had those money troubles, he was on the verge of having to dump a lot of the unprofitable subsidiaries. That would have greatly decreased the overall value of Cole International."

"God! That would have killed him. That corporation was his lifeblood. He always said it was a testament to what you could do with no money but a lot of grit and determination. If he lost it, well, you can imagine."

The pounding inside her skull got louder. She closed her eyes and tried to will the pain away.

"Here, Devon. Take this."

She opened her eyes to see Avery standing there holding a glass of water and three tablets.

"Acetaminophen. Take them. If you rub your temples any harder, you'll have holes in the sides of your head."

She popped the tablets in her mouth and drank almost the entire glass of water. "Thank you. That should help. It's just turning into a bitch of a day."

And it started so nicely.

"Back to your father." Avery settled behind her desk again. "The red ink explains why he was so desperate. The infusion of cash from the private investor allowed him to pull those subsidiaries out of the red and before long they were all showing strong profits."

"What else?" Devon asked. "I can tell by your tone of voice there's something wrong here."

"We know the money was filtered through a company called SMX." Avery cleared her throat. "I had one of our agents who happened to be in the area check on it. I'm sorry, but it's nothing more than a one-room office, manned by a woman whose sole job is to monitor the computer and answer the phone. It's just a shell corporation."

"But that's absurd." Devon swallowed. "If everything was being funneled through this shell corporation, where did the cash come from in the first place?"

Avery set her tablet on the desk and leaned forward.

"Our point exactly. I'm betting the answer will be our friend, Cruz Moreno. It's even possible that Pellegrino was the one who set it all up to begin with. He was vice president for corporate finance, right?"

"Yes." Devon had the feeling she'd suddenly landed on a very slippery slope. She tried to take another sip of the coffee to steady her nerves, but the liquid had gone cold so she set it on the little table next to her chair.

"Moreno needed a place to clean his money from the sale of drugs and guns. Make it grow even more. Cole International was tailor made for him."

Devon thought she might faint.

"Drugs? Guns? My father?" She swallowed. Hard. The coffee she'd managed to get down threatened to roll back up from her stomach. "That— that he was involved in those things? God."

She was damn glad she'd taken the pills from Avery. Otherwise her head might have exploded.

"Drugs seem the biggest and more logical possibility," Logan said.

"So you're saying the money came from Moreno?" Devon asked.

Logan nodded. "Remember the men who waylaid you on the highway? The one who spoke had a Spanish accent."

Devon curled her hands into fists in her lap, holding herself together by a thread. She couldn't fathom that her father was in bed with a drug dealer. That he'd accepted money from him.

Avery leaned forward. "It's a good bet your father has every bit of data on the cartel on those hard drives, information that could crucify them. It was his protection and he let them know it. That's what everyone is looking for."

"Of course! You're absolutely right. You think Alford and Bodine were sent by Moreno to get it?"

"That, and I'm sure there's stuff on there about them, too."

A chill raced along her spine.

"And then," Logan added, "it becomes a question of just how Cole International got into financial hot water to begin with. And whether it was your father who somehow dragged them into it or they did the dragging."

Devon pressed her fingers to her mouth. "I never even thought he might have been set up. But then, why would I?"

"We still don't know who Cruz's money man is," Avery reminded them. "If it was Pellegrino, how and why was he killed? Was it Alford? Bodine? As attorneys, they'd be in a prime situation to broker deals. Or someone we don't even know?

"We're going to figure it out," Avery assured her, "and find the right threads to pull. I promise you. That's what we're doing." She slid a glance at Logan. "Let's wrap it up for now. Go home." She grinned. "Have a drink." Then her face sobered. "And Devon, write down everything you can think of. Even the smallest detail can be a help. Computers can give us all the raw data we want, but only you can give us an idea of his physical and mental state."

"I'll do what I can. I have to have some answers here and find out where he's gone."

Avery came out from behind the desk. "Take her home, Logan. She's had two days that would wreck anyone. Make her get some rest. The minute I have anything to add to this I'll call you."

"Good idea." He tugged Devon out of the chair. "I think a nap might be just what's ordered now."

"I'm not sure I can sleep," she mumbled.

"Hold on." Avery went to a cupboard against the wall, took something out, and handed it to Logan. "Peppermint tea bags. They do wonders for anything that ails you, including a bad case of nerves." She winked at Devon. "And if all else fails, have that drink."

"I'll take care of it," Logan assured her.

Devon noticed Avery raised an eyebrow when Logan put an arm around her to lead her out of the office. If he didn't care, she guessed she didn't either. Right now, all she wanted was to get out of here.

"Do you want someone following you back to the house?" Avery asked.

Devon's stomach cramped. "You think they'll be waiting out there again for us?"

"Anything is possible. Well, Logan?"

"No. I'm prepared for them this time. Remember, my car is bulletproof. Theirs isn't."

"Okay. Make her get some rest," Avery repeated, as she ushered them to the front door. "Sleep, Logan. Sleep."

Devon caught the edge to Avery's voice. If she discerned something going on between the two of them, would she replace Logan? She'd somehow have to make sure that didn't happen. Even in such a short time something very intense was building between them. Crazy as it sounded, she didn't want to let go of it.

Then they were in his truck, heading back to the house, and she clung to his hand holding hers like it was the only lifeline out there.

Chapter 9

Logan didn't know if he should try to talk to Devon on the drive home or if silence was better. God only knew he'd seen plenty of people in shock before. Usually it happened when they were confronted by death or extreme violence of some kind. The episode on the road, the phone calls, the explosion on the boat, and someone ransacking *Lady Hannah* were bad enough. Now came the news about her father. Although Vigilance was still digging, it was patently clear Graham Cole had been involved in something less than legal.

Somehow she'd found an inner strength to keep it together, but she looked like she was sliding down to the end of her rope. She sat beside him still as a statue and so pale he wondered if she was going to pass out.

"I can feel you thinking." Her voice was quiet, but stronger than he'd expected. "I'm okay."

"I know you are. You've just had some information thrown at you that would be hard for anyone to absorb."

"I'm good. Really. I think I'm tired more than anything. I didn't sleep well last night. Plus the past two days have been unsettling to say the least."

His heart turned over. Everything she did, everything she said, reminded him so much of Amanda. The same strength. The same determination. The same unwillingness to let situations defeat her. He'd known a lot of women who thought they were strong, yet who either crumbled at the first sign of disaster or lost it altogether.

And he wanted to talk to her about what happened between them... *was* happening. He hoped like hell he didn't scare her off but it was there between them, and he knew she felt it, too.

As soon as they were in the house he reset the alarm, then took a mug down from the cupboard.

"I think I'll combine both of Avery's prescriptions. Just sit at the table for a minute while I get it ready."

He watched her lower herself into a chair, slowly as if she might fall over. He didn't bother with Avery's tea bags, instead using a pod for the fancy machine on the counter. While it brewed, he headed into the den and returned with a bottle of bourbon.

"I spotted this when I was checking out the den yesterday. I think it's just what Dr. Malik prescribes."

She managed a tiny smile. "Dr. Malik writes good prescriptions."

When everything was ready, he set the mug in front of her. "Drink slowly, it's hot. But drink it all down."

He went over to the computer on the counter, tapped some keys, and began scrolling through the camera footage for the time they'd been gone. He tapped a few more keys and the screen returned to normal. "No news is good news. No visitors while we were gone."

"You thought someone might have tried to break in?" she asked.

"Yes." He bit off the word. "They want the location of your father. They probably think he left some clue here."

"But you didn't find anything when you looked," she reminded him.

"Graham scoured this place pretty good, but that won't stop someone from trying."

Devon cradled the mug in her hands, sipping it slowly. Logan fixed coffee for himself and sat down with her.

"Drugs and guns." She said the words slowly. "I still can't get my head around the whole thing. Logan, my father has always been a respected businessman. Even when I was a young child and he was still building Cole International, wherever we went I saw the admiration people had for him, especially those in the business community. When the first articles profiling him began to appear, my mother was so proud. She showed all of them to me. So how does a man so well respected end up in bed with drug dealers and gunrunners?"

"A question only he can answer." He took Devon's empty mug from her hands. "Why don't you lie down and try to nap a little. While you're sleeping, I'll raid the freezer and fridge and throw some dinner together."

Her lips curved in a tiny smile. "Are you going to be the live-in chef until this is over?"

He shrugged. "I like doing it. Unless..." He studied her. "Unless you're saying you want to take care of the meals."

She laughed. Just a little one, but it was a laugh. "Heaven forbid. I'd poison us both. My cookbook consists of takeout menus from every restaurant within a ten-block radius of my apartment."

"No kidding?"

She cocked her head. "You aren't one of those men who thinks a woman's place is in the kitchen, are you?"

"Now it's my turn to say heaven forbid. Or hell no. So why don't you try to catch a nap. I've got some work to do and I'll rustle up a meal."

"Is there some special reason you want me to get in bed? Or are you just trying to get rid of me?"

Why the hell am I always putting my foot in my mouth?

"You said you were tired," he said. "I thought maybe you could stand a little sleep."

She stared as if waiting for him to say something else.

"No ulterior motive," he assured her. "If I—never mind."

"Logan, if you've got something to say just spit it out. We're going to be living in this house together for the foreseeable future. If there's a problem, that won't work. So tell me what's on your mind, because I know something is. You said we'd talk when we got back here, so talk."

When would he ever learn to keep his mouth shut?

"How about if you rest or nap or read or whatever you want to do? I'll do some work on my laptop. Then we'll have a nice dinner, maybe with some wine, and we'll talk."

"Are you saying you need to get drunk to tell me what's on your mind?"

He wanted to snap back at her, frustrated with the situation he'd gotten himself into. Then he looked at her and saw that little smile teasing her lips again.

"You're yanking my chain."

"Mmm, maybe a little. You've been uptight since we walked back into the house."

He had and he knew it. He wanted to tell her what he was feeling and why it happened so fast, but he also didn't want her to kick him out the door. He was counting on the fact that everything indicated she was feeling it, too. But as strong as he did? As intense? And after not even forty-eight hours?

Jesus, Malik.

She laughed again, a soft sound but the first time he'd heard it since he saved her from those two thugs on the highway.

"Never mind. I think I need to occupy my mind more than put it to sleep. I'm going to set up my computer and printer. I need to check my e-mail, and I have clients I can't ignore for too much longer." She pushed herself to her feet.

"I didn't even ask you. What do you do?"

There went that smile again. "I'm sure it's all in whatever file Avery sent you, but it's nice of you to pretend you don't know. I'm a graphic designer. I do everything from book covers to brochures to marketing materials to whatever the client needs."

"No kidding?"

"No kidding." She picked up her purse that she'd dropped on the table. "Listen, Logan. What I heard today is a lot for me to process, and we've probably only got the tip of the iceberg. I need some time to myself to think about it. There's a desk in my room so I'm going to set up my stuff there. Then we can both work on our laptops, only I'm sure mine won't be nearly as interesting as yours. Answering e-mails is mindless enough work that I can let my brain try to sort everything out."

"Sounds like a plan. I'll check on you in a little while."

"Then maybe you can tell me what you wanted to talk about?"

He nodded. "Then we'll talk."

At least it gave him time to figure out what to say. He'd broken his own and the agency rules once already, because he couldn't deny his unexpected feelings for her. His intense need and hunger. If he was smart, he'd just pretend nothing had ever happened. Apparently, he wasn't as smart as he thought he was, because he knew that wasn't going to happen.

He'd never been good about sharing his feelings, not since Amanda. What if Devon looked at him like he was out of his mind?

Listen, Devon. The sex between us is great but it's more than that. You're the first woman I've fallen for in a lot of years since I lost the last woman I loved. I never thought this would happen again so I'm breaking all my rules to see if you feel the same way.

Yeah. That sounded so good.

He was a Marine, for chrissake. Marines didn't get caught in this kind of emotional quagmire. Where was his Marine discipline when he needed it?

Disappearing fast, that's where.

* * * *

While Devon set up her laptop, plugging in her external hard drive and connecting to her wireless printer, she let everything from the past couple days roll through her mind. She could hardly believe it was only yesterday morning she woke up prepared for another day in her very ordinary life. In less than forty-eight hours her life had been upended. She'd been told her father had disappeared, received threatening phone calls, been run off the road, attacked and shot at by two very scary men, and had off-the-charts sex with a mysterious man who pushed all her buttons.

She could hardly accept that her father was involved in anything illegal, but Avery had been very convincing. And his actions the past few years certainly made everyone suspicious. Why hadn't she paid more attention? Asked questions? Anything? Because he'd been very obvious about shutting her out.

Their visits together had become less and less frequent. He had talked a lot about moving from Tampa after her mother passed away and she wasn't surprised when he told her he was selling his house and building a new one in Arrowhead Bay. Whenever he took her out on a Saturday sail, she could see why it appealed to him, especially after she met some of the friends he'd made and realized he was carving out a whole new life for himself.

And rightly so. Everyone needed changes. She'd just been so glad whatever his problems were had seemed to be fixed and he was moving on to the next phase of his life. She'd visited him as much as she could and they always spent time out on either *Princess Devon* or *Lady Hannah*. That was where he seemed the most relaxed.

She began to roll things through her mind, trying to pinpoint exactly when things began to change again. Maybe the couple of times she'd called to visit and he told her he was having a business meeting at the house. How preoccupied he'd become again. She wished now she'd asked more questions and insisted on answers. Of course, that didn't mean he'd have given her any.

Oh, Dad, what did you get yourself into?

When she had everything connected and turned on, she booted up her laptop and went to her e-mail program. Her inbox exploded. Good. She could concentrate on answering messages and forget about this situation, at least for a little while.

But she couldn't stop wondering what Logan wanted to talk to her about.

* * * *

Graham—he had to keep reminding himself he was now Grey—helped himself to another cup of coffee and carried it to the table where Leslie was finishing her late lunch. The afternoon sunlight slanted in through the window, catching the red highlights of her auburn hair. The green of the sweatshirt she wore matched the shade of her eyes almost exactly. Hers was a natural beauty. Something that captivated Grey from the first moment he met her. He thought he could stand here just watching her, drinking her in, forever.

But life moved along and he had things to do.

"Are you coming to the marina with me?" she asked. "I think it would be good for me to introduce you to a couple of the regulars and for people to start seeing you there."

"I agree, but there are a few things I need to do first." He sat down in the seat opposite her. "I want to open a bank account, and also rent a safe-deposit box."

Leslie put her cup down. "Do you have identification to do that? Were you able to get what you needed?"

He nodded. "I'm set. If you can spare the time, I need to buy some clothing. I fit as much as I could into the one suitcase but that won't hold me for long."

"No problem." She swallowed the last of her meal and carried her plate to the sink.

"Leave them. I'll take care of it. I know you have to get to the marina. I'll be along after a while."

He rose to walk to the door with her. Before she opened it, she turned and slid her arms around him.

"Be careful with everything you do, Grey. Please." Her voice was edgy with concern. "You don't know what electronic traps might be out there waiting for you."

"We've discussed this, honey, and I'm good. Really." He pulled her in for a long kiss. "I don't plan to do anything to jeopardize this."

"Okay." She let out a breath. "I trust you and believe in you. But I get to worry about you, too."

"Back atcha. Now go on, before all those people start a riot because you aren't there."

He rinsed her mug and plate and stuck them in the dishwasher and refilled his coffee mug. It amazed him how at home he already felt. It might be a far cry from the lavishness of Arrowhead Bay but he was a lot more comfortable in it. For one thing, he wasn't entertaining members of a drug cartel or helping them to facilitate their shipments of drugs or arms.

How could his friend have done this to him? He realized now the suggestion to move to Arrowhead Bay had been subtly planted in all the months leading up to the financial rescue. With the financial crisis over, he'd had the money to buy the land and build the house he wanted. Or had that, too, been suggested to him?

But the worst had been when, after a couple of years, he'd approached his investment advisor and said he wanted to start repaying the money. Buy back that portion of his company. That's when he'd learned who his "silent" partner really was. Drug cartels were so far off his radar he hadn't ever given them a thought. Discovering who he was in bed with, who had really saved Cole International, was a shock that nearly killed him.

Shock had made him physically ill, along with the blunt little chat they'd had about how he was now inextricably tied to the Moreno cartel. The smartest thing he could do was just run his now very profitable conglomerate and ignore the source of the money. And if he hosted a small group of businessmen at his home now and then, well, that's what big houses were for.

From there it was only a small step to rendezvousing with another boat out in the Gulf of Mexico and bringing "merchandise" back to his house when emergency arrangements had to be made. It hadn't become a regular habit, thank God, but every so often when their regular routes were fucked up, they pressured him to host them at the house. They brought their drugs in their luggage and rendezvoused with the buyer.

The helicopter became the auxiliary transport when their regular routes for gun shipments were impassable. After all, no one thought twice about a high-profile businessman with an impeccable reputation. After each "situation" he locked himself in his den and indulged in a good drink.

By the time a year had passed he felt dirtier than garbage, and he was caught in a trap he couldn't find a way out of. He had lived in fear for so long now, sick with the effort of keeping everything from his CEOs, from everybody. Again he wished he'd made the decision to scale the company back. Sell the units that were bleeding red ink or just close them altogether. His inability to admit failure or defeat was his undoing.

Look where that had gotten him.

He had allowed it to ruin his relationship with Devon because he was such a desperate coward. He managed to make sure none of it touched her, although he knew she was hurt that he was withdrawing from her again. But that was the one good thing he could do. Protect her. And when the situation became intolerable, he hatched his plan. God had sent him Leslie at a time when he desperately needed a woman just like her. Falling in love was an unexpected bonus. The fact that she was willing to hide the hard drive and folders he'd brought with him, that she agreed if anything happened to him she'd go at once to the DEA, told him more than anything about the depth of her feelings for him. How lucky could a man get, to fall in love twice and each time with an incredible woman?

Now, in Leslie's comfortable saltbox house in this typical small Maine town, he really felt he was starting a new life. He just had to clean up a few messy threads from the old one.

As soon as Leslie left, he locked the door, fetched his new laptop along with a flash drive from his briefcase, and set everything up on the breakfast room table. It didn't take long to boot up and access the secure web site and his anonymous e-mails. The moment he'd made his decision to do this—the point in time when he realized if he didn't get out, sooner or later he could end up dead—he'd begun his research. He had to have some way to communicate without leaving any trace, and to receive answers if he needed them. The way he understood it, it was similar to the kid's game with string called Cat's Cradle. Every string only led to another string, and only the originator knew the starting point.

He had money to set up in numbered bank accounts, other arrangements to make, and he'd also wanted to be able to track what went on in Arrowhead Bay once he disappeared. For a brief moment, he'd been tempted to confide in Devon, but they hadn't been close for so long he wasn't sure how she'd react. But he had to have a connection to her.

His research had paid off. Originally called an onion network, it dealt with using encryption to create private anonymous virtual networks. It had the capability to bounce e-mails over a number of servers so anyone trying to trace him would get lost in the chain. He'd also learned to shut down any e-mail address as soon as a message was sent and create a new one for the next message.

He was set up to force all his e-mails to write only in plain text and not to pull in any images. He'd already tried it out, sending to another fake e-mail he'd created through another program. Nothing bounced back. But the real test was when he tried to trace it back to the source and location and he just got an error message. He could use each address once. Period. Obviously nothing was foolproof but if he killed every address after he used it and stuck to the basics, he could be pretty sure he was safe.

He was protecting not just himself but Leslie as well. If Moreno traced him to this little coastal town, not only would his life be worth nothing but Leslie would also be in danger. He'd taken the time to be sure he did this right. Now he was ready to get to work.

The first thing he did after logging on to one of the virtual private networks he'd chosen was access the web site for a shell company he'd set up. The one skill he'd learned well handling things for Moreno. Vince had explained every step to him as he set up multiples of shell corporations and explained how the money washed through them so he knew what they were doing. At the thought of Vince, sadness and regret washed through him.

He moved through the complicated network of entities, each one requiring a different password, until he accessed the one he'd filtered his own money through. The bank account totals were still correct. Nothing had changed. No one had figured out how to get to them. Thank God. After today he'd start sending regular payments from Morton Investment Funds to his new bank account. At some point, he'd figure out how to withdraw larger sums without causing a ruckus but he was a long way from that. He'd calculated what a reasonable monthly annuity would be and that was what he set up. Then he set up anonymous e-mail accounts, untraceable and if anyone tried to reply, they'd get a bounce-back.

That done, he decided to check the Tampa newspaper. His disappearance was bound to be news, even if it was just a mention. If they featured the story, it was probably on the local news channels, too. Although he knew the position Cole International had in the business world, he wasn't arrogant enough to think he'd make the national news. At least not yet. If he found himself forced to blow the whistle on the Moreno cartel, it would be a different story, one he dreaded.

Tracking how far the police were progressing in their search for him was important. He was sure someone would have notified Devon when the boat was found drifting. Hopefully the Coast Guard would write it off as lost at sea, she'd grieve, and life would go on for her. But knowing his daughter, he couldn't be sure. Had she gone to Arrowhead Bay? Was she involved in what was happening? The stories would give him an idea.

What he found made his blood pressure rise significantly.

There had been an attack on Devon and the *Princess Devon* had been blown up. They wanted the hard drive and would go to any length to get it. He couldn't let this go on. But he had to figure out what to do and still stay alive and out of prison.

I need more information.

He went back to the secure virtual web site he'd set up and typed in the name of the Arrowhead Bay newspaper. If there was any place to get detailed news about what had happened since he disappeared, this was it. The moment the front page loaded he saw the story about him, pictures and all. He'd expected that. This was a small town and for them this was a huge deal.

First there was a detailed article on Devon's incident. The thought of that scum running her off the road and attacking her made his blood boil. He was glad to see the man who'd stopped and run them off was an agent of Vigilance. He knew their reputation and that Devon was friendly with the owner. If they had taken Devon under their wing, she'd be well protected. And maybe, in the end, they would be his conduit to release information on Moreno if the scumbag didn't leave Devon alone.

Right along with that was the article about the fire on *Princess Devon* and that the cause was determined to be an explosive of some kind. He read them over one more time, the details burning into his brain.

God fucking damn.

He felt sick to his stomach. Then a boiling rage surged through him. If Cruz Moreno had been in front of him right now, he'd wring the man's fat neck.

Graham had figured—hoped—when he disappeared Devon would just have the authorities keep her informed of the investigation and that would be that. He should have known family was still important to her. No matter how he'd treated her lately, she had jumped in her car and driven to Arrowhead Bay to find out what was going on.

He ground his teeth as he read the details of the incidents yet again. He had to do something. He'd thought Devon would be safe once he was gone, but he'd made a huge error in judgment. He'd hoped everyone would believe he'd drowned and he'd be safe. Obviously that didn't happen, either.

If he contacted Moreno, the man would know he wasn't dead. But just because the man would know he was alive didn't mean he could find him. Graham just had to make sure nothing could trace back here to this town and Leslie.

Damned if I do and damned if I don't. But I really don't have a choice. I have to protect Devon.

He picked up the burner phone he'd brought downstairs with him, activated one of the money cards, and went to one of the secure e-mail accounts he had set up. He wasn't taking a chance using the laptop.

He still had the e-mail Moreno used to communicate with him. It was untraceable, just like the one Graham would use. Opening up a blank message, he thought for a long moment about what he wanted to say, then typed a simple message.

"Leave my daughter alone or I will ruin you."

He read the words over once, then pressed Send. Moreno knew he had enough material to bury the cartel. If he didn't back off Devon, Graham would start dribbling it out a little at a time. The Vigilance involvement was an unexpected blessing. Sending it to them would get quicker action than sending it to the Feds. If the cartel didn't leave Devon the hell alone, he'd destroy them.

At last he closed everything on the laptop and leaned back in the chair. Tomorrow he'd check for a reply to the e-mail. If there was none, he'd keep his eye on news in Arrowhead Bay, hoping Devon's name would not pop up again. Today he would wander through the little town as Grey Callahan, doing his best to blend in. And take the first steps to making a life with Leslie.

Chapter 10

"Knock-knock."

Devon looked up from her desk. Logan was standing in her bedroom doorway. She allowed herself a moment to look her fill of him. The black T-shirt and jeans outlined his lean, toned body with its sculpted muscles. The image of him naked flashed into her brain, heating her body and sending the beat of her pulse up another notch. She was crazy, thinking such erotic thoughts when in the middle of a crisis like this.

"Sheri called."

She tried to read his face. "The Coast Guard? Did she hear from them?"

"Yes, and it's not good."

Oh, God.

Suddenly she found it hard to breathe. "They found a body?"

Logan shook his head. "No. Devon, I don't think they'll find anything. The cutter commander said they'll give it until the end of the day and then they're calling off the search. They think, and so do I, given what we've learned, your father pulled off a disappearing act."

She had to agree with him, but it filled her with such emotional pain.

Oh, Daddy.

"The good news is, that means he's still alive somewhere."

"But we don't know where."

"No, we don't, but tomorrow we'll talk to Avery about options. Vigilance has helped people disappear like that before. She'll have ideas about what to do next." He held up a bottle of white wine and two glasses.

"I didn't know if you wanted red or white, but white is usually a safer choice. I found the glasses in the bar in the living room. The wine was chilling in the fridge. This house is prepared for everything."

She twisted her lips in a wry smile. "Like I said earlier, my father had regular business meetings here. It was in his DNA to be prepared for everything."

A sober expression crossed his face. "Too bad you don't know more about those business meetings, but I can understand him wanting to keep you out of everything."

"With all the stuff that's happening now, I wish he hadn't." She heaved a sigh. "I hope Avery has some more ideas when we talk to her again."

"Me, too." He wiggled the hand with the wineglasses. "Dinner is warming in the oven. I thought we'd take this out on the patio. The sun's going down and it's nice out there."

Devon tried to read the expression on his face. "Are you trying to get me drunk for some reason? To have your wicked way with me?"

Now why did I say that? He probably wants to tell me what a mistake it was, and there are rules and all that. Why don't I ever keep my mouth shut?

His smile was uncharacteristically tentative. "Not quite. And maybe after we…talk, you won't want me to, anyway."

A sudden cramp gripped her stomach and she forced herself to take a slow breath. "Well, um, let's find out."

She shut down her laptop and pushed back from the desk. "Lead on."

The patio as usual looked like a decorator had just left, an artful arrangement of lounge chairs, easy chairs, and a table with six comfortable chairs surrounding it. The last remaining rays of sunlight bathed it with the same golden glow they cast on the emerald green of the lawn and the bright colors of the flower beds.

Logan uncorked the wine and filled the glasses before handing one to her.

"To good thoughts," he said, touching his glass to hers.

"Good thoughts," she echoed, although she had no idea what he meant.

When she was seated at the table, he drank his wine in two swallows, set the glass on the table, and walked to the edge of the patio, standing with his back to her. Despite her edgy feeling, Devon forced herself to sip the cold, crisp drink and wait for him to speak.

"At one point in my life in the Marines," he began, "I was stationed at Camp Pendleton, at San Diego. I was invited to a party one night where I met the most incredible woman. Amanda was the daughter of a very wealthy attorney in San Diego. She was a language expert who often did work for the government. She also taught at San Diego State. She was an incredible person, independent, smart, brave. Really had her act together."

A shaft of pain pierced Devon's heart.

"She sounds…amazing." Devon didn't know what else to say. She was afraid she wasn't going to like the rest of this story.

"Without getting into too many details, we fell in love. She told me her father always worried about her because he'd made a lot of enemies and he was afraid they might go after her. It had happened to friends of his. He tried to have a bodyguard trail her, but she used to tell me how trapped she felt, what a lack of privacy it gave her. She resented sacrificing her privacy for a danger she wasn't even sure existed."

Another pause.

Devon reached for the bottle to refill her own glass. She had a feeling she was going to need it.

"And?" she prompted.

"We spent as much time together as we could. Amanda was good at giving her bodyguard the slip. After all, I was a big bad Marine who could protect her, right? And I always got her home safely."

"What happened?" She whispered the words.

"I was supposed to pick her up one night but I had something to do so we agreed to meet at the restaurant. She was kidnapped in the parking lot." He bowed his head, not saying a word for a long moment. "She was killed before she could be rescued."

"What about her bodyguard? Had she ditched him that time?"

"No. I insisted she not go there alone. Because of an international deal he was involved in, her father had recently received an escalation in threats, warning him what would happen if he did not kill the deal. Her bodyguard drove her to the restaurant. His body was found in the parking lot, hit as soon as he got out of the car. By the time I got there police were all over the place and her father was a raving maniac. Justifiably so."

He paused, swallowed, took a deep breath.

"He tried to have me arrested. Even suggested I was behind the whole thing, to keep her bodyguard away from her so I could have her all to myself. Then he got the message from the kidnappers and hired his own firm, one like Vigilance, to rescue her. But the kidnapper was ready for that. The minute the premises were breached he shot Amanda. Just like that."

Logan stood where he was for a long moment, silent, his body lined with tension. The pain radiating from him was so palpable she thought she could reach out and touch it.

Devon felt the guilt he carried.

She got up, refilled his glass, and carried it back to him. He started to refuse the drink but then changed his mind. He lifted it and drank half in one swallow.

"Logan." She said his name in a tentative voice.

"I know, I know." He slugged down the remainder of the wine. "You can tell me all you want that it wasn't my fault. That her bodyguard should have been more alert, but hell. They were on him the minute he opened the car door. I still can't help thinking if I'd picked her up it wouldn't have happened. It made me question myself as a man and a Marine."

"I'm so sorry. I—" She stopped. What could she say?

"After that I made up my mind love was not for me. It was too painful to lose someone, and besides, I was sure I'd never find another woman just like that. So strong, so independent, so determined no matter what the circumstances. It's worked for all these years." He gave her a piercing look. "Until I met you."

Devon tried to conceal her shock. This was the last thing she expected to hear.

"It's not just the chemistry," he told her. "Although that's pretty damn strong. But you are so much like her it's unbelievable. And when we made love…"

At least he'd said made love instead of had sex.

She cleared her throat. She didn't want to ask him, but she had to. "Are you sure you don't just see me as a replacement for her?"

He shook his head. "The truth? I asked myself the same question, and the answer is no. As much as you're like her, you're that many ways different. Your own person."

"I don't know…"

He held up a hand. "Let me finish." He refilled both their wineglasses. Lifted his and took a swallow. "There are rules, Devon. My rules. Vigilance rules. Top of the list is clients are off-limits."

"I know," she broke in. "That's why I had reservations about…what we did. I have rules, too, Logan. It seems we both broke them."

He nodded. "I just couldn't help myself. I've asked myself every minute if I was imagining this, but the connection we made… Devon, it's been years since I felt one that strong." He stared at her, the look in his eyes piercing. "Am I just imagining all this?"

She shook her head. "No. You're not. At first I thought maybe I was crazy. I mean, thugs run me off the road, a man saves me, and the first thing I feel is an unbelievable attraction for the man who rescues me? I thought to myself, *Am I nuts?* Is it possible for something like this to happen that fast?"

His mouth curved in a lopsided grin. "It must be, because it hit both of us." Then his smile disappeared, replaced by a serious look. "I broke my rules here, because I wanted you more than I wanted my job, which is really saying something." He looked away for a moment, then back at her. "I worry that I'll let myself get distracted and something will happen to you."

Like Amanda. He didn't say it but she knew that was what he was thinking.

She took a slow sip of her wine and tried to collect her thoughts. She needed to take great care with her words.

"Logan, listen to me." She put down her glass, walked over to him, and took both of his hands. "I can't even begin to imagine the pain you carry with you from such a devastating situation. But she could have been snatched at any time."

"I know that's logical," he agreed, "but I never could make myself believe it."

"On the other hand," Devon went on, "if the point of this conversation is to let me know what happened between us is a mistake, that's okay. I can deal with that. I—"

"No." He snapped the word out. "That's not it at all."

She locked her gaze with his. "Then help me understand what you mean. I don't want to do anything that—"

"No. Stop." He blew out a breath. "I'm doing this all wrong. Damn." He rubbed his jaw. "This feels like a scene out of a bad movie. This is not who I am, this kind of dialogue."

Devon had to smile. "No, I'm sure it's not, Mr. Big Bad Marine."

He smiled back at her, although his expression was tentative.

"What I'm getting at is this." He skewered her with his gaze again, as if trying to see beneath the surface. "Unless my radar is way off, we have something going here. The last thing I ever thought was to find this with someone again and I don't want to screw up. You'd think after all these years I'd have enough discipline to put it all in my back pocket until this is resolved, but that doesn't seem to be working for me." He stopped, apparently waiting for her to say something.

"If you're asking do I feel the same way, I think I already answered that." She chose her words with great care. "I know what's going on here. What's at stake. But I'm not a child or an idiot. For whatever reason fate put us together and created something special for us. You've had this once before so maybe you're afraid to take a chance again; I haven't and I don't want to walk away from it. I've waited a long time for someone like you."

He studied her for so long she was suddenly afraid of what his answer would be. "Okay," he said at last, "here's the deal." He raked his fingers through his hair. "Do I think it's smart to put this away until all the danger is past and we can take a rational look at it? Probably. Do I want to do it? Hell, no. But I also have to put your safety first. I don't want to do anything to put you in danger." There was that crooked grin again. "Talk about being a mixed-up mess. I might lose my man card."

Devon took his wineglass from his hand and put her arms around him. "I trust you, Logan. Trust you to use good judgment and to keep me safe. Whatever exploded between us isn't going to burn any less bright because you're here to protect me. How about if we take it slow, one day at a time? If what we feel is real, it won't disappear. If we can steal some alone time without courting danger, let's do it. And let's both be alert, all the time."

"I'll feel a lot better when we know exactly what the deal is with your father and where the danger is coming from."

"Me, too."

He looked down at her for so long and took so much time to comment on what she said that she wondered if she'd said something wrong. Then he tightened one arm around her, slid his fingers into her hair to cup her head, and took her mouth in a kiss so hungry she wondered if he'd ever be satisfied. His tongue plunged and swirled, sliding across hers in an erotic caress. His hard body was pressed to hers, the thick outline of his cock evident against her pelvis, the earthy scent of his aftershave tantalizing her nostrils.

They broke the kiss only when they both ran out of breath. They looked at each other, stunned by the intensity of what was between them. Logan opened his mouth to say something when the landline rang. They both hurried into the kitchen.

"Let me get it." Logan reached for the receiver.

"All right, but I want to hear whatever is said," she insisted.

He held it to give them both access.

"Yes?" He barked the word.

"Tell the bitch if we don't get what we want, yesterday was just a little taste of what we have in store." The voice was guttural, with a Spanish accent.

To Devon it sounded like the same man who had threatened her on the road.

"She has nothing for you." Logan delivered the words in the coldest voice she had ever heard. "And next time I won't be so friendly."

"Don't make light of this," the voice said. "We always get what we want." Then there was a click and they heard the dial tone.

Devon tightened her fists and shoved them in her pockets to halt her sudden trembling.

Logan cupped her chin and tilted her face to him. "Listen to me. They will not get you. Not touch you. Not harm you. You can take that to the bank."

He rubbed his thumb against her jawline and she pressed her head into his palm, seeking strength from his touch.

"I believe you. It's just—" She sighed. "This is all just such a mess."

He winked at her. "That it is, but I'm the best cleanup man you could ever want."

"Do you think they'll try to come to the house?"

"If they do, help is just five minutes away."

"I'm not sure which upsets me more, the idea of guns or of drugs." Then a thought hit her and made her stomach cramp. "Do you think maybe he was into both? Oh, Logan, my God." She rubbed her forehead. "What made him get involved with people like that, if in fact that's what he did? Was he in that much trouble? Did he need the money so badly?"

"Desperate people do desperate things. Avery said they're searching as fast as they can. By morning she expects to have a lot more to tell us. Your father was very good at layering and hiding things, though, making it just that much harder to trace. And now that we think executives of CI were involved, who better to cook the books than the vice president for corporate finance?"

She chewed her thumbnail. "I hope Avery can figure out how this all happened and who all is involved besides a cartel."

"If anyone can, it's her," he assured her. He stroked his thumb over her knuckles. "Vigilance is the best, you know. They can find a gnat in the desert under ten tons of sand. They'll get to the bottom of this and we'll find your father. That's a promise from me to you."

"You know you can't make those kinds of promises."

He lifted her hand and kissed it. "I can, I will, and I am. It just takes time. You saw the setup at Vigilance. Right now Ginger's assignment is to focus on this, nothing else. She's running every program and writing new ones if she has to. It's a little more difficult because it looks like your father created electronic walls and traps to protect himself."

"He knew what he was doing." The thought was so hard to get her mind around. "But was he burying all this for whoever he was involved with or to protect himself?"

"Hard to tell. I'd say probably both. If he was mixed up with some really bad guys, he'd want to give himself an edge. Just in case."

Devon didn't want to ask in case of what.

"What about his phone? Any further news to report on that?"

"We're looking at a form of encryption more complicated than we've seen before." He sighed. "It seems that the moment companies like Vigilance find a way to crack a code, someone invents a tougher one. But they're on it nonstop."

"I know. It's just—" She threw up her hands.

"Come here." He drew her into his arms. "You have my promise that we'll get to the bottom of this, and soon. And that I'll keep you safe." He brushed his mouth over hers. "Meanwhile I prescribe another glass of wine and a nice dinner. And maybe a hot bath." He wiggled his eyebrows at her. "That's Dr. Malik's prescription."

She laughed, knowing that's what he wanted from her. "Yes, sir. I'll do my best to follow doctor's orders."

Devon had trouble concentrating on dinner and even sitting still. She kept expecting the phone to ring again with a call from the men dogging her. And every time there was a noise from outside she jumped, even though she knew every single sound was being monitored. Logan had even set up a laptop in the kitchen so he could keep an eye on things while they ate.

"I think you've pushed that piece of chicken around on your plate long enough." Logan's voice held a touch of amusement. "Let's just say you get an A for effort and leave it at that."

She dug up a smile for him. "I'm sorry. I don't seem to have much appetite. I can't get my mind around everything Avery told us and all the possibilities. It's unbelievable that my father would be involved in stuff like this."

"When we get the details, it may turn out not to be as bad as we think."

"That's nice of you to say, but you don't have to be careful of my feelings."

"What I do have to be careful of," he told her as he pushed away from the table, "is making sure you get enough rest. You've had a traumatic couple of days."

He stacked the dishes from the table and carried them to the sink.

"Wait." Devon rose and picked up the few things still left. "I can do this. You cooked. I'll clean up."

He took the things from her hands and put them on the counter.

"Most women would rejoice at being waited on."

"I'm not most women," she pointed out.

Logan turned to face her, cradling her chin in his palm. "That's for sure. And thank the Lord." He dropped his hand and linked his fingers through hers. "Have a nice hot shower." He leered at her. "Then I'll tuck you nicely into bed."

"Oh, really." She wiggled her eyebrows at him.

He kissed her forehead, then gave her a pat on the ass. "Go on. I'll be in shortly."

She stripped off her clothes, and when the shower was good and hot, stepped under its spray. She couldn't get her mind around the story Logan had told her about himself. To have loved someone so much, and to lose them the way he did was certainly devastating. No wonder he hadn't gotten over it. Had closed himself off from emotion all these years. That might have made him a damn good Marine and now a security and protection agent, but at what cost to himself personally?

She was shocked that his reaction to her was so strong it could make him break his rules. And the agency's. She was equally stunned at her own response. What a time for this to happen, but then it wasn't always possible to predict how and when this kind of powerful emotional attraction would strike. She worried that when everything was over and her life returned to whatever passed for normal, Logan would have second thoughts. He'd regret what he'd done and what he'd told her, and pull back from her.

Okay. She was tough. She'd just go back to Tampa and try to rebuild a life that had come apart before her very eyes.

She turned off the water, squeezed the excess from her hair, and opened the door to get a towel. And gave a little squeak. Logan was standing there, holding the towel for her. She'd been so busy running her brain through hoops she hadn't heard him come in, nor noticed the shadow outside the frosted door.

His mouth curved in a lopsided grin. "I could smell your brain burning all the way in the kitchen. Don't think so much."

She took the towel from him, not the least bit self-conscious about her nakedness, and began to dry herself off.

"I wasn't thinking," she denied.

He gave a short laugh. "Never try to lie to an expert."

She wrapped the towel around her body, and tucked it in beneath one arm.

"Maybe I was thinking about this morning."

"God. I hope so." His voice had a rough, husky sound to it. He leaned in the doorway watching her as she spread lotion on her skin.

"Am I putting on a show for you?" she teased.

"I hope so." His eyes glittered with need.

"So how do I stack up, on a scale of one to ten?"

He moved to lick an errant drop of water from her shoulder. "Possibly an eleven. We'll see."

She stripped away the towel and took her nightshirt from the vanity where she'd placed it earlier. After she slid it into place, he took her face in his hands and brushed his lips over hers.

"I haven't been able to get this morning out of my mind." His eyes, that mysterious stormy gray/blue, darkened almost to navy as heat sizzled in them.

"Me either."

He tipped her head up so he could look in her eyes again. "It was... unbelievable. But it can be just as good if we are a little less hasty and frantic." He took her hand. "Come on. Let's get you into bed."

Lifting her as if she were nothing, he carried her into her bedroom and turned back the covers and eased her down onto the sheets.

"Don't go to sleep," he warned, giving her another light kiss. "I'll be right back."

Devon tried to settle herself in the bed but she couldn't seem to find a comfortable spot. She thought how strange it was that the bed seemed so empty without him.

He was as good as his word. In five minutes he was back in her room, a towel wrapped around his waist, his hair still damp from a shower. Tossing the towel aside, he slipped into bed beside her and drew her against him, spoon fashion. Despite the shower, his body was still like a furnace. She could feel it even through the thin material of her sleep shirt.

She could feel something else, too, the hard, thick length of his cock nestled against the crevice of her ass. She wriggled her butt against him, pressing back against his body.

His arm around her waist tightened.

"Unless you mean business you better cut that out."

"Oh, I definitely mean business." She blew out a breath. "I need to wash away today and blot out all the bad images in my head."

"It's been a tough day for you." His breath was a soft breeze against her ear. "I didn't want to push you into something you were too wrung out to enjoy."

"I don't think I would ever not enjoy this."

He didn't say another word, just nibbled on the rim of her ear as he tugged up her sleep shirt and slid his hand up to cup a breast. She loved the feel of him and the way he touched her. His hands had a slightly rough feel to them, the touch of a man who used them for less than delicate things. She also knew he could use those hands to kill, but that didn't detract from them at all. The moment he cradled her breast in his palm she felt her nipple go hard. When he brushed the pad of his thumb over it, she moaned, and Logan's low, sexy laugh rumbled in her ear.

"Feel good?" he asked.

"I don't know," she teased. "Keep doing it for another three or four hours and I'll let you know."

"You just lie there," he whispered in a low growl, "and I'll see what else I can do to make you feel good."

He was unhurried, slow moving, as he stroked and teased her body. When he had tormented one nipple to his satisfaction, he slid his hand to the other one and gave it the same treatment. When she tried to wriggle her butt against him, he threw one muscled leg over both of hers and pinned her in place.

"No moving." His voice was low and warm like molasses. "This is my show. Just relax and let me give you pleasure."

Lying still was one of the hardest things she'd ever done but she drew in a deep breath, let it out slowly, and willed herself not to move.

When both nipples were hard and aching with need, he slid his hand down lower on her body, pausing at her navel to trace a fingertip again and again over the curled flesh there. Spears of electricity stabbed everywhere on her body, stealing her breath, and making her pulse accelerate until it felt like a jungle drum at the hollow of her throat, her wrists, and most important, between her legs.

Just as she tried to squeeze her thighs together to still the throbbing deep in her sex, Logan eased his hand down over her mound, nudged her thighs apart. As he eased a finger between her outer lips, gliding over her clit, he bit down lightly on her shoulder, intensifying every feeling in her body. She tried to push down on his hand but he held her in place, teasing her with his finger. One of his legs hooked over hers and tugged to inch her thighs apart, giving him full access to her.

She knew what sheer torment was now. It was the very slow glide of his finger over her clit in a touch as soft as a fairy's kiss, just enough to torment her but not enough to give her the relief she wanted. With the palm of his hand pressed over her mound he rubbed and swirled and rubbed some more. When he finally slid one finger inside her she wanted to cry with relief. Only the moment she tried to press down on it, he eased it out of her hot, slick channel and concentrated only on stroking her clit with those lighter than air touches.

"Feel good, baby?" His voice was a low rumble in her ear. "Like that? And this? And this? You know what I'd like to do to you?"

And while he worked her clit like a master he proceeded to whisper in her ear details of every erotic act he wanted to commit with her. The more he stroked and the more he whispered the hotter and more aroused she became. When he removed his hand, she cried out in protest, but in the next moment he eased his middle finger, slick with her juices, between the cheeks of her ass. As lightly and gently as he'd done everything else he stroked up and down, pressing against the opening there before sliding his finger up and down again.

Devon thought she would go mad with need. She wanted him *inside* her, his finger *inside* her, his cock *inside* her, and she wanted it now. When he traced the shell of her ear with his tongue over and over, shivers raced down her spine and the walls of her sex throbbed and pulsed.

When she was at the point of begging, pleading, he nipped her shoulder again and shifted position for a moment.

"Hold on a minute. I made sure I was prepared."

She felt him roll partially away from her for a moment. Then she heard the distinctive tear of foil, felt his hands against her ass as he rolled on a condom. Then he lifted her leg to slide his cock between her thighs, resting the head just at her opening.

"Please," she begged again.

He eased himself in so slowly she wanted to scream. But she was good and ready for him, inner walls pliable and slick with her cream. When he was fully seated inside her, he pressed his hand against her abdomen to hold her body to his and began to move.

Devon never realized before what slow torture was but she knew it now. She tried to signal him to go faster but he was obviously determined to take his slow, sweet time. With every glide and thrust, in and out and forward and back, her desire ratcheted up another notch. He was hard and thick inside her, filling her completely, matching the strokes of his finger on her clit to the rhythm of his body until she wasn't sure she could stand it another minute.

She was perched right on the edge of release, her body humming with need, nerves firing.

"Please." She whispered the word. "Please, Logan."

As if her plea triggered a reaction in his body, he pressed his hand hard on her mound, finger on her clit, thrust once, twice, then bit down on that sensitive spot where neck and shoulder joined. They exploded together, their bodies glued so tight together they might have been one person. Everything disappeared except the pulsing of her inner walls as they milked his cock and the spasms rocking her entire body.

At some point the frenzy subsided, the tension easing from their bodies. Devon struggled to catch her breath, even as she felt the beating of Logan's heart against her and heard the rasping of his breath mingling with hers. Finally Logan eased from her body and rose from the bed to dispose of the condom.

"Back in a second." His voice was deep and raspy.

"Not going anywhere," she managed.

Devon couldn't move if she wanted to. She just lay there, reveling in the incredible afterglow until Logan slipped into bed again and once more curled her body into his.

"Sleep," he murmured, trailing kisses along her jaw.

And she did, falling at once into a deep sleep where everything from the past two days disappeared.

Chapter 11

Cruz Moreno wanted to throw the damned cell phone on the floor and smash it. Could no one do anything right?

Cole's disappearance, without a trace, was a shock to him. He'd totally underestimated the man, something that still rankled. And now Cole, from wherever he'd disappeared to, had sent him a threatening e-mail. Leave Devon Cole alone or else. Well, fuck that. No one threatened Cruz Moreno and lived to talk about it. One way or another he'd find the man, or find a way to smoke him out. He hoped the two *pendejos* he had sent on this assignment got their act together. Getting rid of them and sending in another team would take time, and that was something he did not have. With one phone call, Graham Cole could bring down the entire cartel and Cruz was not about to let that happen.

The e-mail had sparked a nearly uncontrollable fit of temper. He had immediately typed *"Chinga usted, pendejo."* *Go fuck yourself, asshole.*

He had waited for an answer but none was forthcoming. He had ordered Emilio, his nephew with a university degree in computer science, to trace the e-mail to determine Cole's location, with no results.

"He is using an anonymous server, *Tío*," Emilio said. "He has much the same setup we do. It's impossible to trace."

"Nothing is impossible," Cruz shouted. "Find him."

His rage only increased tenfold when Emilio told him it would take some time to get a geographic location.

Emilio had rubbed his hands nervously. "I'm not saying I can't crack it, but it will take a lot of time."

Now he clutched the cell phone in his hand hard enough to break it. He listened to the man on the other end of the call, anger seething through him as he heard excuse after excuse.

"So you failed." He bit off each word. "Again. You were unable to capture Cole and I still don't know how the fuck you let him get away. Then you made an incredible mess of the situation with his daughter. Now she's had a look at you and gave your description to the police." Pause. "What *absolutamente* bad luck that an agent from Vigilance, that thorn in everyone's side, happened along at the exact wrong time. The same agent now living in her house. Perhaps your luck is too bad for me to keep you on this project."

More squawking. He heard the panic in the man's voice. Everyone who worked for him was well aware that screwing up could result in their execution.

"Then fix this. I don't care how. He has to have left something at the house that will lead us to him. A clue. Find it. Today. And take Luis with you. He's just sitting on his ass doing nothing. Maybe three of you will have better luck than two. Remember. This is your last chance. *Comprende?*"

He drew heavily on his cigar as he listened to protesting on the other end of the conversation. He could feel his blood pressure rise with each word.

Cruz curled his lips in a sneer. "Then you should be inspired. Call me when it's done."

He punched the button to disconnect and tossed the phone on the little table next to him. He leaned back in the large armchair in his living room, reaching for control, and blew out a stream of smoke from his hand-rolled cigar. The building of this house and complex had taken two years but everything had been done to his specification. Everything was custom designed and manufactured, from the furniture to the floor tiles to the crystal chandeliers. The pool was Olympic size and the patios on either side could hold a party for a hundred people. He had chosen to build on top of a very high hill, so that access was either by helicopter or up a very long, winding road that allowed him plenty of notice when anyone approached.

If others criticized it as being too opulent, well, that was too bad. He had the money and he loved spending it. He was, after all, *el Jefe*.

But today nothing in the house could soothe the anger bubbling inside him. His carefully laid plans that had worked for such a long time had developed a glitch that needed to be fixed at once. Cole International had been an ideal target to use as a conduit to launder money. Careful plans had been made, people put in place or seduced by the promise of large rewards. Fancy bookkeeping had put Graham Cole in a desperate situation. Everything would be cloaked in respectability and he wouldn't have to worry about the operation garnering unwanted attention.

When Cole wanted to repay the money, he'd been told that was not possible and informed where the funds came from. When Cole objected violently and wanted out at once, Cruz's anger rose to the surface. Others were on board with the plan. He failed to see what the man's problem was. He had a steady flow of capital through his conglomerate, 10 percent of which went into the corporate coffers. Wasn't that enough for him to look the other way?

Okay, Cruz was willing to admit he might have pushed the envelope when he'd demanded the use of Cole's house several times for an exchange of goods, or for a meeting that could not take place at the Moreno property. But at the time, circumstances had permitted him very few options. He offered Cole an additional 2 percent of the money, a sum that would have satisfied anyone else. He should have been suspicious when the man agreed so readily, after digging in his heels.

"You really want to send them, after the mess they already made?"

He looked at the man sitting on the couch, the one he called Vato. "I need to find a clue as to where he's hiding. He can ruin all of us, including you, if he lets it out."

"People will be watching for them," the man said. "Besides, Vigilance installed a new security system at the house."

"Nothing I can't handle." He drew on his cigar and blew a thin ring of smoke in the air. "You are as much at fault as they are, *mi amigo*."

Cruz was only too happy to call Vato friend as long as he continued to provide avenues to launder the vast sums of money the cartel received for the drugs and arms they smuggled. Today, with Cruz's careful plan unraveling, he had sent his helicopter to fetch the man for this meeting. At this level, he preferred to deliver his ultimatums face-to-face. He'd always found that to be more effective.

Unfortunately, it hadn't worked with Vincent Pellegrino. Who knew the man would grow a conscience? There was no room for one in this business.

Vato frowned. "At fault for what? Without me you wouldn't be using Cole International to launder your money with such success. Or have any of the other deals I put together."

"Don't puff yourself up too much. You aren't the only one who made this happen. You should have taken better control of this entire situation. No loose ends, however you had to do it." He flicked a ring of ash into a crystal ashtray. "You assured me you had him under control."

"I told you Cole freaked when he discovered the reality of the situation. I had to really talk him down off the ledge. We've never had a problem with anyone else."

"But it's been months since he found out. You had plenty of time to be sure nothing like this would happen." He glared at Vato.

Vato shifted in his seat. It was obvious to Cruz he was trying to appear as unruffled as possible. "When Cole was desperate to save his company, I knew he'd take anything, since other doors were closed to him. I never thought he'd want out."

Moreno took a puff on his cigar and blew another smoke ring. "Did he ever discover how it all came together?"

"Hell, no. That *really* would have been a disaster. Once he got used to the income, I didn't think anyone in his right mind would want to terminate an arrangement that brought in that kind of money without lifting a finger."

"You obviously misread the situation, *amigo.*" Moreno nearly spat out the last word, robbing it of any sense of friendship. "Now he has disappeared with records of everything and he has the nerve to threaten me. *Threaten me!*"

He repeated the words with venom and glared at the man sitting across from him. He was impeccably dressed in slacks, a gray sports shirt, and a bad case of nerves.

"I want to find him," he continued. "No, I *need* to find him. And you are going to help me."

"Me?" The man spread his hands in a helpless gesture. "How do you expect me to do that? No one knows where the hell he's gone, including his daughter."

"But if we have to, we can use her to force his hand."

"Did you read what he said? If you don't leave her alone, he dumps all that information out there, probably to the Feds." He snorted. "Besides, she's got that damn fucking Vigilance agent stuck to her like glue. I have to be real careful there." He leaned forward in the chair. "You should hire better help, Cruz. Then you wouldn't need me. They couldn't even destroy a boat without making a major incident out of it. And sending that kid to search? A mistake."

"If you had gotten to the boats when I told you, it would not have been necessary."

"With a hundred eyes on them?" The man shook his head. "Anyway, I'm too visible to go sneaking around at one in the morning."

Cruz shook his head. "I should have all of you eliminated."

It did him good to see the other man lose all color in his face.

"A good option," Cruz added.

The man shifted in his seat. "But sending those thugs to the house again? I don't mean to tell you your business, Cruz, but Vigilance will have both her and the house locked up tight with security. High-end security. This could create another disaster."

"This is their last chance. They'll be well motivated." He stared at the man opposite him. "Hear this, *mi amigo*. If I go down, I take everyone with me. It might be in the best interest of you and the others to get me the information I need."

"I'll do my best."

"Your best better leave no room for error. I want results. If nothing else works, we may have to use the daughter for leverage."

"I think that would be a big mistake."

"Then it falls back on you. Get me results."

Cruz watched Vato through narrowed eyes as he left the house and headed toward the helipad in the back. He meant what he said. There was enough mud to dirty everyone, and he knew just how to do it.

* * * *

The ringing of Logan's cell phone on the nightstand woke Devon. He slid his arm from beneath her, rolled over, and scooped up the phone.

"Yeah? Uh-huh. Yeah. Okay. We're moving." He set the phone down and gave Devon a light tap on her ass. "Time to hustle, babe."

Devon sat up, shoving her hair out of her eyes. "What? What's up?"

"That was Avery."

Devon scrambled off the bed. "She found out where he is?"

"No, unfortunately." Logan tipped her face up to his and stroked her chin with his knuckles. "Come on. Let's get ready and see what she's got."

She showered quickly and pulled on jeans and a T-shirt. A quick twist of her hair into a ponytail and she was ready. No makeup. Not a necessity today. Logan made sure the alarm was set before they left the house, and fifteen minutes after Avery's call they were headed toward Vigilance.

Devon sat rigidly upright during the ride, her body stiff as dead wood. She was just as glad they hadn't had time to eat anything. She didn't think she'd have been able to swallow anything, much less keep it down. Whatever she heard this morning, she knew it wouldn't be good and she wasn't sure how she'd deal with it. She might have had her ups and downs with her father but she still loved him. She just couldn't imagine him mixed up with anything that would cause him to disappear. Or send people like those two men on the road after her.

Avery must have been watching for them because she opened the door as soon as they pulled into the parking area.

"I have coffee and reports ready. Come on."

When they were seated in her office, everyone with full coffee mugs, she opened a folder on her desk.

"It took Ginger quite a while to track all of this down," she began.

Devon gripped her coffee mug so hard she hoped she didn't break it. "Avery, I don't mean to be rude but can we just cut to the chase here? *Is* my father involved with drug dealers?"

Avery hesitated for a moment before she nodded her head.

"Yes. We already know four years ago your father was in a tough financial spot. If he went to one of the major financial institutions, they might hesitate to lend him the money, worried the cause of the red ink was bad management. And if they did process the loan, there'd be a chance word would get out and that wouldn't be good for business either."

"Enter the private investor," she guessed.

"Yes." Avery flipped through a couple sheets of paper in front of her. "We still can't find where and how he made the original connection, but like I told you before, the cash was washed through SMX."

"The one with the fake office in Aruba?" Devon asked.

"Yes. Ginger is really good at digging out money trails. We now have proof SMX is the major funnel for the Moreno drug cartel." Her mouth curved in a dry smile. "To let you know how good she is, not even the Feds have been able to identify this up until now. Whoever set this up for the cartel did an excellent job."

Devon was sick at the thought that popped into her head. "Vince Pellegrino."

"Maybe. For the moment we'll assume so. It looks like he was involved with the cartel for a long time, before he even came to Cole International."

"He was a Trojan horse," Logan guessed.

"What?" Devon looked from one to the other.

"Someone who appears to be one thing but when they are successfully in place turns out to be something else entirely."

"We think they maneuvered to get him the job at Cole International in the first place. Manufactured a portfolio for him. Then, when he was in place, it's even possible that he cooked the books to show the company losing money when, in fact, it might not have been."

Devon's jaw dropped. "Are you serious?"

"As a heart attack. Ginger's found all kinds of things. It's going to take a really good team of forensic accountants to trace it all and straighten it out."

"Oh my God." She felt suddenly lightheaded.

Logan reached over and took the mug from her hands. "Breathe, Devon. Slowly. In through the nose, out through the mouth."

He watched her until she managed to get control of herself again.

"What about Alford and Bodine? If they used to work for Moreno's attorney, they also have to be involved."

"They were. Are. Pellegrino recommended them to your father when he suggested the corporation change attorneys. Hire someone in house. They structured the fake legal work on a lot of the deals so they'd look legit."

"Damn," Logan said.

"How does it all work?" Devon asked.

"It's really very simple. The cartel securities firm poses as a private investor. They seek out situations where an infusion of cash is imperative and they have someone in a position to direct people to them. Once the deal is struck they start funneling it through the pipeline. On paper it looks like a straight business deal—so much cash for a percentage of the business."

"I can't imagine anyone would be that anxious to in effect hand over part of their company."

"But what if they couldn't get the money anyplace else?" Avery asked. "What if they didn't have a choice? Moreno's done this a lot. He provides the cash, Alford and Bodine draw up the so-called legal papers, and redefine the structure of the business."

"In the beginning, it's a hands-off situation, with a few suggestions here and there," Logan guessed.

Avery nodded. "The investor is satisfied with his monthly return on investment. By the time someone like your father figures out who their investment partner is, the cartel has its hooks in them so deep they have no choice but to continue the arrangement.

"I'm pretty sure your father wasn't aware in the beginning where the funds came from," Avery continued. "It's all very well hidden. It took Ginger a long time and a lot of knowledge to find the answers."

"The deal would have looked like a straight financial contract," Logan added.

"But we found changes in vendors and suppliers after the loan was made. That's common. It's how the cartel washes their money through shell companies."

Logan nodded. "And your father didn't really think much about it."

"That's another area that Alford and Bodine handled. They oversaw all that."

"Until there was a problem," Avery agreed. "My money says your father reached a point where he wanted to pay off the investor. That's probably when he was told where the money came from and that there was no paying it off. Just a lot more of what was going on."

Devon swallowed back the nausea threatening to break loose. "But we still don't know who approached my father about this. Could it have been

Pellegrino, put in place well in advance to be in that position? Or one of the two attorneys? Someone had to be the point man."

"Good question," Avery answered. "Did your father spend a lot of time here before the move?" Avery asked.

"A fair amount." Her eyes widened. "Do you think it's someone from Arrowhead Bay?"

Avery shrugged. "Or it could be someone who sails in here and that's how they met. Sharing a common interest. Anyway, I'd like to think we would have sniffed it out long ago if someone here was washing money for the cartel, but anything is possible."

Logan looked over at her. "Do you think you could make a list of everyone you remember your father being friends or friendly with for the past few years? Business as well as personal? This has to be someone he trusted a lot."

Devon nodded her head. "I'll do my best, but you know there was a lot about his life I don't know." She rubbed her face. "God. I can hardly take in the whole thing."

"One more thing." Avery looked at some of her notes. "We don't think Pellegrino's death was an accident."

"What?" Devon jumped out of her chair. "What are you saying?"

"If the cartel got wind of your father's plans and Pellegrino had lost control of him, then he became disposable."

"Holy God, Avery." Devon closed her eyes and swallowed. "This is a nightmare."

"Pellegrino's accident happened the same day your father disappeared," Avery said. "We think Moreno demanded a meeting that day."

Devon was still trying to get her head around it all. "So he just up and left?"

Logan shook his head. "To do a Houdini the way he did required a lot of advance preparation. He was ready to bail. This may just have pushed up his timetable. I'd guess that—"

Whatever else he was going to say was interrupted by a squealing sound from his watch at the same time Avery's office phone rang.

Devon jumped, startled, then looked from one to the other. "What—?"

Avery was hanging up her phone before Devon could get another word out.

Logan was already on his feet. "It has to be those two jokers from the other day."

"You're right." Avery punched a button. "Mike Perez is in the electronics room. He's just off an assignment and free. Grab him and get going. Now."

"She stays here." He pointed at Devon. "Eyes on her at all times."

"Done. No one can get to her here. Go." She waved a hand. "Now. And be sure you guys have your radios with you. I'm calling Sheri."

"Tell her no sirens."

"Hey, I'm the boss, remember? I know this stuff."

But by that time Logan was gone, leaving Avery punching speed dial on her cell and Devon in a high state of nerves.

"What's happening?" Devon stared after Logan. "Avery, what's going on?"

"Just stay calm, kiddo. That's the signal someone broke into your house. There's an alarm receiver on Logan's watch as well as the one here in headquarters. We use them all the time. It goes off whenever there's a breach of the property."

"I should—" she started again.

Avery shook her head. "You should stay right here, where you're safe. Logan and Mike will be there in a few minutes. And they won't be expected. Logan set the alarm on silent before you left, so it won't tip anyone off in case of something like this. If they think they neutralized it, we have a better chance of catching them."

"Are you—"

Avery held up her hand and spoke into her phone.

"Sheri? Yeah, a breach at the Cole house. Logan and Mike Perez are on their way. Can you grab one of your officers and head out there? Uh-huh. Yeah. Okay." She looked at Devon. "Okay, she's on her way."

"I hope they catch those bastards." She could still see them standing on either side of her car, trapping her inside, shattered glass all over her.

"So do I. I want to turn my people loose on them and shake their brains to see what falls out."

* * * *

"So what kind of shit are we facing here?" Mike Perez asked, as they raced up Seacliff Road.

Logan had worked assignments with Mike before and trusted him 100 percent. Tall and built like a football player, he was also a crack shot.

"At least two guys, we think sent by a drug cartel, to search the house."

"Drug cartel?"

"Yeah, it seems somehow Graham Cole got himself tangled up with Cruz Moreno."

"Holy shit!" Mike said. Moreno was well known as one of the most vicious cartel leaders alive.

"In spades. Graham Cole disappeared on them and they want the information he has. They're stupid to think he left it at the house, or even left a clue as to where he was going. Otherwise, why disappear? They're after something they aren't going to find, and that's going to make them very mad."

"Do I need to know what?" Mike asked. "Never mind. We just need to catch these guys, right?"

"Right."

Across from the Cole house he pulled off the road into the thick trees lining that side.

"Hell-o." Mike pointed to a black SUV hidden not far away. "This must be their ride."

"Sure is." Logan turned off the ignition. "That's the car they forced Devon off the road in."

"Devon?"

"Cole's daughter. Come on. We need to sneak around on the far side where they can't see us. Thank God that's where the garage is." He picked up the tiny handheld radio he'd taken from the office. "Avery? We're here and it's definitely them. I recognize the car. We're on our way. Out." And he slipped the radio into his pocket. "I'll take point," he told Mike.

He led the way past the next curve of the road, up the slope of land past the scattering of fiddlewood and pigeon plum trees until they reached the garage. There were no windows here. Logan pulled the key ring Devon had tossed at him as he left Vigilance out of his pocket. The second key he tried unlocked the side door to the garage.

"Come on," he whispered, opening the door.

They crept across the nearly empty garage to the door into the house. Logan slipped the key into the lock, turned it, and eased the door open. When they were through the opening, he spotted a guy in the foyer watching the front of the house. He turned to Mike, signaling one person he had eyes on. In one smooth movement, he went up behind the thug, wrapped his arm around his neck, and clamped a hand over his mouth.

"I'd snap your neck without hesitation," he whispered in the man's ear, "so don't make a sound."

The man nodded but the moment Logan eased his hold he opened his mouth.

"Idiot," Logan cursed, exerting pressure on the man's neck until he sagged against him, unconscious.

Logan lowered him to the floor as Mike slid past him, moving slowly through the house to search for the man's friend. He had just finished fastening zip ties on the man's hands and ankles when he heard two shots, fired in rapid succession. At once he moved toward the kitchen where the sound came from.

Mike was standing over the other asshole, now on the floor holding his stomach and writhing in pain.

"So much for being quiet," Mike complained. "The jerk turned around just as I came in and went for his gun. I aimed for his hand and his stomach got in the way."

He handed the radio to Mike. "Tell Avery to call Sheri to come up to the house. And tell her we need an ambulance. I'll check the rest of the house but if there was anyone else, he's gone by now."

Moving slowly and carefully, Logan cleared each room, one at a time, checking for all possible hiding places. He was convinced there weren't any others until he got to the den and found the French doors to the garden wide open.

"Son of a bitch." He looked all around the small patio area, especially the flower beds bordering it. Sure enough, there were footprints in the soft earth. He looked across the yard, hoping whoever it was had run to the highway and Sheri would spot him, but no such luck. The preserve in the back was too tempting and a better way to disappear.

"I radioed Avery," Mike told him as he walked back into the kitchen. "Sheri will be up here in seconds."

"Well, there was a third one but he's long gone." He took back the radio and punched the button for Avery. "There were three this time and one of them is out there. He ran back toward the preserve so he's in the wind. Tell Sheri to put out an all-points bulletin on him. The problem is we have no idea what he looks like."

"She'll be there in a second."

Shit, shit, shit.

He looked at the man on the floor. "Your friend sure ditched you in a hurry."

The man just scowled at him, his face lined with pain.

He went to check on the man in the hallway and found him awake. When he saw Logan, he began swearing in Spanish.

"Yeah, yeah, yeah," Logan snapped. "Whatever. Your friend took a powder real quick and left you guys holding the bag."

More swearing.

Just then the doorbell rang and he cut the alarm to let Sheri in.

"Lost one, did you?" Sheri shook her head. "Don't worry. I've got everyone out looking for him. Ambulance is on its way."

"Thanks."

"Just to be safe, my officer let the air out of the SUV's tires. I hope they don't try for your truck."

"If they do, the alarm will sound. No sweat."

She eyed the man on the floor in the hallway. "This one of the same guys from the other day?"

"Yeah. His partner in crime is in the kitchen. Gut shot. He thought he could move faster than Mike."

Sheri gave an unladylike snort. "Stupid jerks." She headed for the kitchen to take a look. Then she was back. "Okay. We'll get everyone processed and out of here fast. You might want to clean the blood up before you bring Devon home."

"I'll take care of it."

He was still pissed off at himself, feeling like a rank amateur. It was especially bad with Devon's safety at stake. After this he'd be surprised if she let him in the door. Some protector he was.

Chapter 12

Devon couldn't sit still so she paced the office, her heart beating a rapid tattoo. How many were there? Were there more than the two from the other day? Logan had told her that her father really sanitized the house. If there had been anything there, she was sure he would have discovered it by now. If these men didn't find what they were looking for, would they come after her again?

She stopped in front of the desk and faced Avery.

"What do they want from me? What makes them think I know anything? I've hardly been in the picture the last couple of years." She held out her hands. "I have no idea where my father is."

"I'm sure they've been told to check the house for any clue at all," Avery said. "They're frantic to find a trace of him."

"But there's nothing there," she insisted.

"Right, but they don't know that. And my instincts are telling me something else must have happened to prompt this."

Time crawled. At one point Avery's cell phone rang, and Devon wondered if Logan might be calling instead of using the radio. Did that mean everything was taken care of? They'd caught whoever it was?

"Sit down. I mean it, Devon. I know this is a tense situation and your nerves are all over the place, but you aren't doing either of us any good wearing a hole in my rug. Now sit. At least for a minute."

Devon sat, but she perched right on the edge of the char, her hands balled into tight fists as she fought for control.

"Okay. I'm sorry. I'm just—"

"I know. I really do. Believe me."

"How do you do this?" Devon rubbed her hands on her jeans. "Sit here like this. Waiting."

"It's one of the second hardest parts of this job. But I've learned to trust my agents and that helps." She gave Devon a sympathetic smile. "And Logan's one of my very best. I have full confidence in him."

More time passed. To occupy her mind, Devon distracted herself by surfing the web on her phone, looking for anything else in the media about her father. Her little episode was still getting a fair amount of play, too. Crap.

"Avery?"

At the sound of Mike's voice coming over the radio she jerked her head up.

"I'm here," Avery told him.

"Call Sheri and tell her to get on up here. And to radio for an ambulance."

"On it."

Devon listened while she called Sheri and relayed the message, then told Mike it was all set.

Another minute or so later, while Devon stood hands clenched and jaw tight, she heard Logan's voice again, explaining there had been three men this time.

Devon's stomach knotted. A third man out there? Would he be after her, too?

Devon desperately wanted to speak to him, but this was not the time. At least hearing his voice calmed her a little.

"So what happens next?" she asked.

"Logan and Mike will follow the ambulance to the hospital. Sheri will go, also, and take their reports there." She picked up her tablet. "The one requiring hospitalization will need a guard twenty-four/seven. I'm going to offer to handle that for Sheri. Her staff isn't really big enough for her to take that on." Her lips twisted in a wry grin. "This is actually a little more excitement than Arrowhead Bay is used to. Vigilance usually takes its action out of town."

"Those men. They're the same ones from the other day, aren't they?"

"Yes. Moreno's men, I'm sure, as is the one that got away."

"Why won't they leave me alone?" She ran her fingers through her hair, then tucked it behind her ears. "I don't know anything. I don't have anything."

"This was a desperation move. Something must have happened to trigger it."

"But what?" Devon stared at the other woman.

"I don't know. Let's hope one of these guys talks. Listen, you could probably use a cup of coffee. Let me get you some. Then I need to check everyone's schedule and see who I can tap for hospital duty with Tyson."

"I can get it myself. Really." Devon walked over to the coffeemaker.

"Do what you have to. That's more important."

She refilled her mug and forced herself to sit down again. She wondered if she clicked her heels like Dorothy in *The Wizard of Oz*, this would all disappear and she'd be back in her apartment in Tampa.

But then I wouldn't have Logan.

So she sat, drinking her coffee and trying not to check her watch every five minutes.

* * * *

Although Logan checked in, it seemed forever until he finally walked back into the office. Devon jumped up and threw her arms around him. Without even thinking about how it would look and ignoring the others, he wrapped her in his arms. She fell into him without hesitation, and he leaned into the feeling of her warm, soft body.

In a moment he took a step back and looked hard into her eyes. "You okay?"

She gave a nervous little laugh. "Oh, I'm fine. Just another normal day, right?"

After a long moment, he set her away from him.

"I guess you're glad to see me." He smiled, even though the situation troubled him.

"Uh, sorry. It's just—" She lifted her hands and let them fall in a helpless gesture. "I was worried about you." She glanced at the others. "Sorry."

"Damn, Logan gets all the luck," Mike joked. He held out his hand. "Mike Perez. And you must be Devon."

She nodded. "The focal point of all this trouble."

"Not really, babe." Logan gave her hand a squeeze. "You're just the one caught in the trap."

"Let's all sit down," Avery told them, "so I can get up to date. I take it Sheri has the one guy in her jail?"

Logan nodded. "She'll—"

Avery's phone rang, interrupting everything.

"Sheri? What's up?" Avery went completely still, her face a hardened mask. "Son of a bitch. Maybe we should double up the guard at the hospital. Okay, I'll talk to Logan about it."

"Now what?" Logan asked.

"As they were moving the prisoner from the patrol car into the jail, someone fired from the trees across the street. The guy is deader than a doornail."

"Holy shit." Logan smacked his fist on the arm of the chair.

Avery skewered him with her gaze. She knew what he was thinking. "Quit beating yourself up over it. Whoever this guy is, he heard the gunshots, didn't hear his friends tell him it was all clear, and got his ass out of there. We'll all do our best to get him. Shit happens. Let's move forward."

Logan nodded. "They refused to give their names. Sheri printed both of them, including the one with the gut shot before they took him into surgery. She wants to know who has jurisdiction over him, considering the circumstances. Should we call DEA?"

"I think so." She looked at Devon. "This is beyond Arrowhead Bay now. I'm sorry, and I know if your father *is* alive, this probably won't be good for him."

Logan could almost feel her body tighten, but she nodded her head. "It is what it is. I'm hardly the expert here but I agree with what you said."

"Tyson's waiting for the one remaining thug to come out of surgery. They'll let him stand guard in recovery as well as when he gets to his room. I insisted on a private room, by the way. If someone wants to off this guy so he won't talk, they'll have to get past Vigilance."

Avery nodded. "Which means not at all."

"Still," Logan went on, "I'd feel a damn sight better if we got our hands on the guy who's in the wind. By now I'm sure he's called Moreno, or one of his lieutenants, and who knows what the hell they'll do. They sure don't want their boys talking to us."

Mike snorted. "Would you?"

"My fucking fault," Logan spat out. He still couldn't believe he'd been that careless.

"Enough already," Avery snapped and held up a hand. "Do not say this is on you again. There's nothing you could have done to prevent this. You and Mike were busy with two of the men, there was no hint of a third, and I—" She threw up her hands. "Get it out of your head or you'll be useless to both me and Devon."

Devon. He reached over for her and was happy that she gave his hand a reassuring squeeze. Avery was right. He had to get his shit together and do what he was supposed to do—keep Devon safe. He had a lot more reason to want that than when he'd just been her bodyguard.

"But this shows us the lengths they'll go to," Mike put in, "to keep their boys from talking to us."

A knock on the doorframe caught everyone's attention. Del, their crackerjack tech guy, who was working on Graham Cole's phone.

Avery motioned him into the room. "Got something for us? I hope?"

"I finally cracked all but two passwords. I think, based on time spent so far, we're pretty close. I wanted to let you know. I'm running it through two sophisticated programs right now."

"Okay, Del." Avery nodded. "But some things have happened to escalate the situation. This is very encouraging but time is critical here. Get back to it and push it as hard as you can."

"Avery?" Devon cleared her throat. "What do you think is on there besides numbers and texts?"

"Those will be a big enough help by themselves," she answered, "tracing the numbers those calls and texts went to. People have the mistaken idea that burner phones can't be traced. A good tech person like Del can find anyone, anywhere. If the phones haven't been destroyed, that is."

"I hope we get somewhere before someone else comes after me." She looked at Logan. "They might not want to kill me, right? They might think I know where my father is and—"

"Whatever they want they won't get it," he said, fierce. "I promise you that."

Devon dropped her head into her hands. Logan leaned over and cupped her chin. "Look at me, Devon. We'll find the bastard. I promise you. Despite what happened today, letting people get away just isn't in my wheelhouse."

He was still sitting with her when Sheri walked in. He looked over at her. "You okay?"

"Pissed as hell but otherwise all right."

She fixed a cup of coffee for herself, took a long, slow sip of it, then went over the details of the shooting again.

"I'm trying to think if there was a different way we could have handled this. And where the hell did that fucker get new transportation and a rifle so fast?"

"Probably called Moreno," Mike told her.

"Well, I've got everyone, including the sheriff's department, looking for him in every nook and cranny."

Avery nodded. "Good. And there's a BOLO out?"

"Did it first thing."

"Good. Is the Cole house presentable so Logan can take Devon home?"

Sheri nodded. "Taken care of."

"Presentable?" Devon looked at each of them. "What—? How—" Logan saw the look on her face when she realized that of course there was blood from the shooting and someone had been sent to clean it up. He was afraid any minute she might throw up.

"Easy, honey." He put his arm around her. "Deep breaths, okay? It will be fine."

Avery cleared her throat. "Get her out of here, Logan. Take her home and give her plenty of TLC. She needs it."

"No problem there."

"I'm okay," Devon protested.

Logan knew she'd say that. She'd fall on her face before she gave in to what she saw as weakness.

"Not hardly," Avery said. "Go home. You look like death warmed over."

Devon managed a grin. "Gee, Avery, you sure know how to make a girl feel good."

"I promise we'll call Logan with even the tiniest bit of news, okay?"

"Okay."

Logan took Devon's hand and hauled her out of the chair. "We're out of here."

Chapter 13

Logan glanced sideways at Devon as he headed the truck up Seacliff Road. Her head was pressed back against the seat with eyes closed and fingers pressed against her temples. He'd bet all his money that she was fighting a motherfucker of a stress headache. And no wonder. Her whole life was turned upside down and she was in constant jeopardy. Today was the frosting on a rapidly deteriorating cake.

"You need to eat something," he told her as he pulled into the garage.

"I don't know if I can. Pardon the inelegance, but I feel like crap." She rubbed her temples again.

"And with good reason." He took one of her hands and brought it to his lips, placing a soft kiss on her knuckles.

"I keep thinking this is all a bad dream. That I'll wake up any minute and it will all have gone away."

"If only." He climbed out and went around to her side of the truck. "Come on. I prescribe some of my famous chicken soup."

"Okay," she gave in. "I'll try. I don't think I could eat anything else."

When they walked into the house, he watched her look around as if expecting to see blood still on the floor, the house in disarray, and God knows what else. He'd made sure they put everything back the way it was. He didn't want her walking into chaos.

"Come sit down. I'm going to make you some tea to drink while I heat the soup."

"You must have brought some big ass kettle of that soup."

He was glad to hear the teasing note in her voice.

"Sure did." He winked. "It's my way to a woman's heart."

She gave him a serious look. "Are you working your way into my heart, Logan?"

Damn straight he was, despite his history and a truckload of misgivings.

"You know I am. And I hope to stay. But that's a conversation for another day." He took her small hands in his larger ones and gave them a gentle squeeze. "I'm pissed at myself for letting that guy escape today, Devon. He's out there without our eyes on him. My bad. But I promise you, I will not let him get near you."

He'd give his life for that if he had to.

"I know you won't." She turned and pressed herself against him, her arms going around his torso to hold him close to her. "I trust you and believe in you."

"Good." He kissed the top of her head.

He settled her at the table with a mug of tea, noticing how she wrapped her hands around it and leaned forward to let the steam heat her face. He was sure all the stress had made her chilled and tired.

He had just dumped the sweetener in the way she liked it when the landline rang. He looked at Devon but she just shrugged.

"I have no idea."

"Well, the two assholes are definitely out of commission," he said, "so it can't be them."

"Unless it's the one who got away. Answer it and find out."

Logan picked up the receiver and held it so they both could hear. "Hello?"

"This is Cash Breeland." The heavy drawl cut across the wires. "Can I speak to Devon?"

"It's okay," she whispered and took the phone, holding it so he could also hear. "Hi, Cash. What can I do for you?"

"Just checking on you, honey. With your dad missing and the boat being blown up, well, I wanted to make sure you were okay. And then I heard about a dustup at your house today. Something about someone breaking in."

Devon's eyes widened and he knew what she was thinking. Was it all over town already? Is that how he knew?

"It was really nothing," she assured him. "Chief March took care of everything."

"Still, a good reason why you shouldn't be alone. Marian and I thought you might want to come stay with us."

Logan frowned. "Are you that close to them?" he mouthed.

"No," she whispered. "Not at all."

"Devon? You there?"

"Yes, sorry, Cash. It's been a rough couple of days."

"All the more reason why you should come stay with us. You pack a bag and I'll come out and pick you up myself."

Devon frowned and looked at Logan. "Strange," she whispered. "Cash, that's very generous of you, but I have my bodyguard here with me and he'll make sure I'm taken care of."

"Now, Devon," he drawled. "I don't want to tell you your business, but what do you really know about this man? I mean, your daddy and I were best friends. I know he'd want me looking after you."

Logan frowned and she mouthed, "Not no but hell no."

"Cash? Again, that is very lovely and generous of you and Marian, and if I change my mind, I will be sure to let you know. Thanks so much for calling."

"Oh, sure, sure, sure." He cleared his throat. "We're just checking up on you, is all."

"Thanks for your concern. I need to go now. Bye."

She replaced the receiver in the cradle gently but Logan saw how rigid her body was. He'd have smashed the damn thing if it were him.

Devon stared at him.

"That is just the strangest thing in the world. Best friends?" She shook her head. "Uh-uh. I'm not so sure about that."

"Were they close?"

"Sure. And maybe he was closer to my dad than anyone else here, but my father still kept his distance." She wrinkled her forehead. "And to tell you the truth, the few times I saw them together the last year or so, I got a feeling that relationship was strained."

"Maybe Cash wanted your father to move some of the corporate money to his bank."

"Why would he do that? It doesn't offer near the advantages he got with the national bank."

"Just sayin'. Hey, you'd better get to that tea before it's stone cold."

He saw her visibly relax, even gift him with a tiny smile. "And it's just what I need."

As soon as he had her seated with her tea again and the soup heating, he pulled his cell out of his pocket and began punching buttons.

"I'm texting Avery to run a profile on Cash. I don't like the way he's behaving. Let's see if he's hiding something."

"I can't see him involved in my father's disappearance," she protested.

"You'd be surprised at who gets involved in what. I don't want to take any chances." He finished typing and hit Send.

He had managed to get a bowl of the soup and some toast into her when his cell rang. He looked at the readout. "Avery. What's up?" he asked, putting the phone to his ear.

"Del didn't even need another couple of hours," she told him. "He cracked the code not ten minutes after you left."

"And?"

"Everything we found confirms what we thought. He's in deep with the cartel. We even have names and numbers, although the numbers probably aren't good anymore."

"Damn."

"Right. I'm going to e-mail all this information to you. If she can handle it, go through it with her, see if by some unbelievable chance anything rings a bell. Can she handle it?"

"She's a trouper." He looked at her sitting at the table, her body vibrating with tension. "She'll do it. Can you send it to my laptop?"

"No problem. I'll be sending it in just a few. Unfortunately, there's not a damn thing on there that gives us a clue to Graham Cole's current location."

"Crap."

"Indeed. Oh, and I got your text about Cash Breeland. What's that all about?"

"Just crossing all the Ts." He told her about the phone call. "So send me anything you find."

"Will do."

Devon pounced as soon as he hung up. "Tell me."

He repeated his conversation with Avery.

"I can hardly believe all of this."

He hated the look on her face, a mixture of hope and dread. "Whatever it is, we'll handle it together. Okay?" He lifted one of her hands and kissed her knuckles.

"Okay," she said at last in a weak voice.

He fixed another mug of tea for her and coffee for himself, then went to fetch his laptop from his room. By the time he had it set up on the table, the e-mail had arrived. He opened the attachment and moved next to her so they both could see it.

"It's nothing different than we suspected," he said after they'd skimmed through the first few pages.

"You're right." She sounded so depressed he wanted to push away the damn computer and haul her into his arms.

"It just confirms everything Avery told us earlier. Looking at the dates of calls and texts, I'd say your father started making his plans the moment he learned for sure who his 'investor' was and that there was no way out."

Devon studied the screen as Logan scrolled through the report.

"I'm not very good with finances or financial charts. I don't know what half of this stuff means."

"I'm not much better." Logan scrolled down to the last page again. "Here's Avery's analysis, though, based on the texts. This was all set in motion long before Cole International began to bleed red ink. Vince Pellegrino was put in place at CI and made himself your father's right-hand man. And see here?" He pointed to a section on the page. "The dates when Bodine and Alford were hired. I'll bet if we dig into CI's employment files, we'll discover they were recommended by our good friend Vince."

"What are these documents? Is it possible to store documents on a cell?"

"Yes. These are spreadsheets. They look like duplicates but—" He leaned forward and studied them, switching from one to the other. "If I'm not mistaken, this is how the books were cooked to make your father think the company was bleeding red ink. They needed a way to get him on board."

"But why CI?"

"Because Cole International is a company that operates internationally and provides the opportunity to ship drugs from country to country, and move money to international bank accounts."

"I feel sick." Devon leaned forward and dropped her head into her hands. "What a nightmare."

"One thing's missing from here." He gestured toward the screen. "Moreno puts Vince in place to manipulate the books. Crisis arises. Vince says get an investor. SMX is the investor. But someone had to make the marriage between SMX and CI. That's not part of Vince's job. Did he still do his banking in Tampa?"

"I guess. He liked working with big international banks. Damn." She rubbed her forehead. "I'm no help whatsoever."

"I'm pretty sure a bank like that would not be working as a money launderer for Cruz Moreno."

"You're right. So what happens now?"

"Avery takes it from here. My guess is she'll sit on this until we have a definitive answer about your father, one way or another."

"If everything Avery's found is true, and he really is in bed with the cartel, I can see why he'd do this. But Logan?" Tears rolled down her face.

The day was finally taking its toll on her.

"Hold on a sec. I have just what you need." He hurried into the den where he'd spotted a fully stocked bar and grabbed a bottle of Jack Daniel's. Back in the kitchen he poured two fingers into her mug of tea and nudged it toward her hand. "Drink up. You need it."

She sipped, tentatively at first, then took a healthy swallow. In a moment color began to return to her face and her eyes weren't quite so glazed over.

"This is better than putting milk in my tea." Her mouth turned up in a ghost of a smile. "I'll keep it in mind."

As he sat and watched her, dredging up bravery to battle shock, he was overcome with a desire to just load her into his truck, drive south, maybe to the Keys, and hide her away until all this nastiness was over. Of course, as independent as she was, she'd probably fight him tooth and nail, but damn! It hurt his heart to see her going through all this.

As she lifted the mug to take another sip, the alarm in the house sounded. Her eyes widened and she gripped the mug even harder. Logan checked the laptop on the counter and saw a car moving slowly up the driveway. Now what? He waited as a man climbed slowly out of the car and walked up to the front door. Logan had no idea who he was.

"Anyone you know?" he asked Devon, showing her the camera shot on the laptop.

"Not me."

"Stay in the kitchen," Logan ordered. "Strangers make me nervous right now."

He pulled his gun from the small of his back but held it down at his side as he headed for the doorway. Then he pressed the intercom button.

"Who's there?" he asked. "Identify yourself."

"Jesse Rogers, crime reporter for the Tampa paper." He held up his wallet to show his credentials.

"What can we do for you, Mr. Rogers?" No way was he letting a stranger in the house, not with a killer on the loose.

"I wondered if I could have a few minutes of Miss Cole's time. I want to do a personal interest story on her father."

"Sorry. We've had all the personal interest we need for the moment. Thanks anyway."

Logan kept his eye on the screen in the security panel. It also received a feed from the cameras.

"The newspapers are going to write the story anyway," Rogers protested. "The television reporters will be here before you can blink. Doesn't she want to get out ahead of all this? Tell her side?"

"Her side of what?" Logan had to restrain himself from opening the door and ripping this guy's head off. "Good-bye, Rogers."

The reporter's face reddened. "I'll get my story; you can't stop me. And I'll get it before the other—"

"Before what?" Logan snapped. "Is there another reporter from your paper here? You looking to scoop him and make your bones? Go on. When there's something to tell, we'll let you know."

He watched as the reporter stormed off to his car, then drove off with tires squealing. Then he walked back into the kitchen.

"Are you sure I'm safe here?" Devon asked.

"We're in a fortress, babe. Best security system around." He grinned. "Including me. No one gets to you."

"Thank you." She blew out a breath. "I think I'd like to lie down for a while."

"Sounds like a good idea. Today hasn't been a lot of fun."

"No kidding." She carried her mug and soup bowl to the sink, then walked over to where he stood. "It would be great if you could lie down with me for a while and just hold me."

He cupped her chin and studied her face, saw how drawn she looked, the troubled look in her eyes. He placed a light kiss on her lips. "I think that can be arranged."

Her smile warmed his entire body. For that smile alone he'd slay dragons.

He walked into her bedroom with her. Watched while she tugged back the covers and slipped out of everything but her T-shirt. Then he put his gun on the nightstand where it would be in easy reach, kicked off his shoes, and lay down beside her.

"You're not getting undressed?" she asked.

"In a while. I want to hear what Avery has to say after she gets to the hospital. Then I'll check the entire security system again before crawling into bed with you."

"Okay." Her eyes were already closing, emotional fatigue laying heavy on her.

He slid his arm around her and pulled her against him, feeling her curves even through the covers. He knew he'd never be able to shut his own eyes, nor did he plan to. But if Devon could get just a little bit of sleep, she could recharge her batteries. After today she definitely needed it.

He lay there with her for a long time, just watching her sleep, the occasional flutter of her lashes and the rise and fall of her beautiful breasts. One thought was front and center in his mind.

I will not let any harm come to her, no matter what.

Chapter 14

Devon came awake slowly. She had no idea what time it was, although she could see between the blinds that it was dark outside. Logan was still with her, his body warm and comforting. She could feel the muscular length of him, and the hard thickness of his cock pressing against her buttocks. One arm was curled over her, his hand cupping her breast.

"Mmmm." She wiggled back against him. "You feel good."

"So do you." He squeezed her breast to emphasize it.

"How long was I out?"

"About two hours." He brushed her hair back from her face. "You needed it."

"I guess I did. No more phone calls or visitors at the house?"

"None. Sheri's had one of her officers doing regular drive-bys so that's probably kept everyone away."

She turned over to look at him, studying his face. Trying to read him. "Can I ask you a question?"

"Sure." He stroked his thumb over her cheekbone. "Ask away."

"With the way my life has turned upside down in a few days?" She spoke slowly, weighing her words. "I'm not sure what's real anymore and what's in my mind."

"I can understand that. Go ahead. What's your question?"

He continued to rub his thumb over her cheek and along her jawline. She loved that soft touch of his. For a tough guy he could be surprisingly gentle. And he treated her as if she were the most precious thing in the world. She'd never had sex with a man who was so completely focused on her. God, he was something else. Those long, muscular legs and the toned body. The soft hair sprinkled on his chest. Hands that knew exactly how and where to touch her. She wanted him to bury himself in her and stay that way until all the goblins were gone.

Did he feel any of that? She knew he hadn't been emotionally involved with anyone since Amanda, and she was afraid when he stopped to think about it, he might feel disloyal to her memory. She wasn't sure how she'd even handle that. She hoped like hell her question wouldn't trigger that.

"Is this real, Logan? What's happening to us?" She rubbed her thumb along his jawline, loving the rough feel of his late-day scruff. "I don't want you to do this just because...well, you know."

"No, I don't know." He frowned. "What are you talking about?"

"Everything's happened so fast. One day we don't know each other, and the next..."

"And the next it's like we've known each other forever." His voice was a soft caress when he spoke.

"Yes." She searched his eyes for answers.

He stroked her back, his hand warm on her body. "Sometimes danger escalates a situation. It's a time when all your emotions are running closer to the surface. For me, it's strong enough to make me break my own rules, and I'm not a bit sorry."

"I'm not a needy person, Logan. It's important that you know that. I guess I'm a little scared because this happened so fast and it's so good."

Emotions swirled in his eyes. "You can be scared about a lot of things but not this. Did this happen fast? Damn straight. And is it totally inappropriate for this situation? Absolutely. Do we just walk away from it because of that? Not if I have anything to say about it."

"Me, either." Her lips curved in a hint of a smile. "This is crazy. Insane. All those things. But, Logan, to me it feels right. I just know it. Here." She pressed her hand to her heart.

"I know it too, babe."

He pressed his mouth to hers in a sensuous kiss. He thrust his tongue into her mouth and his taste was delicious. She wanted the contact to go on forever. Her hands moved over him, soft but strong, stroking his back, sliding across the late-day stubble on his jaw, following the muscular line of his arms.

Then he rolled off the bed and quickly shed his clothes. When he grabbed a condom from his wallet, he looked at it and cursed.

Devon wrinkled her forehead. "What's the matter?"

He gave her a lopsided grin. "I'm always prepared, except I wasn't prepared to meet an amazing woman, fall for her, and have incredible sex. I'm definitely going to need more condoms."

She gave a small laugh. "Do you think we should stop?"

"Hell to the no. But I'll need an emergency run to the drugstore. This is the last of my emergency stash."

Then he was back, naked and hot, under the covers with her.

"I'm so greedy for you," he said in a low, rumbling voice. "I want to taste every part of you, inhale your incredible essence, and touch every part of your body. Damn it, Devon, you make me toss away all restraint."

"Good," she whispered. "Very good. This is what I really want, what I really *need* from you. Please don't stop."

"But first we need to get rid of this."

He tugged her T-shirt up and over her head, then tossed it to the floor. Then he started with her mouth, tracing its outline with the tip of his tongue before slipping it softly over the surface. He nipped, just tiny bites, tugging her lips gently with his teeth.

But Devon had her own ideas of how she wanted this to go. Threading her fingers in his hair, she held his head as she thrust her tongue into his mouth again and slid it on the slick surface. His own tongue was hot and sweet, and when she sucked on it, he answered in kind.

He broke the kiss, moving his mouth from hers, and trailed tiny kisses along her jaw. Logan stopped to nip her earlobe and gently suck the skin beneath her ear before moving his mouth down the slender column of her neck. At the place where her neck and shoulder met he bit again, not hard, just enough to make her groan with pleasure.

She arched up to him, her fingers pressing hard against his head as she tried to drag it down to her breasts. But it seemed he wasn't in any hurry.

"Today was a pisser," he said, his lips against her skin. "We both need this, so be prepared, I'm going to take my time."

He slipped his mouth along the line of her collarbone to the hollow at the base of her throat, pressing the tip of his tongue against the frantic beat of her pulse there.

"Mmmm." The sound eased from her as a soft moan and again she arched up to him.

Finally, he captured one hard nipple between his teeth and tugged on it.

"Ohhhhh."

"God. I love those sexy little sounds you make."

She did it again and felt his cock harden and pulse against her body.

He grazed her nipple with his teeth before soothing it with his tongue and then sucking it into his mouth.

"Oh! Oh! Oh!"

He sucked even harder before giving it a final lick and turning his attention to the other one. When her nipples were aching and tingling, he slid his mouth in a line between her breasts and down to her navel, trailing kisses punctuated with little nips. He paused a moment to trace the curled flesh of her navel before running the tip of his tongue along the top edge of her bikini panties.

Sliding his hands beneath the cheeks of her ass, he lifted her slightly and lapped at her mound through the flimsy material.

"I need more," he growled. "I need you really naked."

He dragged the panties down with his teeth, exposing her soft curls before shifting enough to yank them down and off completely. He pressed her inner thighs so she widened her legs for him. The hot bud of her clit was swollen and throbbed. When he flicked it with his tongue, she gasped and lifted herself to him. So he did it again. And again. Pressing his face to her sex, he inhaled, making her squirm and press herself up to his face.

She moaned as he used his tongue on every inch of her sensitive flesh. It amazed her how he could take her from zero to a hundred in seconds.

He paused to look up at her. "I think you've bewitched me."

"Oh?" She didn't think she'd ever bewitched a man before.

"I always prided myself on self-control, my ability to hold back until I gave my partner the ultimate in pleasure. With you, my little witch, my control is shot to shit. It's taking every ounce of restraint I can muster not to rush through this."

Her pulse ratcheted up at his words. "Oh, yes, please don't rush."

Exposing her clit, he flicked his tongue over the swollen bud again and again, punctuating the strokes with tiny little nips. She rocked against him, urging him with her body for more and more. He slid two fingers into her wet, slick channel, curling them just right to hit her sweet spot and drag the tips over it. He added one more finger and stepped up the pace of his in and out strokes, his mouth still tormenting her clit.

Finally he increased his pace and she came, screaming, pouring into his hand. She was still trembling when he sheathed himself and slid inside her.

"Oh, God!"

She was wet and hot and so very ready for him. She closed her eyes as he thrust in slow motion into her slick passage and her inner muscles clamped down on him.

Oh, sweet Lord!

"Look at me," he commanded, his voice so rough she almost didn't recognize it. "Look at me, Devon."

She opened her eyes and did as he asked, locked her gaze with his. The passion and emotion she saw there answered all her questions.

"I'm not thinking of anyone else." His voice was rough with need. "Just you. Tell me you believe me."

"I do," she whispered.

And then there was no more thinking. He drove into her again and again, telling her how he felt and all the erotic things he wanted to do to her.

"Yes, yes, yes." She met every thrust with an upward arch of her body, taking him so deep she felt completely filled by him.

The climax, when it came, was like a fierce explosion that shook them both. Her inner muscles gripped him like a vise, and she raked his back with her fingernails. His shaft pulsed inside her over and over, until she had milked every drop from him. Then he fell forward, catching himself on his forearms.

Her heart thudded inside her chest like a bass drum gone mad. Or was that Logan's she felt, beating so hard against her?

She stroked the damp skin of his back. "All I can say is, wow!"

He smoothed the hair back from her face. "Amen to that." His face had such a serious look to it. "But, Devon? My sweet, sweet Devon, I can do so much better. And I will, when all this shit has gone away."

"I'm not sure I could stand better," she teased. "Oh, and I feel a lot better now."

He laughed. "I know *I* do."

He eased from her body and went to dispose of the condom. Then he crawled back into bed and pulled the covers over both of them, cradling her body against his.

"Let's hold on to this for a few minutes. The world is going to intrude again soon enough."

He was right about that. She was still processing everything she'd learned from Avery and there were people out there who wanted to do her harm. But right now, this was what she needed—what they both needed—and that topped everything.

* * * *

"You haven't done badly for your first couple of days," Leslie teased, as Graham followed her into the house.

"I have a good teacher," he told her.

She closed her office every day at five thirty, but the gate had a keyless lock and the people who rented slips had the code. Her cell number was posted on the office window for emergencies, and she had underlined the word *emergency*. For those just passing through who needed a slip overnight, the town maintained a small pier at the end of the harbor. For two days,

Graham had spent time with her at the marina, meeting people, learning the ropes so to speak. People were reticent at first, much as he'd expected. He was a stranger, an unknown quantity, and they had a protective air where Leslie was concerned. He liked that. He was doing his best to assure them that he hadn't come here to take advantage of her or steal from her. He expected as time passed all of that would ease. Leslie was certainly doing her damnedest to help.

"I'm going to shower and spend a little time on my laptop while you make dinner." He brushed a kiss over her cheek. "Unless you need me to help."

"I think I can handle it." She turned and looped her arms around his neck, studying his face. "You want to see if there's any more about Devon in the papers, right?"

He'd shared everything with her about what was going on. The one promise she'd extracted from him when she agreed to be part of his new life was that he never lie or keep anything from her. That was a tough one because he hated for this to touch her any more than it already had, but he understood why it was important and agreed.

"Yes." He paused. "I haven't heard anything back since I sent that e-mail to Moreno."

"You're sure he can't trace you if he does respond?"

"Positive. I tested this out when I set it up." He touched his forehead to hers. "I feel like shit, Leslie. I never thought any of this would blow back on her."

"You have leverage here. Use it."

"Damn straight." He dropped a brief kiss on her lips and stepped back. "Okay. Shower and computer. Then food and drink. You're sure I can't do anything?"

"Positive. Besides, you won't be any good to either of us until you check your e-mails and surf the news."

"Thank you."

He showered and dressed in sweatpants and sweatshirt, then set up his computer on one end of the kitchen table. He logged on to his virtual network and searched his ghost e-mails. Nothing. Not a damn thing. Hell and damnation.

Next he plugged Devon's name and Arrowhead Bay into the search bar and hit Enter. The first thing that came up was a short story in the Tampa newspaper online. When he read the details of the break-in, his heart nearly stopped, afraid that Devon had been home. Thankfully she'd been out of the house.

"Police chief Sheridan March, along with agents from Vigilance who

have been providing protection for Miss Cole, responded to the silent alarm. One of the intruders was shot and taken to the hospital under guard. Assumptions are made that this is all connected to the disappearance of Arrowhead Bay resident and business giant Graham Cole.

"Watch for updates when further information is available."

Fuck!

He wanted to throw the computer across the room. Of course, then he'd have nothing to get his news with.

"I need a drink," he told Leslie.

After fetching the bottle of Jack Daniel's he'd bought and one of Leslie's rocks glasses, he poured himself a good amount and took a healthy swallow.

"Don't get drunk or drink yourself into a heart attack," she warned. "Then you won't be good to anyone, including me."

"Don't worry. I'll sip the rest."

Okay. If Moreno wanted to play that kind of game, Graham would follow through on his threat. He opened his mail server again and typed in a new message.

"I warned you. You didn't listen. Today I am sending a small amount of information to the right people. Stay away from my daughter or I'll give them everything."

He hit Send and waited until the e-mail was gone. Then he did a search for Vigilance. They were protecting Devon so they were invested in this. He didn't know how that happened but he was glad for many reasons. Not the least of which was it gave him a conduit for the information. He hadn't wanted to send it directly to the Feds and open himself up to their probing, and he wasn't sure who else he could contact. Vigilance would know how to handle this while protecting both him and Devon.

He found their e-mail on their web site, as innocuous as he'd expect it to be.

"For information contact vigilance@vigilance.com."

He thought a minute about how to phrase his message. Finally he wrote, *"I have information that can help Devon Cole. If you know who I am, reply to this message."*

He hit Send, then sat back and waited. He didn't know what to expect. How closely did they monitor their e-mail? How fast would someone answer him? Would they even answer him at all?

The bell on his computer dinged scarcely a minute later.

"What was the reason your wife passed away?"

He was stunned. Someone other than a techno hack was watching this system. And they wanted to make sure it was him. Okay, then.

"She had stage four breast cancer. Progressed rapidly."

He waited for a reply. It came within seconds.

"Send your information to the following secure e-mail."

"Fine. But only a small amount. My only bargaining chip for my daughter's safety."

A longer pause this time.

"Fine. A small amount."

"Give me a minute."

He sat there in thought for a long moment. He was positive the Vigilance computers were safe, that they were hackproof, although nothing was really protected under some conditions. He had no idea what they'd do with it, but from what he knew about Vigilance, they had contacts everywhere. They'd get it to someone who would move forward with it, a signal to Moreno that Graham Cole didn't make empty threats.

He jogged upstairs to get the external hard drive from the locked briefcase he'd stashed in the back of the closet. Leslie watched him as he sat down again and plugged it in.

"You found something you didn't like," she guessed.

"Those fucking assholes broke into my house. It's a damn good thing Devon wasn't home or she might be dead." He felt sick to his stomach. "This is all my fault. I was too interested in saving my own hide."

Leslie wiped her hands and came to stand beside him. "You wouldn't be any good to her or anyone if you were dead," she reminded him. She gave him a long hug. "What are you going to do?"

He told her about Vigilance and how it was his best hope, especially since they were protecting Devon.

"I'm sending them a teaser, but enough that they can go after the cartel or at least rattle their cage."

He accessed the external drive, selected what he wanted, and attached it as a file in an e-mail.

"I hope you can use this to protect my daughter."

He hesitated only a moment before hitting Send. There. It was done. If they went after the phony investment firm, the word would get back to Moreno. Then things would start to happen. Graham only hoped they were good things.

He lifted his glass and took another swallow of the liquor. He had no one to blame for this whole clusterfuck but himself. He wondered how soon he'd hear from Vigilance.

Chapter 15

Logan was still lying in the darkened bedroom, holding Devon, when his cell rang.

"I need to get this, babe." He rolled away from her to grab his cell from where it sat next to his gun on the nightstand, and saw Avery's name on the screen. "What's up, boss?"

"We have big problems, Logan." Avery's voice was tight with anger. "I'm at the hospital."

He sat up straight in bed, raking his fingers through his hair. "What now, for God's sake?"

"The guy Mike shot is dead." She spit the words out as if each one were poison.

Logan's jaw dropped. "How the hell is that possible? Tyson was there, right? And he's no slouch."

"Not a bit. It happened right under his nose. Goddamn it," she exploded. "This is one big clusterfuck."

Logan had never heard her this irate. "Tell me what you found out."

There was a moment of silence during which Logan could almost visualize her reaching for her self-control. What the hell had happened to make her this enraged?

"A male nurse was attacked entering the hospital for his shift," she told him. "We found him out cold by the staff entrance, with a major head injury. He was stripped down to his boxers, his scrubs and ID missing."

"Shit." Logan wanted to smash his hand against the wall. No wonder Avery's anger level was so high. Then something occurred to him. "All the staff at that hospital have photo IDs. That means whoever did this came prepared with his own picture and ID tag."

"You got it. Shit, Logan. Before it was just a theory but now I'm positive someone locally is pulling the strings for Moreno. And that person was able to make a proper ID tag, most likely for the piece of shit that got away at the Cole house."

Logan pushed the covers back, sat up, and swung his legs over the side of the bed. "That's how he got past the guards. Which means," he said, "it might not be Alford or Bodine. Where would they get the equipment so soon?"

"Unless they have a local contact."

"But what did he use to kill him?" He began to gather his clothes. "Hell, he had to do it right under Tyson's nose."

"Exactly. He injected something right into the guy's IV line. Tyson even watched him do it and thought nothing of it. Nurses had been coming in and out on a regular basis and giving him meds that way, since he's still unconscious."

"Damn it all to hell, anyway. Okay, what can I do?"

"Stay there. I don't want Devon out of the house and I don't want you more than two inches away from her at any time." She paused. "Do you think you need reinforcements?"

"Not unless someone is planning a major attack on the house. In that case I'd see them coming and can send an emergency call."

"Okay. I can—hold on, I have another call coming in."

Logan sat there holding his phone while he waited for Avery to get back to him.

"What's going on?" Devon, obviously awakened by the call, sat up behind him. When she touched his shoulder, he could feel the tension in her body. "It doesn't sound like anything good."

"It's not. I'll tell you as soon as I get off this call. I—"

"Logan?" Avery's voice broke in. "You still there?"

"I am. What's going on? You sound strange."

"We have a situation here that we have to figure out how to handle. Either someone is yanking our chain in an effort to locate Graham Cole or he's found a way to contact us."

"Avery, what the hell?" He sat back against the pillows so he could pull Devon in close to him, stroking her arm in a soothing motion.

"Del just called to tell me the agency got an e-mail from Graham Cole. He says—"

"An e-mail?" He started to say Cole's name before he caught himself. "Are you shitting me?"

"No, and listen to this." Her voice dropped, obviously to shield her conversation. "He sent us a tiny block of information about Cruz Moreno and the cartel. Hard goods. He wants us to use it to find a way to protect

Devon. To let Moreno know we have it and he'd better back off."

"There's only one thing wrong with that. It might backfire and piss him off enough to make a move we don't want." He wasn't about to voice his fears about Devon's safety with her sitting next to him.

"I'm aware of that and we'll take precautions. I'd love to keep her locked up tight in that house but I have a feeling that won't fly."

He snorted. "You got that right. Avery, we really need to meet to discuss all the ramifications of this. And Devon needs to be included. I don't want to keep secrets from her."

He sat through a beat of silence.

"Okay," she said at last. "I guess you're right. Sheri and I will come out there as soon as we're done here. Sheri's seeing to the handling of the body and she's going to call her liaison with the sheriff to ask for some manpower. We need to get this piece of shit rounded up."

"What about an autopsy?"

"On the list. We're asking the sheriff for his medical examiner to do it. They can pick up the body and take it to their morgue. They'll also have deputies to guard it both on the way and once it gets there."

Logan sighed. Things just went from bad to shit at the drop of a hat.

"Okay," he told her. "Call when you're on the way. This place could feed an army, so I'll fix something to eat."

"Fine, although I'm not sure how hungry anyone will be. Later."

He disconnected the call and put the phone back on the nightstand.

Devon moved around so she was face-to-face with him. She had the sheet pulled up to her breasts, which was a damn good thing, because he didn't need a distraction right now.

"Okay, Malik, spill it."

He nodded. "I'll tell you everything, but let's get dressed and go in the kitchen. I could use a cup of coffee and you need something more substantial than soup. I told Avery we'd have dinner when she and Sheri got here but that could be a while."

In the kitchen Logan fixed coffee for himself and pulled out a tea pod for Devon but she shook her head.

"I think I've had enough tea for a while."

Sitting at the kitchen table, he gave it all to her, chapter and verse. To her credit, she sat quietly and listened to everything he said, not interrupting him the way a lot of people he knew would have. For a moment panic flashed in her eyes but then he could practically see her pull herself together. Damn, the woman had strength. But, as he'd told Avery, she had a right to know. She was the lynchpin in all this and her safety was of prime importance.

Giving her full knowledge was a way to help ensure that.

She took a swallow of coffee and set the mug on the table.

"My father is putting his own life in jeopardy to protect me." A statement, not a question.

Logan nodded. "I'd say that shows he loves you very much. Just because he got his nuts caught in a wringer and vanished, leaving you holding the bag, doesn't diminish that fact. And think about this. Maybe he thought by doing a disappearing act, he was taking the heat off both of you."

"Did—Did he say where he was?"

Logan shook his head. "No. Nor would I expect him to. I think it took a lot of guts for him to reach out to us the way he did. Del tried to pinpoint the source but he's been smart enough to use phantom servers."

"But why now? And why Vigilance?"

"His e-mail said he read online what was happening, especially to you. He'd sent an e-mail to Cruz Moreno warning him off. When that didn't happen—when, in fact, things escalated—he decided to make good on his word. He knows it's a much safer bet for him to go through us than directly to the Feds, especially since the paper stupidly printed that you have a Vigilance bodyguard with you. He's leaving it to us to decide the best way to handle it."

Devon rubbed her forehead. "This is all such a mess. When will Avery and Sheri be here? I want all the details from them."

"And you'll get them. I'd say at least another hour. You hungry? I can fix you a snack."

"No." She shook her head. "Who has an appetite? But I'd sure love another drink."

He reached over and squeezed her hand. "Another shot of Jack Black coming right up."

* * * *

"This is your mess. You'd better clean it up."

Cruz Moreno growled the words into the telephone. He drew on his cigar and blew a perfect smoke ring into the air. He needed to focus on something like that to control his escalating rage.

"What do you think I'm doing?" Vato asked. "If you had sent someone with one iota of intelligence, none of this would have happened."

"Don't try to throw this back on me. You failed to keep Cole in line." His big hand tightened on the phone. "You assured me he was controllable, like the others. I think you misjudged him from the beginning."

There was a long moment of silence.

"I didn't misjudge his desperation," Vato protested.

"This is a business operation." Cruz ground out the words. "I am a businessman and someone is fucking with my operation. It needs to be fixed. Now."

"Before I do anything else," Vato said at last, "I have to clean up the mess those idiots made here. Luis's body was turned over to the medical examiner. I think—"

"Which might lead back to me if they identify him," Cruz interrupted. "And what about Agustin? Is he safely away?"

"How the hell should I know?" Vato spat the words. "You had me tell him to disappear right after he did the deed, so he's in the wind."

"I instructed him to ask for your help in that." Cruz ground his back teeth. "If he's picked up…" He let the words trail off.

"Well, he's gone. And I can't exactly round up a crew of people to look for him."

"*Mierda!*" Cruz wanted to kill someone but he had no one handy.

"I'll see what I can do about locating Agustin, but my guess is he's halfway to Tampa by now. He can get lost in the Hispanic community there."

"If he knows what's good for him, he'll stay lost." He blew another smoke ring, using the focus it took to pull himself together. "I have to know if Cole made good on his threat to release information about the cartel."

"Just how the hell am I supposed to do that?" Vato raged. "It's not as if whoever received it is going to take me into their confidence."

"What if he sent it directly to the Feds?" He tightened his hand into a fist, wishing it was closed around someone's neck.

"Jesus, calm down, Cruz. If he sent anything to the Feds, they'd be crawling up your ass by now. And probably mine, too."

"Then who? Find out for me."

Vato gave a short laugh. "Exactly how should I do that? Take out an ad in the paper?"

"Your sarcasm is out of place. Remember. If I fall, I take you right along with me."

Cruz was silent for a moment, thinking. "I think we need to shut down SMX before they get to it. Do it now," he instructed, "and set up a new one."

"Shit. I can't do it with one stroke and you know it. It's a complex arrangement. Let me see what I can do. And quietly," he added. "No sense stirring things up if Cole never outs us."

Cruz thought for a long moment. "The key is the daughter. We need to grab her. She'll be our leverage."

"Oh, sure." Vato snorted. "She's got more protection than the damned president."

"I don't care. You're so fucking smart. Find a way. I can contact Cole by e-mail. I have the address, even if I can't find the location. I'll bet every dollar he'll exchange himself for her."

"Cruz." Vato's sigh came over the connection. "You're playing with fire here."

"Then it's your job to see I don't get burned. Here's what needs to be done." He outlined exactly what he had in mind. "You'd better get busy. We both have a lot to do. I will call you at the same time tomorrow. Have answers for me."

He hung up on the man's outrage. Then he sat for a few minutes, mulling the whole thing over in his mind. At last, when he had his thoughts straight, he went in search of Mateo, his lieutenant, his right-hand man.

"I have a project for you," he told the man when he found him. "I can't trust anyone else with it. Don't make me sorry I trusted you."

* * * *

Logan opted for the easy route and made sandwiches for everyone, but no one seemed to be very hungry. They sat at the table, plates in front of them but the food mostly untouched.

Sheri filled them in on the dead cartel member but had no information on the killer.

"The sheriff's all over it," she reported. "And he's got the word out at all the airports around here. But truthfully? The chances of finding him are fifty-fifty."

"I can't believe all of this." Devon raked her fingers through her hair.

Logan was watching her carefully, worried at how she was absorbing all this and its effect on her. He could have made her eat something when they came home, but she needed him more than food, and one thing led to another. He nudged her plate a little closer.

"Do me a favor and eat more than a bite or two. You've hardly eaten all day. Getting sick won't help things."

"I just don't have an appetite," she protested. "Sorry. Avery? Did you say you have people tracing that e-mail? Have they gotten anywhere yet? Is it hard to trace?

"I'm not going to lie to you. The answer is yes. Your father's pretty damn smart. He set up a network of anonymous e-mails on a virtual server that makes it almost impossible to backtrack. That doesn't mean we won't try."

"Why didn't he take me with him?" She tightened her hands around her mug, as if the warmth from the hot liquid could seep into her body. "Never mind. That's a stupid question."

"So what's next?" Logan asked. He wanted action. A plan. The sooner they put one in place, the closer he'd be to neutralizing the danger to Devon.

"I e-mailed Graham Cole to let him know I got his information and tell him my plan." Avery looked around the table. "He wants them to back away from Devon, so the smartest thing is to hit them where it hurts."

"The money," Logan guessed.

"Right on. I'll contact a friend who is a DEA special investigator and send him the info on SMX Group. They can disrupt the money trail, forcing Moreno to set up a whole new system. The DEA can monitor it and when the process begins, shut it down and move in on Moreno."

"I don't mean to sound like a ninny," Devon said, "but shouldn't they arrest them?"

"Easier said than done," Logan told her. "Moreno's undoubtedly well protected in a heavily guarded estate, and we don't have the actual proof yet to nail him."

"Your father said he has every bit of information on the cartel that he can send us," Avery told her. "Right now what he wants is someone to rattle their cage so they'll leave you alone. As soon as he acknowledges my reply to him, I'll turn everything on SMX over to the DEA and let them do their thing. Your father e-mailed Moreno and warned them there's more coming unless they stay away from you."

Devon's head was spinning with the complexity of the situation. "And they'll just do that?"

"That's what we hope. If not, your father's prepared to dump everything about them in the DEA's lap."

She blew out a breath. "So we just wait?"

"I gave him my cell number so he could reply directly. I'm expecting an answer any minute. I'm pretty sure he was waiting at his computer to hear from me."

Even as she spoke, her phone chimed with an incoming text. She tapped the screen to open it, read it, and nodded.

"What did he say?" Logan asked.

"He said to do whatever we think best as long as the cartel leaves you alone. So to make that work, I've got to get this stuff to the DEA right away. Let me contact my friend."

At that moment the landline rang.

"I'll get it." He stood and reached for the receiver. "Hello?"

"Yeah, hello." The familiar deep drawl made his hand tighten on the receiver. "Cash Breeland here. Can I speak to Devon?"

Logan frowned. What the hell did he want now? "She's really busy, Cash. Can I give her a message?"

"Oh, well, no." There was a brief pause. "I was just checking again to make sure she's okay and ask her if there was anything I could do for her."

What the hell was up with this guy, anyway?

"She's just fine. And well taken care of," he added.

"Earl Flannery and I were talking and wondered again if she should really be out there in that house all by herself." He lowered his voice as if they were exchanging the most intimate information. "We thought she might be better off in town. Like I told her the last time, Marian and I really want her to come stay with us. But if not, at least at the B and B."

Logan felt a little thread of something cold wriggle through his system. This was way out of left field.

"I'm sure she would appreciate it, but she's fine here. And she's definitely not alone. But I'll pass along your concern." Breeland was still talking when Logan hung up the phone.

He turned to the table and found everyone staring at him.

"What is it?" Sheri asked. "You have the strangest look on your face."

"That was Cash Breeland."

Devon raised her eyebrows. "Again?"

"What do you mean again?" Avery asked.

"Oh, he called before and wanted me to come stay with him and his wife." She snorted. "As if. He's nothing to me except one of my father's friends."

Sheri snorted. "That old busybody? He thinks he's the unofficial mayor of this place and responsible for everyone and everything. Anything the least bit interesting happens, he's got his nose stuck in it."

Avery leaned forward toward her. "Devon, did you ever spend much time with him?"

"What?" Her eyes widened. "No. Hardly at all. My dad spent time with him. Cash was one of the first friends Dad made when he started sailing into Arrowhead Bay. But me?" She shrugged. "Maybe five or six times over four years."

"Something about him is bugging me." Logan refilled his mug with fresh coffee and sat back down at the table. "I wish I knew what."

"It's just Cash being Cash. He's one of those people who thinks he has the right to mix in everyone's business," Sheri said. "He's always been like that."

"Maybe. Something just doesn't feel right but I can't tell you what.

Avery, did you run a profile on him?"

She nodded. "At first blush he looks clean, but I told Ginger to dig deeper." She pushed back from the table. "We'll see what she comes up with. In the meantime, I'm heading back to the office. I'm going to have Graham Cole call me so we can strategize. It's important for Moreno to think Cole is serious about his threat but make him believe he can still save his empire if he backs off of Devon. I'm also contacting my DEA friend."

"Call and keep us in the loop," Logan reminded her.

"I will."

Sheri also rose. "I'm off to get back in touch with the sheriff and find out when the autopsy is. I asked him to put a rush on it. Told him we had exigent circumstances."

When they were gone, Logan cleaned up the kitchen. Then he poured them each a small drink and sat down at the table. He placed his cell in the center and turned on the record feature.

"Now. Let's see how much of your dad's life the past four years we can reconstruct. Hopefully it will give us a clue as to how he got into this mess and with who."

Chapter 16

Sipping her bourbon slowly, Devon made it last until halfway through the session with Logan. She switched to hot tea, and Logan pushed more cookies on her. She nibbled on them as he asked questions to pull out everything she remembered about the last four years as it related to her father.

He had just called for a break when his cell phone rang.

"Yeah, Avery? What? Okay." He looked at Devon. "She wants me to put this on speakerphone." He tapped the speaker icon and placed the phone on the table between them. "Okay. You're on."

"Devon? You there?"

"I am." She tightened her hands into fists. "Did something else happen?"

"First, let me get this out of the way. I sent Sam to the dock to see if she could get anything else out of Gary. She flashed a little money and his tongue loosened up."

"And?"

"A little surprise here. When he told us two men had been asking about Graham Cole? We thought it was the cartel thugs."

"It wasn't?"

"No, it was our two buddies from Cole International."

"What the fuck?" Logan shook his head. "They were in town long before they made themselves known to us."

"Uh-huh. It could even have been them showing up that hastened Cole's disappearance. If in fact they went to see him."

Logan wanted to pound something. "This whole thing just keeps getting more convoluted."

"No kidding. Anyway, Graham Cole said he'd call me, but only on a phone that is secure and not a cell phone. Too easily traced. And…"

"And what?" he prompted.

"He wants to talk to Devon."

"To me?" She almost squeaked the words. "Really?"

"He wants to explain, he says. He never expected this to happen. You'll have to bring her here so we can use the secure Vigilance line."

"She's pretty wiped, Avery."

"Do we want to get this done or not?" she reminded him.

"Yeah, yeah, yeah. Okay, when?"

"As soon as you can get here."

"Got it."

"Also, Cole agrees with our DEA plan, too, so I put a call into my contact. He's in Tampa and he's on his way."

"So are we," he assured her and hung up.

"I can't believe this." Devon scrubbed her hands over her face. "What did Avery mean, she might want you to take me someplace else?"

He took her hands and pulled her closer to him. "When all the cards are on the table, she may decide you're safe out of this war zone completely. Someplace where Moreno has no idea you are."

She leaned into him for a moment. "It's like a nightmare that never ends." She sighed, then moved away from him. "Okay. Let me just wash my face and throw on some shoes and I'm ready."

Before they left the house, he made sure the alarm was properly set and synced with his watch. He looked carefully as they headed down the drive and onto Seacliff Road, but he didn't see any cars. Although by now it was dark and with no street lights out here they'd be easy to miss. He'd just have to be hyperalert.

"I'm going to stop and get gas. I'm lower than I like to be." There was a gas station conveniently at the end of the road at the turn into town, but Logan bypassed it.

"You missed the gas station."

"I know. But that corner is kind of isolated and on two sides the roads are heavily treed. I want one with more people around and a lot of lights."

She glanced over at him. "You don't really think they'd make a try for me here in town, do you?"

He grunted. "No? Have we seen anything so far that tells us they're afraid of being caught?" Then he reached over and took her hand. "Don't worry. I plan to take excellent care of you." Then he softened his voice. "In more ways than one."

She squeezed his hand, and said in a soft voice, "I know. I trust you."

He drove to a convenience store just one block off Main Street, but still well lit, and pulled into one of the pumps. There was more traffic here, too, more people around.

"This should just take a few minutes."

"Okay."

He climbed out of the truck and locked the doors. He had pulled up as close as he dared to a pump that he could make a quick exit from. He swiped his credit card, selected his gas, and began to pump. There was hardly any room between him and the truck, and as he pumped he constantly looked to the left and the right.

God, he thought, the fucking pump was so slow. Or maybe it was just his edginess and impatience.

A car with two men in it pulled into a pump in the next lane but they didn't seem to pay any attention to him. Then a car with a woman in it pulled in behind him. She looked to be having some kind of trouble with the pump. His brain automatically cataloged them from force of habit, although they all looked harmless enough. Still, he'd learned that what looked harmless was often lethal.

Hurry up and get the fuck out of here.

His pump had just shut off and he'd replaced the nozzle when here she came, in jeans and a T-shirt with ridiculously high heels and a perplexed look on her face as she studied something in her hand.

"I hate to bother you," she said, "but I have a problem here."

"Ask inside. Someone there can help you." He started to move away from her.

"Oh, I don't think so," she said, and brought up her hand.

As the jolts of electricity stabbed through him and he fell, he thought, *Taser.* He wanted to tell Devon to get the hell out of there but he couldn't speak.

Then blackness washed over him.

* * * *

"Logan." A voice came at him out of the dark. "Logan, wake up."

He forced his eyes open but everything was blurry. The first thing he realized was he wasn't at the gas station. Whose voice was that?

"Avery?"

"Oh, thank God he's awake." He could hear the relief in her voice.

He squinted, trying to focus. "Where the hell am I?"

"At Vigilance." Mike Perez's voice. "How do you feel?"

He tried to sit up, then fell back. Every muscle in his body felt as if he'd been kicked by a horse. Even his bones hurt. There was a sharp pain in his side but when he slid his hand down to see what it was, Avery grabbed it and pulled it away.

"Don't touch. There's a bandage there."

He tried to frown but even his forehead hurt. "From what?"

"You were hit with a Taser," Mike told him. "A heavy dose. We had to get an EMT here to remove the barbs."

"Shit." Again the scene flashed back to him. "Devon. Where the fuck is Devon?"

Avery just looked at him. "I'm sorry, Logan. She's gone."

"Dead?" He felt as if the electricity had jolted his heart. "Please tell me she's not dead."

"No." Mike crouched down beside him. "But she's gone. We figure Moreno has her."

"Fuck, fuck, fuck."

"Can you tell us what happened?" Avery asked.

He told them about stopping for gas, picking a well-lit station. The two cars that pulled in after he did. The woman who asked for his help.

"She had the Taser, but her hand covered most of it until the last minute." The nausea he felt had as much to do with Devon missing as with the aftereffects of the electric shocks. "Those two guys in the other car. Shit."

"Sam made the owner of the convenience store let her watch the security tape. Too bad we couldn't catch the license plate of the car that parked behind you. And the woman knew enough to look away from the camera. We've got sort of a picture of the guy who took Devon but none of us know who he is. Sheri's going to take a look."

"Where's my truck?"

Avery shook her head. "Gone, with Devon in it. They obviously had one of those electronic things that unlocks vehicles."

With Mike's help, he finally managed to pull himself to a sitting position.

"Get me some aspirin," he told Avery. "How long have I been out?"

"An hour. When you didn't get here in a reasonable amount of time, I tried calling you. I didn't get an answer so we pinged your cell phone's GPS. When we got to the gas station, two people were trying to revive you."

"Could they tell you anything?"

"No," Mike answered. "They were busy with their own stuff. Oblivious, like most people."

"Sheri's got an APB out," Avery told him. "So does the sheriff, and he asked the highway patrol to keep an eye out. We have no idea where they'd take her."

"And Tweedledum and Tweedledee at the B and B?"

"Also gone."

I promised to keep her safe and I let her down. If she dies, it's all on me. Someone should just shoot me.

"You get one minute for a pity party," Mike told him, as if reading his mind. "Then we've got work to do if we're going to get her back."

"How the hell did they know you'd be at the gas station?" Avery asked as she helped him to his feet.

He took a moment to fight back the nausea and get his balance. He'd had worse than this in Iraq, he reminded himself. And a light bulb went on in his scrambled brans.

"Cash Breeland."

"What?" Avery and Mike both stared at him.

"It's the only thing that makes sense. He's a friend of Graham's. Probably his best friend here. And…wait for it…owns Arrowhead Bay Community Bank. We were looking for a conduit? There it is. And he could have made the hospital badge, too. Damn." He smacked his forehead. "Why didn't I think of this before? Because I'm stupid."

"Don't beat yourself up, Logan," Avery told him. "I think we all made the mistake of thinking nothing like that would be based in sleepy little Arrowhead Bay."

"Which is why it's the best place for it," Logan said. "Fucking damn. My gut told me there was something weird with him. I should have listened to it. I bet he had cars watching for us to leave the house, no matter how long they had to wait. I just made it easy for them."

"You know when we checked him out he came up clean, on first sweep."

Logan made a rude noise. "As good as he's been at covering up cartel money I suspect he'd do the same for himself."

"I'll call Sheri and get her to make a little visit to him." Avery reached for her phone, dialed Sheri, and relayed the information to her.

"I guarantee you he's not home."

"But maybe we can get something from his wife. What about Cole?"

"He's waiting for our call. He's already texted me twice." Avery twisted her lips in a grimace. "He's not very happy with us. By the way, when we found you, I decided some things couldn't wait. I called my DEA contact, Chuck LaValle, and gave him the info on SMX. He said with that they could move right away. But they will need whatever else we have to help with the case."

"Then let's hope Graham Cole still wants to play ball with us."

* * * *

"They're into my money," Moreno screamed.

Vato held his cell phone away from his ear. *Shit.*

"What do you mean, they're into it? How could they be into it? It's covered up six ways from Sunday."

"Your fucking friend Graham Cole has given them the information, that's what." His voice grated on Vato's nerves. "They froze SMX Group assets."

Vato felt a sinking sensation in the pit of his stomach. "That's impossible."

"Don't tell me impossible. It's happening. We monitor those accounts all the time. They're set up to give us an alert if anything like this happens. I want my money back. Now."

Vato dropped into a chair, forcing himself to be calm. How the hell had this happened? He'd made it very plain to Graham what would happen if he tried to pull back from the arrangement or monkey with it in any way. For a while it had strained their relationship. Then one day, it was as if a switch had been flipped. The man had decided to go with the flow. His own coffers were being enriched, although not as much as Moreno's. But he liked his lifestyle and the corporation was doing well.

How was Vato supposed to know it was all an act? That Graham was collecting and storing information, bit by bit, that he could one day use as a weapon? Some fancy financial maneuvering would be required, pronto, to save any of the cartel's money. Even then nothing was guaranteed. Maybe he could find out where Graham was and hide away there himself.

"Calm down, Cruz. I'll get on it right away. You know we have some emergency traps in there."

"I want that man," Moreno snapped. "And I'm going to get him. You've gotten rich on our relationship. If you want to keep that lifestyle and stay out of jail, here's what I want you to do."

When Vato hung up, he had his assignment, one that he'd have to figure out a way to execute under the circumstances. And do it fast. He opened his desk drawer and took out the little pouch he kept for situations just like this. He stared at it for a long moment.

Fuck!

How had he allowed himself to reach this point where he was no better than Moreno? Where he was about to do something that went against every sense of reason?

Because I fell in love with the money.

At first it has been a game, a way to use the smarts he'd acquired all these years. Manipulating Cole International. Getting their own people in place. And now he was in it up to his neck. He had no idea how he was going to accomplish his task, considering the circumstances, but he had a feeling his own life was on the line. Maybe he'd have just a little bit of luck come his way and he could do what he had to. But he was sick to his stomach just thinking about it.

* * * *

Graham booted up the computer and went to his anonymous e-mail. The icon in the status bar told him he had a message waiting. He clicked on it, and when the e-mail opened, his hand froze on the mouse. For a moment he was afraid he'd have a heart attack. Had he caused this? Dear God. All he'd wanted to do was keep them away from Devon.

"It does not pay to fuck with me, mi amigo. We will trade her for you, and everything you have on the cartel. Watch for instructions. Meanwhile, keep this picture as a reminder."

There was a photo of Devon sitting in a chair, hands and feet bound and a blindfold across her eyes. Propped against her body was a newspaper with today's date. How the hell had he done this when she had a bodyguard? And a highly regarded one if what he'd found out was true.

Graham wanted to scream, to smash things, to throw the computer against the wall. Every possible scenario ran through his brain, none of them good. One thing he did know, whatever he had to do, even if it meant sacrificing his own life, he had to get Devon away from this maniac. It took a supreme effort to get his rage under control. He swallowed back the bile that surged in his throat and tried to clear his brain, to think what to do.

He was smart enough to know he couldn't handle this by himself, and to realize he had only one real choice. First he hit Reply to the e-mail.

"I'll take the deal, you piece of shit, but if one hair on her head is harmed, you are dead and so are all your people."

Next he fetched a new burner phone from his stash and plugged in Avery March's number.

"This is Graham Cole," he said when she answered. "I've made a huge mess here and I need help."

* * * *

Logan watched as Avery disconnected the call to Graham Cole. She'd had it on speaker so they could all hear. He was seized with a vicious desire to try to find the man and smash his face in, except it was really his own face he should be pounding. This whole disaster was his fault. He should have taken Devon to Vigilance first, then gone to get gas. It was a rookie mistake and he wanted to shoot himself for making it. He felt so sick he was afraid he'd vomit right there on Avery's fancy rug.

"Logan."

Her sharp voice, like the end of a stick, grabbed his attention.

"What?" He sat up straighter in his chair.

"Get your shit together, will you?" she snapped. "We'll deal with mistakes later but right now we don't have time for self-flagellation."

"Damn it to hell. They have Devon, right?"

"Hold on."

Avery studied her cell. When it chimed an incoming message, she accepted it and held up the screen for him to see. When he saw the picture of Devon, bound and gagged, a pain lanced through him so sharp he nearly doubled over.

"God." He raked his hands through his hair. "If she dies, how will I ever live with myself?"

Amanda and Devon. Two women he'd failed.

"Cut it out," Avery said. "I told you we don't have time for this. We have to get Devon back and we need you to do it. Just pull up your big boy pants and get with the program."

She was right. Wasting time beating himself up wasn't going to resolve this situation. He'd have plenty of time afterward to go somewhere and hide. He certainly couldn't go back to Vigilance. Or to Devon. Not when he was responsible for this disaster. Not that she'd want to see him anyway.

He sucked it up and with the discipline of long years, pulled himself together. He almost welcomed the pain that still lingered, a reminder that he had one goal now—get Devon back.

"Okay. Where are we and what do we need to do?"

"I told Graham we'd come up with a plan. They want to exchange her for him. We're going to help him do that, only we'll be calling the shots. Let's put this plan together."

Chapter 17

Devon opened her eyes and tried to focus. Her head ached and her eyes burned, nausea bubbled up in her stomach, and for some reason she couldn't move. The last thing she remembered was some woman talking to Logan at the gas pump and a strange man jumping into the truck. He sped out of the gas station, with her screaming and trying to jump out of the vehicle.

"Shut the fuck up," he'd yelled, and pulled something out of his jacket. She felt a tiny prick in her neck and then she lost consciousness.

Now she blinked and forced herself to take a look at where she was... and looked right into the face of Cash Breeland.

Oh, God!

"It was you! You're the one who got my father into this hell. I should have known it."

"So you're awake." His heavy drawl couldn't disguise the venom in his voice.

"This your idea of keeping me safe?" she spat at him.

"Too bad you didn't buy my solicitous act." His laugh was anything but humorous. "We wouldn't have had to use a stun gun on your lover and leave him on the concrete."

Logan!

"Is—Is he alive?"

Cash shrugged. "Maybe yes, maybe no. People react differently to the Taser."

Logan! Please be okay. Please, please, please.

"You just couldn't leave things alone, could you?" He rubbed a hand over his face. "Just like that fucking father of yours. He could have been richer than he ever dreamed if he'd just kept his mouth shut."

"You used him." She looked directly into his eyes, appalled at the rage and cruelty she saw there. "You put him in a bad situation and trapped him into making money for the cartel."

"Money is money. He'd have been set for five lifetimes. Too bad he had a conscience."

"I'll bet he was pissed off when he found out what his good friend had gotten him into."

"Ungrateful is what I called it. I helped him out of a bad financial situation. Too bad he didn't appreciate it."

"That he was in bed with a drug lord?"

"Money is money. It all looks the same to me."

"And your bank was the perfect conduit to move the money from SMX to Cole International."

Breeland's face hardened. "So you know about that."

"I know everything," she told him. "My father thought you were his friend."

"And I was," he said. "I got him the money he needed, didn't I? And a lot more. Goddamn Vince was supposed to handle the whole thing, but he fucked up royally."

Devon tried to figure out what time it was. "How long have I been here?"

"A while. Why? You aren't going anywhere until I say so."

Devon tried to move her arms and legs and discovered she was in a chair, her hands bound behind her and her legs tied to the chair. She did her best to push down the thread of fear wriggling through her. Whatever Cash had in mind, it wasn't killing her, at least for the moment. She dug deep for the courage she knew she needed.

Devon blinked again to clear her eyes and looked around. They were in some kind of cavernous warehouse, with a concrete floor and bare walls, and smelling of motor oil. Three chairs, one of which she was tied to. The only light was a bare bulb hanging from a cord. The air was musty and dank, as if the place hadn't been used for a while. She had no idea where it was or how anyone would find her here.

Logan will find me. I can hold on.

There were two men with Cash, the one who'd kidnapped her from the gas station and another who could have been his brother. They looked a lot like the thugs who'd forced her off the highway and she wondered in a hysterical moment if Cash hired only men who looked like this. They didn't seem to be doing much except hanging back, although one cradled a rifle and the other had a handgun riding on his hip.

"You going to shoot me, Cash?" She tilted her head up, chin out defiantly. "Or are you planning to keep me here indefinitely?"

The look on his face was so evil it chilled her blood. Was this the real person beneath the friendly southern "gentleman"?

"I would," he told her. "The men might enjoy a new plaything."

Oh, God.

But then he laughed, and there was nothing jovial about it.

"Where am I?"

"Tampa. A friend of mine owns this property. Has a house and a hangar where he used to keep his plane. And tarmac for a landing strip."

Tampa?

"Why did you bring me here?"

Cash laughed again, a really unpleasant sound.

"You father must love you a lot, chickadee. He didn't like us messing with you and he's offered to exchange himself for you."

No! She wanted to scream the word. They'd kill him.

"That doesn't explain why I'm here."

"Señor Moreno is flying up here to meet with your father, and requires your company on the plane."

Damn. Moreno himself was heading this? Why? Didn't he trust Cash and the others to do this?

She wet her lips. "My father is coming here?"

"No." Cash shook his head. "Just outside Arrowhead Bay at the little private airport. But this was the closest I could get you for him to pick you up."

They'll kill him, she thought. *And then they'll kill me. They'll never let me go. There has to be a way out of this.*

"Forget whatever you're thinking." He snapped his fingers in front of her. "We control the situation. *El Jefe* himself will take care of this."

Devon hoped Logan had a few ideas of his own. And that the Taser hadn't done any permanent damage.

I trust you, Logan. I'm here. Come and get me.

She had no idea how long they were there after that. They gave her water twice, and allowed her to use the restroom in the corner of the hangar. A couple of times, despite her efforts to keep them open, her eyes closed, but then she shook herself awake. Cash Breeland had walked out, leaving one man to guard her, and it seemed like hours before he returned.

"Well." He rubbed his hands. "It seems we're all set. Our ride will be here shortly."

Another few minutes passed and then she heard the sound of a plane drawing nearer. Cash walked to the door that led outside, and the noise grew louder before shutting down altogether.

"Time to get going."

He walked over to her and waited while one of the other men released her from the chair. Cash gripped her upper arm in a pinching grasp and practically dragged her to the door. When he pulled her outside, sure enough, a small plane sat on the tarmac outside the warehouse.

"Your coach awaits." He laughed, a sound with no humor in it. "Come on. Don't make trouble or I'll have to kill you here and that would spoil the party."

Someone opened the cabin door and pushed out the stairs. Cash urged her upward from behind and the strange man dragged her in. Then Cash climbed in behind her. In the next minute, she was strapped in to one of the seats in the luxurious cabin. Cash and the other man settled in their own seats. The man in the seat across from her gave her a smile as humorless as Cash's had been. He held an unlit cigar in his fingers.

"Well, well. Señorita Cole. Welcome to the party."

The rotors whined as their speed increased and in seconds they lifted off and banked into the night sky.

Oh, Logan. I hope you're prepared for this. I have every bit of faith in you.

"This is a nice ride, no?" Moreno looked at her. "We will be at the main party shortly."

"I don't expect to be having much fun." She lifted her chin in a defiant gesture. "Señor Moreno, I assume? I'm shocked you left the security of your estate to come on this ride."

"Your father is a very important man, especially to me. I want to welcome him myself."

And kill him.

"And what will you do after that?"

He shrugged. "He loves you very much. He has agreed to exchange himself for you. A fair trade, no?"

She studied him for a long time, fear and rage boiling in her stomach.

"You aren't going to let either of us go, are you?"

He reached out and grabbed her chin with his fingers, gripping it tightly. It took every bit of willpower not to flinch and try to pull away from him. Instead she stared him right in the eye.

"Well, well. A fighter." Another of those cold smiles. "I might enjoy this after all."

"What do you want?" Although she knew exactly what he wanted.

"What is rightfully mine as well as my pound of flesh for the trouble I've been caused. I think that's fair, don't you?"

"You tricked him. You and that asshole Cash Breeland."

"A little business maneuvering is what I call it," he told her. He glanced sideways out the windshield. "Well, well. It seems we are there already. Just do as you're told and everything will be fine."

For you.

They were barely up in the air before they were setting down at a small airfield, one she'd seen a couple of times outside Arrowhead Bay. Some residents used it for private planes or helos. Surely they wouldn't be landing with people around, would they?

Then they were on the ground and she was pulled roughly from her seat. Someone pushed the cabin door open and one of the men lowered the stairs again. He yanked her from the seat and stood her in the doorway. She could make out a small building that looked like it might be an office and off to the left planes were in their tie-down slots. An SUV and a van were parked by a chain-link fence, with two other vehicles close to the building.

What was waiting for her out there? Had her father really shown up? Was Logan out there, hiding? Did he know what was happening?

The man behind her dug his fingers into her arm in a punishing grip, a rifle pointed over her shoulder. Devon swallowed and straightened her back.

Showtime.

* * * *

The night was still, without a breath of air moving. Nothing stirred on the little side road leading in to the tiny airport from the two-lane highway. The only sound was that of the occasional night bird. Logan was about to check the time on his watch when he heard the faint drone of an incoming plane. He looked up in the sky and saw the plane's winking lights.

"I'm hitting the lights," came Avery's whispered voice in his earpiece.

He clicked his throat mic twice to acknowledge. In an instant she flipped the switch inside that lit up the small runway. The plane swooped down, landed, and coasted to a stop near the building. After what seemed an interminable length of time, the door slid open.

Then there she was in the doorway. Standing behind her was a tall, muscular man holding an assault rifle and scanning the area. Logan's heart rate tripled and he had to force deep breaths to slow it down.

Please don't let this get fucked up.

"Cole," the man shouted. "*El Jefe* wants to be sure you are here."

"I am," Cole shouted from the shadows of the overhang. "But I'm not moving until my daughter is off that plane and out of range. He knows the deal. When she's safely in the SUV, I'll come forward. Shoot me, and everything I have on the cartel goes public."

"How do we know you haven't already given it up?" the man yelled.

"Because it's my only trump card, you idiot. Now let my daughter off the plane."

The man started to lift his rifle, then apparently thought better of it and stepped back into the cabin. Logan ground his teeth in impatience. He held his breath as the man nudged Avery forward, causing her to stumble a little as she descended the stairway.

I'll kill every one of those fuckers if they harmed her in any way.

"Go on," the man called to her. "We need to get your father and be out of here."

He saw her look around the airfield, then spot the SUV and the van and head straight toward them. Her walk was a little unsteady but as she got closer she picked up a little speed. The van blocked the view of the SUV so when she got close enough, Logan reached a hand out and jerked her toward him, clapping his hand over her mouth.

"It's me. Don't scream, okay?"

She nodded. "Logan?" she whispered.

"Get in. Quick." He had the door open and shoved her into the front, over to the passenger side. "Get down and stay down." He looked at the agent sitting in the driver's seat. "Get her the hell away from here. Now."

The SUV was moving almost before he finished speaking.

Logan jumped into the van where another agent waited, the man gunned the motor, and they raced toward the small plane. The moment they began to move, two agents raced from the building, grabbed Cole, and yanked him back into the building. Logan lowered his window, stuck out the rifle that had been waiting for him, and shot out the tires on the plane. At once the plane's nose dipped toward the ground.

Agents dressed in full riot gear dashed toward the plane. The man who had first appeared in the doorway lifted his assault rifle and began firing but in seconds he was down, shot by one of the agents.

Another man moved into the doorway, spraying the area with his rifle. Bullets zinged everywhere. But then DEA Special Agent Chuck LaValle and his men were up the stairway and boarding the plane. Logan leaped from the van and ran over to the plane, right behind them. He wanted to see for himself the bastard who'd started this whole thing and make sure he was secured. Agents from Vigilance stood at the foot of the stairway, guns at the ready if needed.

He'd always wondered what evil personified looked like, and now he saw it in the face of Cruz Moreno. As the DEA agents cuffed him and his friends, Logan glanced at Cash Breeland, also cuffed, his face ashen, his shoulders drooping. Logan hoped all of them would suffer a special kind of hell for what they'd done. He had to restrain himself from taking a punch at Cash as the agents moved him out of the plane, along with Moreno and the others.

Everyone was herded toward the vehicles except for one man who took a moment to slap a sticker on the nose of the plane: Property of the Drug Enforcement Agency. Then he hurried to catch up to the others. LaValle escorted Graham Cole to the vehicle with Sheri and Avery in the back seat. In seconds they were headed toward Arrowhead Bay and Vigilance.

The only one left was him. The SUV Devon had ridden away in pulled back in through the open gate and right up to the building. When the passenger door flew open and she jumped out, Logan ran to her and gathered her in his arms, holding her close to his chest. For a long moment all he could do was stand and hold her.

He looked at the driver. "You were supposed to take her to the office."

"I checked with Avery to get an all clear. If I hadn't brought her back, she threatened to jump out of a moving vehicle and walk back here. Sorry."

Okay. He'd allow himself the pleasure of holding her for one last time and making sure she was okay.

"Did they…hurt you in any way?" He was afraid to ask the question. Afraid of what he might hear.

"Not really. They tied me up and left me alone for the most part. Brought me water, I guess so I wouldn't die of dehydration, but that was all."

In his mind he'd imagined the most terrible things happening to her. It was a small measure of relief that they hadn't. He wanted to kiss her, but then he remembered if not for him she wouldn't have been in that situation.

"Okay." He took a step back. "I'm taking you back to Vigilance. Your father will be there, and he wants a few minutes with you. Are you up for it?"

"I hope so. I'm not sure I know what to say to him." She touched Logan's arm. "Thank you for saving me."

Her soft words were like a knife to his heart.

"Saving you? It's my damn fault you got taken to begin with."

"How can you say that? You did everything right. You locked the doors to the truck when you got out. You pulled up close to the pump and wedged yourself between them. You kept looking in all directions."

"I remember." He ground out the words. "I should have taken you to Vigilance first and then gassed up the truck. It was a rookie mistake. I didn't—" He swallowed, hard, unable to get the rest of the words out.

"It wasn't your fault," she insisted. "Any more than what happened to Amanda was your fault. Will you please get that through your head?" She reached up and cupped his face with her hands. "What about all the things you said? Things we said to each other? I can't believe you didn't mean them."

"You're better off if you do."

He had to get her back to Vigilance before he gave in to the emotion swamping him and told her what he really felt. She deserved better than him. Period.

He was through talking. He just didn't have anything else to say to her, weighted down as he was by guilt. He wanted to hand her over to Avery and get the hell out of Dodge. Find a place where he could hide away from everything. Go someplace where he'd never see Devon again and be reminded of the fact she almost lost her life because of him.

They climbed into the SUV, the agent who'd been driving now sitting in the back. Devon finally gave up trying to get him to talk and they rode the rest of the way in uncomfortable silence.

* * * *

Devon was beyond frustrated. The moment they arrived at Vigilance and he took her inside, Logan had done a disappearing act. She tried to ask Avery about it but everyone else was there—the DEA agents, her father, and the Vigilance agents.

Her father stood in Avery's office, a tentative look on his face. She just threw herself into his arms and hugged him as if she never wanted to let him go.

"I'm so sorry," he said over and over. "I would have killed myself if anything had happened to you."

"But you didn't know what kind of a deal you were getting into," she reminded him.

"I should have. No one gives out that kind of money at a favorable interest rate unless there's something underhanded about it." He cupped her chin. "I love you, Devon. You're my little girl and always will be. It's my job as a father to take care of you, and I almost got you killed."

She wanted to stamp her foot, tired of the men in her life telling her that. Logan was busy wearing his hair shirt and her father was wallowing in guilt and stupidity.

"But you contacted Vigilance," she reminded him. "That was the smartest thing you could have done."

Then she hugged him, not sure how long they'd have together or when she'd see him again. Avery had told her about the deal with the DEA. Just because Moreno and his top henchmen were either dead or in custody didn't mean someone else wasn't running the cartel. Her father would have a target on his back for a long time.

"I wish you could meet Leslie," he told her after he explained his situation. "You would love her."

"If she's good to you and makes you happy, and you're safe, that's all I care about."

"Maybe some day..." He shrugged. "Who knows, right?"

"Right."

It seemed they had barely spent a minute together before Avery was there along with DEA Special Agent Chuck LaValle.

"We owe you thanks for the information," LaValle told Graham, "no matter how we came to it. And thank you for putting yourself at risk for us."

"I did it for my daughter," Graham said, "but hell, it was also the least I could do after realizing I was in bed with the devil."

"You know this isn't the end of it for them," he said. "We got the head honcho but he's got lieutenants who will take over and they won't stop looking for you."

"Is there any way to get their hooks out of Cole International?"

"I think with Moreno out of the picture, and SMX Group closed up, the corporation could phase out the operations they were involved in and move those people into other divisions."

"I'll give you the information on my new attorney." Graham pulled out his cell phone. "He's an old friend and I trust him completely. He has power of attorney to make things happen. He can also facilitate the appointment of a new CEO."

"Good." LaValle nodded his head. "Very good."

"What about Alford and Bodine?" Bitterness edged Graham's tone when he mentioned their names.

"We picked them up earlier today. And of course Cash Breeland was taken off the plane with Moreno."

Graham scrubbed his face with his hands. "I feel like the stupidest person in the world to be taken in by them. Hell, I didn't even suspect a thing when Alford and Bodine and Vince Pellegrino were slipped into Cole International."

"They're very good at what they do," Avery reminded them.

"Do you have any idea why Vince was killed? He was one of their people."

"As we dig through everything I'm sure we'll find the answer," LaValle assured him. "My guess is he asked for a bigger cut of the pie. They also had a sense you were getting ready to disappear and held him responsible for not keeping a tighter hold on you."

"It'll be a long time getting over that," he said. He lifted the satchel he'd brought with him and handed it to LaValle. "The external hard drive. I threw the other one overboard along with the laptop. Everything you want to know about the Moreno cartel is on it."

"For that alone we'll figure out how to extricate Cole International," Avery told him. "Right, Chuck?"

The agent nodded.

"I also have the information he sent us," Avery told the agent. "We created reports and spreadsheets. I'll forward them to your e-mail."

"Much appreciated." He turned to Graham. "We'll be taking you someplace secluded tonight. Then tomorrow and maybe the day after we'll be asking you a lot of questions. Everything you can tell us will be another nail in Moreno's coffin."

"After that I go back to…where I was, under my new name, so they can't find me, right?"

LaValle nodded. "I'm sorry it has to be that way, but we don't want to take chances with your life."

"What—what about Cash Breeland? He's the one who got us into it. Will he get hit as hard?"

"No question about it. As we speak federal agents have taken possession of his bank and brought in a team of accountants. The bank is closed." He shook his head. "Everyone whose accounts are on the up-and-up will get their money, but we have to sort it all out first."

"They were great buddies," Graham told him. "Moreno used to call him Vato."

LaValle snorted. "It means 'dude' in Spanish. I think Moreno didn't respect him as much as you think."

Devon frowned. "Why not? Cash is the one who set up all his money laundering systems."

"That doesn't mean there was respect there," La Valle said. "We'll go over all the records, but I believe they've been doing this together for a long time. I think it probably started when Moreno opened an account in Breeland's bank and deposited a large sum of money."

"I need to make a call." Her father looked at Avery. "Someone's waiting by the phone, I'm sure."

"We can take care of that." She looked at Chuck. "And tomorrow let's let him have some time with Devon, too."

The agent nodded.

And suddenly, with a flurry, they were gone.

Devon looked at Avery. "I should feel a lot better about this, but I just feel…empty. I'm happy I'll get to spend some time with my dad tomorrow but then he's gone again." She looked around. "And where did

Logan disappear to?"

"He has some issues to work through." Avery smiled although it was obvious she was concerned. "Give him a little space and it will all work out."

"I don't know." Devon bit her lip. "He feels so guilty. Did you know he had another incident in his past?"

Avery nodded. "I have to know everything about my agents when I hire them. But he never wanted to talk about it and I didn't want to pry."

She swallowed back tears. "I care about him."

"I'd say it's a little more than that. You're in love with him. It may have been fast but I've always believed when the right person comes along you don't need months to realize it."

"So what do I do?"

"Like I said, give him some space. If he stays away too long, I promise I'll step in. Okay?"

"I guess it will have to be." Devon rubbed her forehead. "Right now I'm unbelievably tired. I need to shower and change my clothes. And sleep, if I can. I'd like to go back to the house, just in case…in case Logan decides to show up. But I don't think I'm up to staying there by myself."

"No worries." Sheri had entered the room without her even noticing. "We discussed it. Avery and I are both going to stay with you. I'll take you home and Avery will be along shortly. Will that work for you?"

Devon nearly lost it then, at the kindness of these people.

"I don't know how to thank you." She swallowed. "Maybe you'd better get me out of here before I lose it altogether and start bawling like a baby."

But as exhausted as she was, it took her a long time to fall asleep without Logan's arms around her and his hard, muscular body curled around hers. She cried silently, not wanting to disturb the March sisters. Finally, just before dawn, she fell into an exhausted sleep.

* * * *

Devon took a deep breath and let it out slowly. For a moment she was tempted to forget this, turn around, and drive back to Arrowhead Bay.

No. This is too important. If I leave now, I'll always regret not taking this chance.

Avery had given her the directions to the little cottage at Ft. Myers Beach.

"I bought it a few years ago to stash a client and decided to keep it. It's proven to be a good place to decompress without having to hide up in the hills."

She'd hugged Avery. Hard. Then left before she lost her nerve.

She knocked on the door and when there was no answer, she knocked again. Still no answer. She peeked through the windows and didn't see anyone and when she checked no one was on the back porch. Sighing, she hoofed it down to the end of the little street where a small park bordered the beach and Estero Bay.

Once she got into the park, Logan wasn't hard to spot. He was standing in the water, the waves lapping his ankles, hands shoved in the pockets of his shorts. He was staring at the water so she didn't think he was aware of her walking toward him in the sand.

"Your perfume gives you away all the time." His voice was ragged, as if he'd been shouting for a long time. "I'll never be able to smell vanilla and jasmine without thinking of you. If you really want to sneak up on somebody, you should change it."

"Maybe I wanted you to know I was here." She slipped off her sandals and walked forward to where he was.

"What do you want, Devon? You should stay as far away from me as you can. Haven't you figured that out yet? I'm poison to the women I love. It seems I can protect everyone but them."

"See. Now that's where you're wrong." She walked up to stand beside him. "You protected me just fine."

"Coulda woulda shoulda."

She flipped a hand at him. "I knew you'd save me, Logan. I had every bit of faith in you."

"I don't know how you could." He stared out at the horizon. "I let the first woman I loved die and almost did the same to the second one. I'm useless, Devon. You're better off without me."

Devon stared at him, the anger building inside her. On impulse she hit him on the side of the head with her sandals.

"Enough with the pity party." She hit him again.

"Hey!" He held up his hand. "That hurts!"

"Good. Maybe it will knock some sense into you." She got ready to do it a third time when his hand snaked out and he grabbed her by the wrist.

"You trying to knock my brains out?"

"I would if you had any." She sighed. "Logan, in life shit happens. Did I think my father would get himself involved with drug dealers? Did he? Did I ever imagine any of this would happen?" She shook her head. "Not in my wildest nightmares. My father is beating himself up even worse than you, saying it's really his fault I was kidnapped. It took me a long time the other day to convince him shit happens."

"How could you ever trust me to take care of you again?" He held his hands out. "How could anyone?"

"Well, I'd say Vigilance would. Avery's got an assignment waiting for you, but I told her it had to wait because you and I had some unfinished business." She took a deep breath and let it out slowly. "You said you loved me. Were you lying?"

"No, but—"

She held up her hand. "You said we'd see what we had together when this was over. Was that a lie?"

He shook his head. "That's not the point."

"Now that's where you're wrong. As far as I'm concerned, it's the whole point. If you can look me in the eye and tell me, truthfully, that you don't love me and what we have isn't the beginning of something strong and lasting, I'll get back in my car, drive back to Arrowhead Bay, and you'll never hear from me again. So look at me, Logan. Can you do that?"

He looked at her, his eyes full of anguish, but something else lurked in there. The feelings she'd seen from the first time they made love. They were there, and the fist clenching around her heart loosened.

"Well?" she prompted.

Without any warning he stepped close to her, grabbed her, pulled her against him, and kissed her so hard she had a hard time breathing. But she didn't care. All she cared about was his warm lips on hers, his tongue dancing with hers, his strong fingers cupping her cheeks as he held her head in place for his plundering. At last he lifted his mouth from hers, but he still cradled her face in his palms.

"I tried to get you out of my mind," he said in a gravelly voice, "but I couldn't. You were in my dreams every night and in my head every day. I don't think I even felt this much for Amanda. But Devon—"

She touched his lips with a forefinger. "No buts. We both have issues to deal with, but we'll do a lot better if we deal with them together."

He studied her face for a long time. "I don't know why or how I got so lucky but if this is what you want, you're stuck with me. Period."

"It's what I want," she whispered. "It's *all* I want."

They walked back to the cottage holding hands. She told him about her father's new life that the DEA was going to get him back to and about his new love.

"The DEA set up a Skype call for the three of us. She's lovely, Logan. And it's obvious she cares a great deal for him."

"I'm glad for him," Logan told her. "Even if I want to kick his balls in for getting involved in the mess he did."

She flapped a hand at him. "He had a problem and didn't look too closely at the solution. It's done now. Over with. They're getting married in a couple of months and Chuck LaValle said he could get me up to Maine for the wedding without leaving tracks." She stopped at the cottage and looked up at him. "I would be more than happy if you'd come with me."

He hesitated for a moment, and she wondered if he was rethinking everything he'd said. Then she saw his body relax.

"I'd be honored to. Maybe by then we could have had our own wedding."

Her heart nearly stopped beating. Then she grinned so broadly she thought her cheeks would crack, and threw her arms around him. "If that's a proposal, I say yes. Yes, yes, yes!" She hugged him, hard. "No taking it back now."

He stroked her cheek with his thumb. "I love you, Devon. Maybe I don't have the right—"

She clapped her hand over his mouth. "We're done with that, at least for today. I know you'll be dealing with it for a while, because that's the kind of person you are. But we'll deal together. Okay?"

His laugh had a rusty sound to it, as if he hadn't used it much lately. "Okay. I guess I find it hard to say no to you."

"Good. Because from now on there's going to be a lot of yes in our lives."

They held hands at they climbed the stairs to the door of the stilted cottage. Logan punched the code into the lock and opened the door for her. They were barely inside before he lifted her in his arms and carried her to the bedroom.

"I have to have you right now," he rasped. "Right. This. Minute."

They were frantic tearing their clothes off. Logan yanked back the covers on the bed and lowered her to the cool sheets. They were both so aroused, so turned on after being apart, that foreplay almost wasn't necessary.

He locked his gaze with hers as he slid into her, holding still as her muscles clenched around him.

"This is forever, Logan. No changing your mind now."

"Forever," he agreed, and took them both over the edge in a whirlwind release.

When they could catch their breath again he brushed his mouth over hers. "Forever," he repeated.

She nodded. "Forever."

In case you missed it, please enjoy an excerpt from Desiree Holt's

FORWARD PASS

Get Ready to Play Rough

Shay Beckham grew up idolizing her brother's best friend, star quarterback Joe Reilly. There was no one in their Texas town who had the moves to match Joe on or off the field. Years later, he's still a player who has what it takes to drive any hot-blooded woman wild. But Shay isn't a kid with a bad case of hero-worship anymore. She's grown-up and independent, with her feet on the ground and a serious head on her shoulders. If she could just say the same for Joe.

It's been fifteen years, but Joe Reilly hasn't forgotten the skinny little kid who used to follow him around like a shadow. What he can't get over is that the skinny shadow has grown into one hell of an incredible woman. One any man in his right mind would kill to get his hands on. And one who seems to be completely immune to him. He knows he and Shay could have something special together. If he could only convince her he's about more than just the game.

A Lyrical e-book on sale now.

Learn more about Desiree at http://www.kensingtonbooks.com/author.aspx/31606

Chapter 1

"Damn it, Hank. Why don't you answer?"

Shay Beckham pressed End on her cell phone yet again and sighed. She and her brother had been playing telephone tag for two days. When he called, she was in meetings. When she called, he was out of signal range. The only voices talking to each other were their voice mails. How godforsaken could it be in Wyoming, anyway? It was still in the United States, right?

And why was he trying so hard to reach her? They exchanged texts now and then, but they were both so busy they only called each other in case of emergency. The places he went, cell reception was spotty at best and talking to him was like playing leapfrog. Wait! Was he okay? Her heart stopped for a moment at the thought he might be hurt, but then she relaxed. If something had happened to him, his boss would have reached out to her. So what was on his mind that had generated this flurry of aborted phone calls? Obviously, he wanted something because he was the one who'd initiated this current game of phone tag.

She leaned back in the taxi as it turned from the airport access road onto the interstate. Less than half an hour and she'd be home, thank God, and she could get out of her sweatshirt and jeans that wore the remnants of her diet cola from the plane.

With the way her luck was running, maybe she shouldn't have accepted her complimentary beverage. On the flight out to New York a week before, a little turbulence had been responsible for her arriving with a huge coffee stain on her favorite yellow sweater. Maybe she should carry a bib with her. Or a large tarpaulin.

On today's flight, she had just set up her iPad and lifted her glass gingerly to take a sip when the plane hit an air pocket and everything bounced. Her iPad. The purse beneath the seat. Worst of all, her drink. Her hand flew up, with it her diet soda and, most importantly, the ice cubes. Up in the air. Over the back of her seat. Into the seat behind her.

She could still hear the man behind her growling. "Shit!"

Then, "Damn it anyway."

She'd used the miniscule courtesy napkin to blot up what she could from her sweatshirt and jeans. Shay had cringed as the man behind her continued to mutter under his breath.

"Hey, you in front. Didn't you ever learn to pay attention on a plane? You got your damn drink all over me."

He hadn't seemed impressed with her mumbled apology so she'd just slid down even farther and buried her nose in her iPad again. And been damn glad to get to the end of the flight without further incident. When it was time to deplane, she'd avoided even looking back at the man, hustling up the Jetway into the terminal as fast as she could. Getting home was all she could think of.

Sighing, she brushed a few wisps of hair away from her cheeks and tugged on the brim of her red ball cap. A lean cougar prowled across the red background, a new graphic she'd created for Dazzling Designs. The company she worked for produced merchandise for college and professional sports teams. This prototype had been waiting for her when she flew in for four days at the main office and she'd decided to wear it on her trip home.

She was worn out from the long, intense days of discussions and brainstorming. This was her third round trip to New York since she'd made the move back to Texas. After five months, she was piling up plenty of frequent-flyer miles, which she hoped to use one of these days.

She realized with a start the taxi, which had slowed a moment ago, had come to a standstill. The driver's two-way radio crackled in the front seat, but she ignored its staticky sound as she checked her phone again. Still no answer from Hank. She leaned forward, seeing rows of vehicles stopped in every lane of the interstate as far ahead as she could see. Shit.

"Is there an accident ahead of us?"

"Yes, miss." The driver was nothing if not polite. "Dispatch radioed me a moment ago. Sorry, miss."

Well, crap. Just what she didn't need. She wanted a hot bath, a glass of wine, and pizza delivery.

She checked her watch again. Was it really only two minutes since she'd tried calling Hank? Maybe a text would reach him. Sometimes she had better success with that.

In cab on way home from airport. What's up? Try a tin can for reception.

She hit Send and waited to see if he answered. In less than two minutes, her phone chimed.

"Good trip?"

"Yes. What's up with you? What's with all the phone calls?"

"Just wanted 2 let you know Laura had 2 vacate condo for repairs for 2 days. Told her she could stay at house. She knows where extra key is."

That was what was so important?

Shay snorted and wrote, *"I'll bet."*

"She'll be gone sometime 2day. Just a heads up." Shay ground her teeth. Damn it. Why couldn't the damn woman have gone to a hotel? And what was with giving out the location of the key? She loved her big brother and was grateful to him for sharing his house with her but she definitely needed to find a place of her own. She didn't need his females driving her crazy when he wasn't there.

"She'd better be out of there when I get home. Want peace and quiet."

"I'll text her now. Just wanted to get yr flight info."

"On my way home from airport now."

"Thx. I'll tell her. How was NY?"

"Same old same old. U home soon?"

"Maybe. Don't know. Take care."

"You, too."

Traffic was still not moving. Shay bit down on her frustration, sighed again, and unzipped the front pocket of her carry-on. She'd grabbed a sports magazine in the airport, planning to check the ads her company was running, but hadn't bothered to read it on the plane. Maybe she could use it to pass the time now.

Flipping it open, the first thing she saw was Joe Reilly's face smiling at her in full living color. Crap. Joe Reilly. Her childhood hero, her teenage crush, and the star of her adult erotic fantasies. The same Joe Reilly who'd called her squirt and pest when she tagged after him and Hank. The football idol who had been a babe magnet since his voice changed.

The man she'd been secretly in love with all these years, a love that stilted every other relationship she'd had. When was she ever going to admit that it was an impossibility? That she needed to stomp on it, bury it, and move forward?

In Texas, where football was the number one religion, high school stars wrote their own tickets. As the star quarterback for the Granite Falls High School Coyotes, Joe had had women hanging over him like so much drapery. During his outstanding career in college and then in the NFL, it seemed every time she turned on the television or checked sports online she saw his picture with one female or another. She was sure he had a black book that rivaled an encyclopedia in size. She might as well have been chopped liver for as much attention as he ever paid to her.

She'd wasted so much of her time studying football, until she could diagram games almost as well as Joe could. She could even point out the percentage of success for each play. Joe had always grinned and winked at her. Only in hindsight had she realized he'd tolerated her because she was Hank's baby sister, with the emphasis on baby, even as she stupidly wanted him to wait for her to grow up.

She needed to find a way to get Joe Reilly out of her head. For good. Certainly her obsession with him wasn't helping her love life. She needed to stop looking for Joe Reilly substitutes. The men she tried to build relationships with may not have been athletes, but they were ardent sports fans and that was what attracted her.

And look how far that had gotten her. One cheated on her with a coworker, one out and out lied about who and what he was, another wanted to move in with her and have her pay the rent. Thank God she'd never said *I love you* to any of them, probably because, in retrospect, she hadn't. All those experiences left her with a strong distrust of the male sex, Joe Reilly being no exception.

Yeah, she was the champion of stupid. What was with her, anyway? She was smart, savvy, successful at her work. She'd braved the Big Apple and found herself a dream job she loved, which paid her extremely well. People would be lining up to be her if she let them. Now she needed to find a way to get rid of this restless, unfulfilled feeling she hadn't been able to shake in years.

For weeks she'd been telling herself tomorrow she'd take the first step to build a new life here in San Antonio, back in Texas where her roots were. Reach out to old friends. Meet new people. Rebuild her life and shake the ghosts of the past. Stop burying herself in the house with her work and marathon sessions with old movies and popcorn. How pathetic was that?

What she needed was the right guy, one who understood emotion and who respected her. One who wasn't a Joe Reilly substitute. It wouldn't hurt if he was really hot and could make every one of her erotic fantasies come to life. And also didn't lie or cheat. Time to finally put the vestiges of her crush, her childish daydreams, where they belonged—in the mental Dumpster. She was through lusting after Joe Reilly.

Enough already.

If she was going to hero worship someone she should have stuck to Joe Montana. He'd be a lot safer. And better. Yes, way better.

She closed the magazine, putting Joe Reilly where he belonged.

In her carryon.

Time to get on with life.

* * * *

Joe Reilly wheeled his rental car out of the parking lot toward San Antonio. Checking his cell phone for traffic alerts, he discovered an accident on Interstate 10 that had traffic at a standstill. He programmed the GPS for an alternate route and headed out.

He could still smell the traces of a soft drink on his slacks. He'd done his best to wipe away the stains but the rental clerk had given him the fisheye, probably thinking he was a real slob. It wasn't his fault some idiot who couldn't walk and chew gum, or manage to hold onto her drink on the plane, had dumped its contents over the back of her seat and onto him. Just another indication of how crummy his day was going.

He'd seen this trip as a chance to spend some quality time with Hank Beckham, who, despite geographical differences, was still his best friend. He didn't get to see as much of him as he'd like to these days. The last time had been three years ago.

Their schedules just hadn't allowed for any time together since then. Hank was an engineer who was always being sent to some assignment for his company while Joe ran around the country for Fox Sports One and for the Coaches Conference business he'd started. The latter was an important project for him, workshops for high school coaches on how to lead as well as coach. How to teach players personal values as well as diagrams and game plans. He'd seen too many kids come out of high school without understanding that playing was only half the deal. Personal responsibility was a big part of it. His programs were geared to help coaches pass that along.

Unfortunately Hank had texted that morning he was still in Wyoming working on plans to build a bridge, but Joe should make himself at home in the house.

"I'll try and catch a quick couple of days while you're there, buddy," Hank had assured him. "But if not, just make yourself at home."

He'd also hoped to spend some time with his parents, of course, who were happy in their new adults-only community, except they were away on a trip. Bad timing, but it couldn't be helped.

So he'd be alone in the house.

Joe shifted in his seat, trying to stretch out his left leg. The ache served as a constant reminder the glory days had come to an abrupt end.

His cell phone rang, interrupting his thoughts. He looked at the readout and swore. Lisa Margolin. No doubt calling for his help with Gina again. God. How had he gotten himself in this pickle anyway? Because his parents raised him to take care of people who couldn't take care of themselves. That was how. He let the call go to voice mail, not in a mood to deal with it right now.

He was aware the most recent company Gina worked for had gone out of business a few weeks ago. Employees had received a one-month severance package and Joe knew Gina was coming to the end of hers. She didn't deal well with uncertainty. Her dysfunctional family had set off her battle with the bottle to begin with and he knew the thread of sobriety was always very shaky.

Ten minutes later the ringtone chimed again and he knew without looking who it was. She was nothing if not persistent. Setting his jaw, he pressed Accept.

"What is it this time, Lisa?"

"You know I wouldn't call you unless it was important, Joe. Really." She always began the calls that way.

Except it was always important. "Yeah, okay. Just tell me what's up now."

"I hope you aren't mad."

She was as good at sounding tearful as Gina always had been.

"Lisa, I'm kind of busy. What's the deal?"

"Well, um…" She paused.

"Look." He chuffed with impatience. "Just spit it out. How much?" It was always money. Of course.

"She's got a few job interviews coming up and she could use a couple new outfits."

Joe squeezed the phone so hard he was amazed he didn't crush it. "What happened to the money I just sent her?"

Pause. "She got sick." Lisa's voice was very quiet. "I mean, really sick. She needed medicine."

He could only imagine. Medicine that came in bottles of cheap booze.

"She really wants to make a good impression at these interviews," Lisa added.

A headache began to burrow its way into his temples.

"Fine. Give me an hour and I'll transfer some money into your account."

"Can't you just meet me with a check?" she whined.

"No. I'm busy. It's the transfer or nothing."

"Whatever." Her heavy sigh was clear across the connection. "Sorry. I just want this to happen for her."

"We're coming to the end of the road here, Lisa. It's time Gina took responsibility for her own life."

"But you're all she has," Lisa protested, a familiar refrain. "You can't let go of her now. I-I'll make sure she stays clean. Gets a job. Goes to work."

"Do that. I'll check back with you to see what's going on." He disconnected the call in the middle of her thanks, grinding his teeth.

Gina Rivera. High school bombshell. Wild child who'd captured his virtue. He hadn't seen her, had even forgotten about her, until his third year in the NFL. She'd shown up at a game, waiting for him at the player's gate, all masses of blond hair and tight clothes. He'd been high enough on the excitement of the win to succumb to her sexiness and spend the night with her.

He hadn't thought much of it, not even when she showed up twice more. Then he'd discovered her secret, answered her one plea for help and after that he was trapped, just because he was basically a good guy. Occasional contact turned into regular contact. And when he'd stopped taking her calls, she'd had Lisa contact him with a sob story that plucked at his conscience.

How long was he expected to offer aid to a raging alcoholic who didn't help herself? He should have told Scott Manchin, his agent, about it from the beginning. By now so much time had passed if word got out, the media wouldn't look at him as doing something kind for a friend. They'd want to know why he'd kept her hidden all this time. Did they have a child together? All that shit. He'd seen it happen to others and hadn't been smart enough to protect himself. It would be gossip fodder for weeks and kill all the work he'd done to clean up his act. He really had to cut the cord here.

Okay, enough of that.

Following the GPS directions, he pulled off the interstate and into an attractive neighborhood of larger homes and mature trees. A little farther on and the GPS directed him to turn left into the long driveway of a two-story colonial. *Nice digs, Hank,* he thought. But the guy was making big bucks. He deserved a good place to come home to.

He parked in front of the garage door. Maybe when he got inside he could grab the opener from Hank's car and use it while he was here. The key was right where Hank had said it would be. He opened the front door, pulled his suitcase inside, and headed toward the room Hank had said was his to use. On the way he passed a room that looked far too feminine to be Hank's. He wondered briefly whose room it was. Hank hadn't mentioned anything about sharing the house with someone.

Too much for him to think about right now. He wanted a shower, and then he'd see about ordering some dinner. Less than five minutes later he was under hot, steaming water, washing away the grime of the day.

* * * *

The taxi moved forward with a jerk and Shay's eyes popped open. She leaned forward and tapped the driver on the shoulder.

"Did they clear away the wreck? We're finally moving, right?"

"Yes, miss." He shrugged. "But slowly."

She rotated her neck, trying to work out some of the kinks. She'd been sitting in uncomfortable seats since she got in the shuttle to the airport and every muscle in her body ached. The hot shower was looking better and better. Or maybe she'd fire up the hot tub Hank had installed on the rear deck.

Hopefully, with all this delay caused by the wreck, by the time she got to the house Laura would be packed and gone. They pulled off the interstate and she mentally crossed her fingers and silently chanted, *Let her be gone*. But bad luck was still with her. When they turned onto her street and she spotted the car parked in the driveway, she swore under her breath. Laura Whoever was still here. Well, she'd better be getting ready to leave. Shay was in no mood to put up with bullshit. Sighing, she hauled her suitcase into the house, closed the door, and headed through the living room to her bedroom.

And stopped.

A hissing sound came from the shower in the bathroom connected to her bedroom and the guest room. Damn it! The least Hank could do was tell his little friends to use the master bath and leave hers alone. He had, after all, promised her that she'd have complete privacy.

"I travel a lot," he'd told her. Then grinned. "And I'll keep the sleepovers to those times you're in New York."

Yeah, yeah, yeah.

So how come this female hadn't gotten the message she was supposed to be gone?

Crap! The door wasn't even closed. Clouds of steam billowed in the bathroom and obscured the figure in the frosted-glass shower enclosure. Okay, enough was enough.

Shay stepped into the bathroom and banged her hand on the glass.

"This is my bathroom," she ground out. "I've had a tough day and you don't want to mess with me. Next time use Hank's bathroom. This one is off-limits. Get your ass out of here in five seconds, or I won't be responsible for my actions."

She turned away, not the least bit interested in a glimpse of Laura Whoever's nudity. She just wanted her out of the house.

The water stopped and the door slid open.

"Okay. I don't want to cause you any more stress. But Hank said I should use this one."

The deep voice shocked her and she turned around before she even thought about it. And nearly swallowed her tongue. A very wet, very naked Joe Reilly stood in her shower stall, grinning at her.

Just when she'd finally made up her mind to stop thinking about him and obsessing over him.

At that exact moment her cell phone chimed. A message from Hank.

"BTW, Joe's in town. Take good care of him."

Meet the Author

Desiree Holt is the *USA Today* best-selling author of the Game On! and Vigilance series, as well as many other books and series in the romantic suspense, paranormal, and erotic romance genres. A RT Book Award finalist, she has been awarded the HOLT Medallion for Excellence in Romance Literature and is a two-time CAPA Award winner. Desiree has been featured on *CBS Sunday Morning* and in the *Village Voice,* the *Daily Beast, USA Today,* the *(London) Daily Mail,* the *New Delhi Times,* the *Huffington Post,* and numerous other national and international publications. Readers can find her on Facebook and Twitter, and visit her at www.desireeholt.com as well as www.desiremeonly.com.

www.ingramcontent.com/pod-product-compliance
Lightning Source LLC
Chambersburg PA
CBHW031421250626
47155CB00004B/1572